LOSERS CLUB COZY MYSTERY BOOK SIX

YVONNE VINCENT

Copyright © 2023 Yvonne Vincent
All rights reserved.

By Yvonne Vincent:

The Big Blue Jobbie
The Big Blue Jobbie #2
The Wee Hairy Anthology

Frock In Hell

Losers Club (Losers Club Book 1)
The Laird's Ladle (Losers Club Book 2)
The Angels' Share (Losers Club Book 3)
Sleighed! (Losers Club Book 4)
The Juniper Key (Losers Club Book 5)
Beacon Brodie (Losers Club Book 6)

For Charlotte and Harry who make me proud every day.

THE FIRST WORD

It's good to be back on Vik with my lovely Losers. They enjoyed their jaunt to Inverurie in The Juniper Key, and there's a shiny new bravery trophy in the cabinet at Vik Police Office, right next to Easy's certificate for best handwriting in Primary 2. But it's time to come home. This book picks up from where we last left off.

In Beacon Brodie, I use a few Scots words that you may not recognise. Most, you'll understand from the context; however, hingin' mince (literally hanging mince) means sausages. There's also claik, which means gossip, and the Broch, which is the local name for Fraserburgh, a town on the North East coast of Scotland.

My thanks go to Michael Strachan from the Museum of Scottish Lighthouses in Fraserburgh, who is the man to ask if you ever want to glue someone to a lighthouse. He is also the author of Scottish Lighthouses: An Illustrated History. Visit https://lighthousemuseum.org.uk if you would like to know more about Scotland's first lighthouse or plan a visit to the museum.

Of course, no introduction is complete without thanking the Angels (Dawn, Louise, Heather, Dianne and Fiona), my sister Anette and the Legend in Tartan Lounge Pants that is Mr V. I really don't know how you put up with me, but I'm very glad that you do.

PROLOGUE

The man sang quietly to himself as he bent to his work, enjoying the warmth of the sun streaming onto his back. There was precious little enough of it these days, he thought. All the bloody climate change nonsense.

He checked the readings and made a note in the small pad he kept for such purpose, scratching the figures in a neat row with the old fountain pen they'd given him when he left the factory, what…it must be coming up to twenty-five years ago now. The Fingavel Engineering logo was barely visible, the gold paint having worn away in pockets and on fingers over the past quarter century, leaving only the ghost of a symbol behind.

Three times a day the man did this - took weather readings. In the evenings, he'd fire up the computer and send the readings off to the mainland, where some boffin would do Lord knows what with them. Sometimes, he'd look back through old readings. That was when you could see the change that time and man had wrought. More rain, warmer temperatures.

All those years ago, when he took the job, nobody had warned him that he'd eventually be replaced by microchips. Truth be told, he wasn't sure why he was still here at all. They could probably monitor the weather remotely if they wanted to. All he did now was fix things, take readings and worry about the state of the world. But apparently, employing him was cheaper than sending a crew out to this remote rock every time things broke, so he supposed he should be grateful to his younger self for making the move to a job where he didn't have to deal with management bollocks all day. This was his little fiefdom, where he ruled the roost.

He made his way indoors and lumbered upstairs, the weight of his toolbox rendering his steps heavy and slow. This may be his roost, but he was getting too bloody old for these stairs. His joints practically sighed with relief as he reached the top and laid the box down with a clunk on the floor. He opened it, checking the contents before selecting a cloth and a spray bottle of white vinegar.

'Mrs Hinch has a lot to answer for,' he grumbled, screwing his eyes against the sun and spraying the window.

He worked slowly, rhythmically spraying and wiping, occasionally tilting his head back to check for smears on the glass. The tourists were a mucky lot. Sticky handprints told of days at the beach and the queues that formed along the path beside Marie Knox's ice cream van. The wind would tear off the dunes to send families huddling into tight groups, goosepimpled arms around each other as they shivered in the shade of the giant Mr Whippy affixed to the top of the vehicle, frantically licking their sand-encrusted cones. The man wasn't sure that was even legal; the big, plastic Mr Whippy, not the ice cream. Although, if he had his way, he'd ban the buggers from taking their cones in here. It was the same every year. Twenty-five times he'd gotten this place ready for the "season." How many more? Not many, he thought. He had enough salted away to buy his own bloody island, where neither man nor ice cream-toting little beast would bother him. Maybe he'd buy a yacht. He squatted down, rubbing at a stubborn smudge of what his mother used to call gulshichs, an old Scottish word for sweets.

Gulshichs on the inside and gull shit on the outside, he thought wryly. Did people still say gulshichs? It didn't matter. Not so long now, and he could say what he damned well liked on his own island…or yacht. A good, working yacht. Nae one of them fancy things with a built-in barbecue and a champagne fridge.

So lost was he in the rhythm of cleaning and his happy imaginings of a solitary retirement, that the man only heard the footsteps when they were directly behind him.

Startled, he looked up. Then his eyes widened when he saw his visitor.

'I…I wish you'd told me you were–,' he stuttered, a smile beginning to form.

He stopped and the smile died on his lips as the figure bent over him and he felt a sharp prick on his neck.

'A decision has been taken, and you're no longer needed,' a rough voice whispered in his ear.

The man put a hand to the side of his neck, panic and confusion setting in.

'What the hell?' he tried to say, but his lips were numb, and all that emerged was, 'Wa wa hey?'.

He put his other hand on the window, using the pressure to help lever himself up as he stared wildly at his assailant, but the glass was slippery with ice cream and white vinegar gloop, and he slid instead to his knees, fingers squeaking as he pushed harder on the glass to slow his descent.

He sat there, looking up helplessly at the figure, unable to understand how or why this was happening. The seconds ticked by, and a trickle of sweat ran down his back. Was it hot in here, he wanted to ask, but his lips and tongue had stopped working and the most he was able to manage was a series of garbled moans.

He once more attempted to push himself to his feet. It was a vain, uncoordinated effort, which left him lying on his side on the floor.

The figure didn't talk. The figure simply watched and

waited. Watched and waited as seconds turned into minutes, and the attempts to stand became weaker and weaker.

The man on the ground wriggled frantically, his eyes wide in terror, his brain urging his body to cooperate. He felt a pair of hands on his belt, the pressure at his waist tightening then loosening as the strip of leather was removed. Fingers fumbled at his waistband, and he heard the sound of a zip. Without ceremony, his trousers were tugged down, his boxers coming with them.

Is this a sex thing, he wondered, as he felt himself slide painfully along the floor, the hands hauling mercilessly on his boots. Then his legs were lifted, bent, straightened, bent, to facilitate the final removal of his breeks.

He'd heard about that serial killer who met folk online and roofied them before killing them, the sick bastard. Jesus, if it was a sex thing, fine. They could have a damn orgy for all he cared, as long as he was alive at the end of it. Although, given that his big legs seemed to have stopped working, he wasn't sure that the little leg would be of much use. The tiny, rational part of his mind that was watching the scene unfold said, 'I can't believe you're desperately hoping that this is a sex thing. It's a murder thing. *Your* murder thing.'

His heart was thumping hard, an arrhythmic jerk in his throat as first his coat was peeled off, then his jumper and vest were manhandled over his ears, leaving him naked on the floor, a line of drool cooling on his face.

He was perfunctorily rolled onto his stomach, where he lay unresisting, awaiting the next humiliation. It didn't take long to arrive. He felt something cold and wet on his back and even though he couldn't see the liquid, the acrid smell told him that it was glue. His thoughts were scrambled. It made no sense. None of this made sense. Was something going to be stuck to him?

He watched white trainers stride confidently across the floor, a gloved hand dragging his window cleaning stool, its wooden legs leaving dark marks in the dust. With a great effort of will, he craned his neck to catch a glimpse of whatever horror was on its way. The figure seemed to be rigging up a pulley. The man could hear ropes being slung over a frame high above him, and he writhed and grunted as it dawned on him what was about to happen. His mind screamed at his useless body to move, just fucking move. Now. His heart seemed to have developed a rhythm of its own and pain shot through his chest. His shoulders strained and his arms crept slowly outwards, then stayed there in a parody of a push-up that he was no longer capable of performing.

The feet came back again. Ropes were tied to his wrists. The feet left, and there was the sound of creaking before he felt himself being dragged along, then upwards. Up, up, up he went, his shoulders racked with the pain of supporting a body grown old and flabby, wrists burning where the knots in the rope dug into flesh.

The man's breath was coming fast, his fingers involuntarily cramping as his heart sent cruel spikes shooting down his arm. He was no longer thinking of why this was happening. He was thinking of his daughter. The daughter he hadn't spoken to since he fled to this godforsaken place. The daughter he'd watched from afar, at first making regular visits to the mainland to wait outside her school, then latterly through social media, combing posts and photographs for any sign of the sickness that drove him to live his secluded life. He cared little for other people, but he'd wanted better for her.

The hands were on his thighs now, gently turning him, and pressing him hard against a cold surface, arms and legs splayed. The man stared into the sunshine that lit the bay beyond the window. Gloved fingers lifted his chin and held his head firmly for a few minutes, while the glue in his short hair bonded with the glass, and he gazed mutely out over a calm sea, feeling his irregular heartbeat slow and fade.

The figure watched as the old man's chest stilled, then

stepped down from the stool, almost disappointed at the anticlimax of it all. They thought they'd feel a euphoric sense of release, yet the thrill had been mild. The guy's heart had given out before the poison had had time to finish the job.

'Never mind,' came the rough whisper, as a pair of grey eyes coolly regarded the dying man. 'Practice makes perfect.'

CHAPTER 1

Freezing mist, thought Hector. Would it ever be spring on this bloody island? Whose stupid idea was it to have a beach party anyway? With an internal harrumph, he answered his own question; it was Edith's stupid idea. If she wasn't his sister, and Mum wouldn't interfere, he'd block her on everything.

Beside him, Edith blundered through the grass, head down and hands shoved deep in the pockets of her thin coat. Danny and Jessica were similarly hunched against the cold, their faces pinched and pale in the dim glow of the lamp.

The four friends continued their slow stumble up the cliff path, Hector lighting the way with the small camping lantern he had found in Grandad's shed. Their insides were warm with the last remnants of the bottle of vodka that now lay buried in the sand at the bottom of the cliff. Their outsides were a different matter. The chill, damp air penetrated the polyester raincoats and the thick hoodies they wore beneath, leaving them shivering and rueful that they'd ignored Granny's advice to wrap up warm. Not that they'd tell her that, of course.

Mary had seen them off on their adventure that afternoon

with sage words of advice about using sat nav thingies and GPs.

'GPS, Granny,' Hector had corrected her. 'We're only going for a walk and a picnic. We'll be fine.'

Granny had declared that Danny should be in charge because he was the sensible one, and Edith had protested that she could be sensible too. She shut up pretty quickly when Granny pointed to Grandad's moustache, which yesterday evening had gone from its usual salted brown to bleached blonde with pink tips.

'I've had to ask the GP...GPS...whatever you call him to remind your grandfather of the perils of drinking whisky on top of sleeping pills. And I shall be having words with your mother when she gets home tomorrow.'

Grandad had slipped Hector and Edith some money and told them to have a good time. Hector suspected that Grandad rather liked his racy new moustache, although he might be less pleased to know that they'd spent the money on vodka and that the picnic had turned into a party involving half their school year.

He tucked his arm through Danny's and tugged him the final few metres to the top of the cliff. They'd emerged near Vik lighthouse, the jaunty stripes of the giant pillar only just visible in the gloom. Hector held up the lantern to illuminate the first few metres of the clifftop path that would take them there, briefly wondering whether it would be a good hiding place while they sobered up. Almost immediately, he dismissed the idea. The climb from the beach had left his legs wobbly, and he didn't fancy hauling himself up hundreds of steps. The place was probably locked anyway, and they'd have to sneak past Keeper's Cottage to get to it. William Brodie was well known for his batlike hearing and supernatural ability to detect any teenager who came within fifty metres of the place after dark. No matter the hour, the kitchen light would come on, and Brodie would emerge from the back door, all grizzled chin and striped pyjamas, waving the big stick and roaring that no little bastard was vandalising his lighthouse. Hector sighed. Old people could be so rude.

'Nobody has ever made it to the lighthouse after dark,' said Danny, his eyes following the direction of Hector's lamp. 'We're too drunk to outrun Beacon Brodie tonight.'

They turned at the sound of female voices. Below them, Edith and Jessica were swearing vociferously in response to the sudden removal of their only source of light. The darkness had combined with the mist and the vodka to befuddle them, and Hector suppressed a snigger when he shone the lantern in their direction to find both girls feeling their way along the path on hands and knees.

'Dickhead,' spat Edith, looking to her right, where just a metre away the path ended in a sheer drop to the rocks below. 'If Mum knew you did that, she'd shit a brick.'

'If Mum knew we'd taken the steep path rather than the long way up, she'd shit a brick,' Hector pointed out.

Edith stood and, taking Jessica's hand, clambered over the lip of the cliff to safer ground.

Panting slightly, she said, 'If Mum knew you got Brian Miller to get us the vodka, she'd ground you for a month.'

'I told him if he got it, you'd let him snog you for ten minutes,' Hector retorted.

'That's disgusting. No, you didn't. Ew, he's an old man. I'm telling Mum you said that.'

Jessica joined in, snapping, 'That's below the belt. For a little dude, you can be quite vicious.'

'Below the belt,' snickered Danny, nudging Hector with his elbow. 'She's right, though. You can't be saying stuff like that about your sister.'

Hector, ever reluctant to admit that he was wrong, especially where it concerned Edith, ignored Danny and grumbled, 'We're too old to be telling Mum on each other. You might still need parental intervention, but I have outgrown such childish nonsense. I'm my own man and I don't appreciate being told what to do. Right, what'll we do next? Can't go home until we've sobered up a bit.'

He looked around as if a suitable suggestion might emerge from the fog. They were on a flat, grassed area at the edge of the village. Nearby, rows of cottages huddled in the diffuse glow of streetlamps, their edges blurred by the haze. Way below them, he could just make out the glow of the fire they'd lit on the sand. He couldn't hear the voices of his classmates, but he knew they were still down there, partying on, ignoring the cold and eking out the memory of the sunshine that had driven everyone to the beach in the first place. It had felt like the first real day of spring, a respite from the snow and wind that had plagued the island for the past week. Winter on Vik could stretch for seven hard months, so the brief burst of warmth that day had lured everyone into the false hope that, finally, the weather had turned.

Hector blew on his hands to warm them, and Danny put an arm around him, pulling him in close to share warmth. He rested his chin on top of Hector's head as he gave some thought to where they could go.

'We need somewhere warm and dry, where there's no risk of running into parents or grandparents,' he mused. 'Chip shop? I think it's open until nine. Margaret will let us sit in the café if we buy food. How much money do we have?'

Pockets were turned out and sufficient loose change was cobbled together to buy a haggis supper. Probably. Perhaps Margaret would take pity on them and throw in a few extra chips.

'Not that you should be eating chips, with your oily skin,' Hector told Edith.

This set off another round of sibling bickery, and it was a moment before anyone paid attention to Jessica.

'Look! Look!' she shouted, one hand pointing upwards and the other tugging on Edith's coat. 'It's the Bat-Signal.'

By the time the others looked, whatever she had seen was gone.

'You didn't take any of the pills that Kyle Trainer was handing out earlier, did you?' asked Hector.

'I'm not stupid,' said Jessica. 'Give it a second…aha! You see?'

Nobody saw. They waited again, then watched in silence as the beacon slowly blinked one, two, three, four times. There, silhouetted against the foggy night sky, was the shadow of a person.

'It's not exactly the Bat-Signal,' said Danny, screwing his eyes and tilting his head to one side. 'More like a…'

'Ghost,' declared Hector. 'Definitely a ghost.'

Jessica gave a short squeal and clung to Edith's arm, trapping her friend's long hair between them and causing Edith to bend to one side.

'Oh, my days. A real live ghost,' she gasped, resisting Edith's attempts to peel her off.

'Ow! It took me ages to do my hair and you're ruining it. For God's sake, it's not a ghost. Maybe something stuck to the window, like a..a…'

Edith's voice trailed away as she tried to imagine what exactly could be causing the shadow.

'Your hair's a mess anyway,' said Hector, the insult delivered on autopilot.

His mind was on the strange phenomenon, his curiosity piqued.

'Although it pains me to say that you're right,' he concluded, 'on this occasion you probably are. Something on the window is being projected onto the mist. It may be something relatively small, but it has been enlarged due to the magnification effect of–'

He was cut short by Danny, who tightened his hold and whispered, 'You're being a pompous English twat again.'

Hector, whose move from posh London private school to the more earthy environment of Vik Academy had not been without its difficulties, gave a stiff nod. He and Danny had quickly become close, and Danny had helped him safely navigate the worst of the bullying. His boyfriend saw beyond the know-it-all attitude to the vulnerable lad beneath; a sixteen-year-old boy whose father was, let's face it, a bit of a useless shitbag and whose mother was distracted while desperately trying to hold everything together in the face of financial ruin. Hector could see that now, even though at the time he'd been a seething mass of resentment towards his mum and had idolised his dad. Danny had been there for him, always happy to have a good moan about parents and use his full six-foot-three height to ward off anyone who thought that Hector being a five-foot-six English "bum-boy" was reasonable excuse for a fight. With humour and a healthy dose of brutal honesty, Danny had cheerfully curbed Hector's tendency to lecture and made him part of a friendship group that didn't care if he was purple with pink spots, so long as he was up for a laugh.

'I'll explain the physics of it later,' Hector said. 'Let's go and find out what's causing it.'

'But I want to go to the chipper,' Edith moaned.

'What about Beacon Brodie?' Danny asked. 'He'll chase us off.'

'My legs are tired,' said Jessica.

'Mine too,' snapped Hector. 'Nevertheless, I want to find out what's causing this. Please, satisfy my curiosity. It'll only take fifteen minutes, then we can go for chips. Come on, the exercise will sober us up.'

'Or make us spew all over the place,' noted Edith. 'Okay then, Twatty McTwatface, we'll check it out. But you have to be nice to me for a whole week.'

'Only if you're nice to me,' Hector retorted.

'That's not part of the deal.'

They grumbled their way along the clifftop path, closely followed by Jessica and Danny. Hector held up the lantern, the light reflecting off the patchy mist, at times making it difficult to see more than a few metres ahead. However, a brief attempt to navigate without it almost sent Jessica over the edge, so it was agreed that the lamp would stay on.

As they approached the lighthouse, their voices dwindled to whispers, each conscious that Beacon Brodie could at any moment come storming from Keeper's Cottage to roar at them. They kept their footsteps light, wincing at the sound of toes grinding on the fine gravel that marked the entrance to the small compound.

Both cottage and lighthouse were surrounded by a high, white wall, built by some enterprising lighthouse keeper many years ago to keep the worst of the wind away. Huddled behind it was Beacon Brodie's squat, stone house, the glow from his kitchen light visible through the gap that was rather grandly termed the visitors' entrance. There was little need for a keeper in these days of automated lighthouses, but Vik was so remote that Brodie had been retained to maintain the machinery. The old man was handy with a spanner, and that included being able to throw the thing with great accuracy at errant teenagers.

As they passed through the gap in the wall, Hector put a finger to his lips and switched off his lantern. In near silence, they stooped beneath the lintel and tiptoed across the yard, using the dim light from the cottage and memory to guide them towards the giant structure that dominated its surrounds.

Hector's stomach muscles complained at the unfamiliar tension, and he consciously relaxed them with a quiet exhalation that earned him a sharp "shh" from Edith. Behind him, Danny swore quietly as his foot caught on a large pebble, sending it skittering across the gravel.

They froze, all four of them listening intently for the sound of Brodie's back door opening and the menacing growl of the man himself. They waited. And waited. Crouching on burning legs for what felt like a full minute.

Nothing.

With a collective sigh of relief, they crept forward, their

eyes straining to make out the shape of the steps that led to the lighthouse door.

Hector couldn't ask the others how they felt as the small group made it into the building, but he couldn't suppress a brief grin of triumph at having successfully outwitted Brodie. He felt Danny's hand on his back and suspected that his feelings were shared.

Surprisingly, the door had been unlocked, and Jessica now closed it with a clunk that seemed jarringly loud in the cold, dark space.

The chill had permeated the wall around them, making the air feel cooler. Wordlessly, they began to ascend, the only sound being four pairs of trainers brushing on the winding stone staircase.

Hector had risked discovery by switching on the camping lamp, but it was flickering now, the batteries beginning to die. He cursed himself for not checking the batteries, but he hadn't intended to stay out until night-time. They'd been going for an afternoon picnic, and he'd grabbed it as an afterthought, in case they went exploring.

'This thing's almost out of juice,' he whispered. 'I'm going to switch it off. Hold onto the rail.'

He was relieved that they weren't in complete darkness. The light from the beacon above filtered downwards, shortening their shadows so that their weary trudge seemed dogged by featureless golems. Hector didn't know if it was his imaginings of folklorish nightmares or the exercise, but his palms were sweating, slippery on the cool iron banister.

'What if it gives way?' said Edith quietly through chattering teeth. 'I can't stop thinking that the rail might give way. How high up are we?'

'Now you're freaking me out,' Danny murmured.

'Me too,' whispered Jessica. 'Who's up for turning back?'

'Nobody's turning back,' Hector whispered sharply, gripping the rail a little more tightly as he stopped and looked back at his companions. 'We're maybe halfway. We got past Beacon Brodie, so we may as well finish what we started.'

They moved upwards, feeling their way across a landing to the next railing, the spiral tighter now as the wall closed in. The light was brighter here, throwing the upturned faces below Hector into relief against the dimly lit steps that corkscrewed towards the ground, where only impenetrable darkness awaited. Hector felt a momentary wave of dizziness as his brain realised that they were high up and that his eyes couldn't see the bottom. He put a hand out to steady himself, his heart hammering to the beat of an irrational fear that he was about to fall, only subsiding when he felt the reassuring solidity of Danny's shoulder.

Hector took a few deep breaths to steady his nerves and moved his hand to the wall, the other still grasping tightly to the rail. His thigh muscles immediately began to smart as he plodded upwards. He lowered his head, focusing only on the next two steps…and the next two…and the next two, lulled by the rhythm of the gentle scrape, scrape, scrape of his toes seeking out the depressions worn into the stone by the thousands of feet that had trodden these stairs over the centuries. The faint groans behind him signalled that he wasn't the only one feeling the burn; however, the light at the top was coming closer and closer. Glancing up, he could see that it shone through a square cut into the upper floor, where a steep, metal set of steps led ladder-like down from the gap. He drew to a halt on the last landing before the final push, leaving room for the others to crowd in behind him.

'We're here,' he said, confident that his voice was unlikely to carry back to Beacon Brodie, safe in his cottage forty metres below.

He felt Danny beside him jump at the sudden increase in volume after their almost silent climb.

'Sorry,' he muttered. 'Good to go?'

Three heads nodded, and they began their final ascent.

The staircase was short and steep. Hector's thighs

continued to protest, and his pace was inexorably slow. So focused was he on looking downwards at his feet, that he was temporarily blinded when he emerged through the opening. He stumbled into the lantern room, pitching forward, hands out towards the floor. A tug at his back told him that Danny had caught his coat, and he felt his feet slide backwards, a heel smacking into something soft while his torso landed gently but inelegantly on the floor.

'You missed the important bits,' wheezed Danny. 'Just as well, or we'd never have children.'

They were all there now, their feet shuffling around him. Hector bent his knees beneath him and hauled himself upright, using the waistband of Danny's jeans as a handhold.

He could hear the steady thrum of machinery as the lens rotated inside the lantern glass. He could smell the salty tang of the sea and…something else. Shit and rotting fruit. So powerful he could almost taste it.

Slowly, Hector opened his eyes just enough to make out the blurry outlines of Danny, Jessica and Edith. Through narrow slits, he could see that they were holding their coats against their mouths and noses.

There was something there, behind them. Something large against the lantern glass. He forced his eyelids up another millimetre. His heart pounded. His mind screamed, 'This is the bit in the movie where you don't go into the basement.' Yet he couldn't help himself. He had to look. He had to see.

The light flashed, dark, bright, dark, bright, casting the scene into slow flickers of carnage. Hector felt his stomach contract as a wave of nausea threatened to overwhelm him. He took a step back, standing on Danny's toes, unable to take his eyes off the figure impossibly suspended on the lantern glass. The man was naked, flaccid skin sagging from his stomach to touch his thighs. His arms were splayed, and a thick sludge of matter ran down the glass between his parted legs. Hector glanced at the face. The man's mouth and eyes were wide in horror, a glassy stare fixed on the grizzled features. He seemed to be floating on the glass, held there by invisible hands. Beyond him, the blinking silhouette of his body projected onto the mist.

'Holy shit,' Hector gasped. 'Is that...it's Beacon Brodie!'

Jessica was the first to scream, her piercing shriek filling the small chamber, bouncing off glass and metal to lance the eardrums of her friends. It seemed she couldn't stop. The screech was followed by another and another, with scarcely a pause for breath in between. Edith hastily removed her coat and threw it over Jessica's head. The sudden removal of sight interrupted the screaming but did little to stem the tide of sobs that followed.

Hector, meanwhile, turned to Danny, automatically seeking comfort but vomiting on his trainers instead. Danny quickly stepped back to avoid the worst of the onslaught and skidded on a piece of half-digested sandwich, sending himself careening back through the hatch and down the steep flight of stairs. Without pause, Edith ran after him, yelling at Hector to call the police and ambulance.

Hector tried to unlock his phone, but it refused to recognise his vomit-flecked face, contorted as it was into an expression of horrified shock. His hands shaking uncontrollably, he finally managed to enter the passcode and hit the digits to summon help. He knew that reception down below was patchy, but here, thank God, the signal was clear.

Somehow, his garbled explanation was understood at the other end, and he was told that PC 'Easy' Piecey and Doc Harris were on their way. What was the condition of the boy who fell down the stairs? Hector didn't know. In his state of fright, he'd forgotten to check.

'He's okay,' shouted Edith. 'A bump on the head, but nothing broken.'

'Teenagers bounce,' said the wry voice in his ear. 'You can stay on the phone and chat with me until help arrives.'

Hector didn't want to do that. Every nerve ending he

possessed was screaming at him to get out of this place as quickly as possible.

Jessica was still standing there with Edith's coat over her head, weeping and sniffing hard through a nose that, thankfully, was too blocked to admit more than a squeak of air. The smell of Brodie was overpowering, and Hector thought he'd never get it out of his own nose, skin, memory.

Gently, he put a hand on Jessica's shoulder and guided her towards the hatch, telling her to lift the coat so she could see the steps. At the bottom sprawled Danny, dazed and shaking, his head in Edith's lap.

By the fading light of Grandad's camping lantern, Hector and Edith helped their friends down the stairs to the lawn outside the lighthouse. Heedless of the possibility of bugs and dog poo, the threat of which would normally have him inspecting every inch of grass before setting his precious designer joggered bottom on it, Hector slumped to the ground. Then he did what all teenagers are far too wise and grand to do. He called his mum.

CHAPTER 2

Penny leaned over the ferry railing, her eyes straining to catch the first glimpse of Vik, the wind whipping her hair into her face where it stuck to the lip balm she'd applied before braving a turn around the deck.

The call from Hector had come mid-evening the night before, just as the Police Scotland Bravery Awards ceremony was drawing to a close. Her elation at receiving a special award had quickly turned to anxiety, and the after-party broke up early, with Sergeant Wilson and some of her colleagues being whisked away by helicopter to police what sounded very much like a murder investigation.

An arm was slung around her shoulders and a paper cup was shoved under her nose. Penny could smell the coffee in the steam wafting up through the small opening in the plastic lid, and she took the cup gratefully, wrapping her cold hands around the scalding cardboard.

'My fingers are so cold, this could be burning the skin off me and I wouldn't feel it,' she said.

'Come inside,' Jim urged. 'You'll be no use to the twins if you get hypothermia. Anyway, blue was never your colour, and you'd look terrible in a foil blanket.'

Penny smiled and allowed him to lead her indoors, where

rows of plastic chairs were filled with excited day trippers and the slumped bodies of hungover islanders who'd gone to the mainland in search of fun the night before and had faced the agonising dilemma of taking the early ferry home or getting kicked out of their hotels at eleven. For those tempted to lie in, the reward was spending the day hauling a suitcase around Aberdeen before braving the Buckaroo Boat at four. The Buckaroos in question were a noisy lot; a gaggle of doughty islanders who hit the big shops a few times a year and returned carrying more bags than could be squeezed onto the average airport carousel. Far better to forego sleep and find a quiet corner on the early boat, where the hangover could be nursed away with liberal doses of caffeine and sugar.

Except things were slightly less peaceful this particular morning. Those pale, timorous, cowering beasties who had anticipated a gentle recovery from their overindulgence now cast doleful glances towards the free space in front of the gift shop, where Mrs Hubbard was teaching Gordon some ballroom dancing moves. Her nimble feet belied the surfeit of cocktails of the night before, and she was steadfastly ignoring the complaints of her dance partner that he couldn't salsa because his dungarees were riding up his backside.

'You shouldn't be going commando, then,' snapped Sandra Next Door irritably from behind her copy of that day's Vik Gazette.

'I'm not going commando,' Gordon shot back. 'I'm wearing Jim's boxers.'

Jim glanced at him, one eyebrow raised, and said, 'Mate, how many days is that now?'

'I turned them inside out,' Gordon protested. 'That way, you get an extra day.'

'Wise man,' said Jim.

Beside him, Fiona snorted and muttered, 'You're not the one who has to sleep with him.'

She raised her voice, startling a group of children who

were competing for the dubious honour of being person who could stand on one leg the longest.

'When we get home,' she told her husband, 'I'm going straight to the supermarket for new underpants for you. And I expect a clean willy when I get back.'

The nine-year-old closest to her lost concentration and toppled over, prompting a bout of tears from him and a stern look from his mother.

'Sorry,' Fiona mumbled, leaning over and proffering the paper bag she'd been clutching. 'Salty nuts?'

The woman opened her mouth to say something but was beaten to the punch by Eileen who, from her perch opposite Sandra Next Door, gasped, 'Mangetout, have you seen this?'

She was pointing at the Vik Gazette, waggling a finger frantically at the headline on the front page, which read "Vik Vigilante Strikes Again."

Penny leaned around to take a closer look and beckoned Jim to join her.

Squatting down in front of Sandra, he read the article to the others.

'The Vik Vigilante has taken a fourth victim in a week. The Gazette's own showbiz reporter, Barry 'The Gossip" Glossop, was made to eat his own words yesterday when a masked intruder broke into his home and forced him to ingest a four-page spread on the secret lives of this year's Vik Ballroom Dancing Championship contestants.

'Mr Glossop, 43, described his attacker as a five-foot-seven babe who showed off her midriff and jaw-dropping cleavage as she strutted around in a tight black number from Balaclavas R Us in Vik High Street.

'The attack follows hard on the heels of that on Harminder Singh, founder and only member of Vik's Welsh Men's Choir. Mr Singh, the manager of the garden centre (the one that does the nice high teas, not the other one), had to be coaxed down from the trellis display after consuming an unidentified substance in his morning coffee and hallucinating Alan Titchmarsh naked in the ornamental magnolia.

'The Vik Gazette has reached out to Mr Titchmarsh for comment. Mr Singh, meanwhile, is considering a return to his native Wales, telling the Gazette, "You don't get this sort of thing in Wales, you don't. I'm not being funny. What it is, is Wales is a wonderful place, with no vigilantes. Just proper criminals. I'm going back there, I am, to experience normal crime."

'On Tuesday, local Vikster driver, Brian Miller, found the wheels of his taxi stolen, and on Wednesday, the parish newsletter contained an article about a wife-swapping ring led by church Elder and high heidyin at the Masons, Alec Carmichael. It was alleged that the church collection bowl was doubling up as the car key bowl.

'Letters were left for all four victims, signed by the Vik Vigilante and claiming to be righting wrongs done by them. The Gazette contacted Mr Carmichael and the other members of the alleged wife-swapping ring for comment, but they are currently out of the country. Whether together or separately, is unclear.

'PC Piecey has advised Vik residents to stay indoors, annoy no one and wait until Sergeant Wilson returns from the Police Scotland Bravery Awards to sort it all out.'

Sandra Next Door snorted derisively, flicked the newspaper with a tight snap then turned a page, ignoring the salacious speculation of her companions. Jim, Penny, Eileen and Fiona set straight to discussing who the vigilante might be and what the victims could have done, save for Carmichael who was such an odious little man that his very existence was an offence. More importantly, who was in the wife-swapping ring?

Eileen was just about to expand on her theory that Carmichael had a third nipple to suckle demons when they were interrupted by a very loud clearing of the throat. Penny looked up and saw Gordon jerking his head towards Mrs

Hubbard so violently that she was surprised he didn't give himself whiplash.

'Just to discreetly tell you, like,' he said.

Mrs Hubbard stood stock still in the centre of her makeshift dancefloor. Her cheeks were red, and tears were glistening in her eyes.

'I think she might be worried about the wife-swapping ring,' said Gordon in a stage whisper.

'It's not that,' said Mrs Hubbard. 'I knew all about the wife-swapping. It's the other thing. The four-page spread on the secret lives of this year's Vik Ballroom Dancing Championship contestants. What have they said about me and my Douglas?'

Penny told Jim to scootch over, leaving a free seat between them, and held out a hand to Mrs Hubbard.

'Come sit here, Mrs H. We'll ring Douglas and ask. It won't have been anything dreadful. He'd have warned you if it was something bad.'

'Assuming he read it, dearie,' said Mrs Hubbard, squeezing her ample bottom between Penny and Jim. 'He threatened to sell it in the toilet roll section last week after that article about Randy Mair being a sugar daddy.'

A voice next to Fiona said, 'Mum, what's a sugar daddy?'

'Shh, I'm listening,' the boy's mother whispered sharply.

'No, but what's a–'

'Scaramouche Patel, if I have to tell you once more to mind your own business, there will be no PlayStation for a week.' The woman glared at her son, then smiled at Mrs Hubbard. 'Carry on. You were saying something about Randy Mair being a sugar daddy.'

'I think somebody else needs to be banned from her PlayStation for a week,' grumbled Sandra Next Door.

Mrs Hubbard settled her second-largest handbag on her lap and explained.

'Och, it was just a silly article about Randy Mair being spotted behind the big tree in the village green with his arm around a lass half his age. It turned out he was helping his niece search for her lost necklace.'

'I wonder who spotted him and told Barry the Gossip,' mused Penny, casting a suspicious glance at her friend.

Mrs Hubbard shifted uncomfortably and said, 'I have no idea, but whoever they are, they clearly jumped the gun and have learned their lesson. That Barry Glossop is a spiteful man, which is why I'm worried about what he's written about me.'

The devil in Penny wanted to ask how Mrs Hubbard knew Barry, but the concerned look on her friend's face made her relent. Instead, she urged the older woman to call her husband, certain that Douglas would provide some reassurance.

Mrs Hubbard hunched over her phone, each click of a number bringing her closer to what she expected to be a monumental row with her Douglas. He'd probably held off on saying anything because he didn't want to ruin the awards ceremony. That must be it. She visibly cringed when she heard his sharp greeting.

'What have you done?'

'Is that you, Douglas?'

'Of course it's me. Who did you think it was? The Saturday boy is off with shingles. It's the risk you take when you employ the over-eighties. I wouldn't let him answer the phone anyway. That one couldn't find a box of cheese straws if they poked him up the–'

'Oh, have you been making a cheese straw sculpture, dearie? Very good. I bet it's lovely.'

Douglas took a moment to reply, and when he did, his tone was wary.

'Are you on the sweetie juice at this time in the morning?'

'No.'

'Have you ordered forty boxes of toilet rolls by accident again? Because I'm telling you, the last lot may have come in handy during the pandemic…and then there was that time you poisoned half the island, but–'

'No. I haven't done anything. I was just phoning to see how you are and, eh, whether there had been anything in the paper about the ballroom dancing competition.'

There was a long silence, and then Douglas' voice exploded through the speaker.

'Don't tell me you were the source of that article!'

'What article would that be, dearie?' asked Mrs Hubbard, failing to keep the quiver from her voice.

'Ben and Marjorie McCulloch. The big exposé in the Gazette. I've had people coming in here asking what we're going to do. Not one of them is interested in my cheese straw railway. All they want to know is what's happening now that Marjorie has been outed as being forty-nine.'

'But she's in the over-sixties category. She looks about seventy. She even had a new hip,' Mrs Hubbard protested.

'Aye, well, it seems she's had a hard paper round. She met Ben on Only Flans.'

'Only Fans? I've heard of that. It must have been difficult getting the angles right for the photos, what with her hip. Maybe that's why she got the new one.'

'Flans. Only Flans. Apparently, she does a grand quiche. And talking about paper rounds, that laddie, what do you call him? Jack? He threw Mr Reid's Gazette into his garden the other day and…'

Mrs Hubbard let her Douglas chunter on, only vaguely aware of such concerns as "Vaseline sales have gone down since the Carmichaels left" and "I could have sworn there was a box of rubber gloves on the shelf under the fondant fancies." The wave of relief she'd felt as Douglas explained about Marjorie had left her quite distracted. When he moved on to the mysterious mess on the bowling green, she muttered a quick goodbye and gave Penny a weak smile.

'Somebody has been letting their dog go on the grass at the bowling club,' she explained. 'At least, they think it's a dog. Douglas has fair got his dander up about it, and I can assure you, dearie, it takes a lot to get his dander up these days.'

The others, who at one time or another had all been on the receiving end of Douglas' wrath, regarded her disbelievingly.

'It's true,' she said. 'Doc Harris gave him pills. White ones for dander down and blue ones for dander up. Or were the blue ones for…?'

Her voice trailed off as she mentally sorted through the various medications in Douglas' pill box.

'No,' she said, with a happy grin. 'The blue ones are the special Saturday ones. Ooh, today's Saturday.'

'Do you think the poo on the grass could be the vigilante?' asked Eileen.

'We have to be careful not to blame everything on the vigilante,' Penny cautioned. 'The article says that letters were left for the victims. Was there a note left on the bowling green?'

Mrs Hubbard thought for a moment, then said, 'No, just a parcel. A big brown one.'

Jim snickered and gave her a friendly nudge.

'Good one, Mrs H. Penny's right, though. There's probably a lot of paranoia on the island at the minute, and we'll need to be erm…what's the word? Objective. We'll need to be objective if we're going to investigate.'

Penny, who was still hobbled by the injuries she'd sustained during their last investigation, shot him a surprised look.

'You'll have to count me out,' she said. 'I've enough on my plate with the twins finding Beacon Brodie glued to the lighthouse and peeing blood.'

'Was it him or the twins peeing blood?' asked Eileen. 'Stupid question. Obviously, he's dead, so it must have been the twins."

'It's me who's peeing blood,' said Penny. 'Why do you want to investigate?'

Eileen gave her a queer look and said, 'I don't want to

investigate. I'd rather not look at your pee, thank you very much.'

'I was asking Jim.'

'I'm not looking at your pee either,' protested Jim.

Penny rolled her eyes and sent up a silent prayer to please, God, save her from these idiots.

'Why do you want to investigate the vigilante?' she asked, enunciating each word slowly. 'That's Sergeant Wilson and Easy's job.'

Nonplussed, Jim replied equally slowly, 'Because that is what we do. Losers Club investigates stuff.'

'I thought we were a weight-loss club,' said Fiona, looking pointedly at Gordon, who had taken advantage of the lull in dancing to avail himself of the shop's snack section.

'I'll be back on the diet next week,' he said through a mouthful of crisps.

'Tomorrow,' Fiona insisted.

'Next week, darlin'. Jim and I have to investigate the garden centre, and I hear they do a nice–'

'Mate,' Jim interrupted with a warning look.

'–macaroni pie.'

Jim's shoulders sagged and, avoiding Penny's eye, he muttered, 'Fuck's sake.'

'Mum, what's a fox ache?' asked a small voice next to Fiona.

'Never you mind,' said the mother, standing up. 'We're nearly there. Let's go down to the car.'

She grabbed her son's hand and pulled him towards the exit, glancing back disapprovingly at Jim.

As they disappeared through the door, the boy's voice drifted back to the passenger lounge.

'Fox ache. I don't want to go to the car. I want to investigate the fox ache vigilante and eat macaroni pies.'

'You and me both,' said Jim sullenly.

Penny gazed out of the window at the harbour in the

distance. The woman was right, they were nearly there. Time to make a move.

No sooner had the thought passed through her mind than Captain Rab's gruff tones resounded from the tannoy.

'Nearly there. Get your stuff and prepare to get off ma damn boat!'

In the subsequent stampede, she and Jim quickly became separated from the rest of the group, but he kept a tight grip on her arm as they jostled with the other passengers heading towards the exit. Penny stood on tiptoe, trying to spot Mrs Hubbard's familiar grey curls. Her eyes raked the sea of hats and straggly morning hair, then paused and swivelled back. She had spied another head. One that she hadn't expected to see.

No. Surely it couldn't be…

She turned to ask Jim whether he too recognised the man, but his grip on her arm was gone, and he had been squeezed further back by the crowd.

Deciding that she must be mistaken, Penny pushed the thought of the vaguely familiar pate away and focused on avoiding the backpack of the tourist in front of her.

Still, the doubt lingered and fifteen minutes later, feet once more on solid ground, she cast an eye around the harbour. Then she shook herself and gave a small laugh.

'What's so funny?' asked Jim.

'Nothing. Just me imagining things as usual.'

Soon, in her rush to reach the car, she had dismissed the man from her mind. All that mattered was getting to her parents' house and giving her poor babies the biggest, squeeziest hug ever.

She didn't see the figure in the dark Audi, his hungry gaze following her progress through the car park.

CHAPTER 3

Operation Macaroni Pie began bright and late on Sunday morning. Jim and Gordon, both of whom were under strict instructions to increase their vegetable intake, sat at a plain, beech table in the vast, crowded garden centre café, patiently awaiting the arrival of their sausage sandwiches.

'Sorry for letting the cat out of the bag yesterday,' said Gordon, fiddling anxiously with the button on his dungarees.

'Forget about it,' said Jim. 'You'd think they'd do pies before lunchtime. What sort of place only sells pies from midday onwards?'

Gordon grinned. They were back in familiar territory.

'Aye, having sausage sandwiches is such a chore. Important question. If Penny was a sausage, which one would she be?'

Jim sipped his tea while he gave this due consideration.

Eventually, he said, 'Chorizo. Can be surprisingly sweet but often comes with a spicy kick. What about Fiona?'

'Oh, that's easy. Square sausage. No fancy ingredients. No wrapping. What you see is what you get. What about Sergeant Wilson?'

'Fun fact,' mused Jim. 'In France, they make a sausage

with pig intestines wrapped in colons that smells like decay. It's called an andouillette.'

'Did I hear my name?' said a stern voice, and both men whipped their heads around to see Sergeant Wilson sitting at the next table. She nodded slowly in greeting.

'Wank Boy. Weasley. Now, if I were to describe you as sausages, I'd say you're a couple of red puddings. What are you doing here?'

Caught out, both men flushed guiltily. Gordon's mouth was opening and closing like a startled goldfish, so it was left to Jim to come up with a plausible excuse.

'We thought we'd come for a macaroni pie, but they don't start serving them until twelve.'

He tried to maintain a blank expression but could feel the tips of his ears becoming hot. Sergeant Wilson was giving him one of her Paddington Bear hard stares, normally reserved for the worst of miscreants. She sat unusually still, which in itself was unnerving. Eventually, her lips twisted into a facsimile of a smile, and she gave him a lascivious wink.

'See when you lie, Wank Boy? I can always tell because you get an erection.'

Jim hastily looked down at his crotch then back up at Wilson. She was grinning triumphantly.

'Made you look, made you poop, made you into tattie soup' she said, reciting the old playground jibe in a gleeful, sing-song voice. 'Now we've established that your pants are only metaphorically on fire, do you want to try again? Tell your Auntie Sergeant Wilson the truth.'

Jim gulped and kicked Gordon, hoping to jolt him into action. For his part, Gordon emitted a squeak, dropped his fork and disappeared under the table. There was much scrabbling, but he didn't reappear, so Jim surrendered to the inevitable.

'We thought you'd be too tied up with the murder of Beacon Brodie to investigate the vigilante. We were going to have a chat with Harminder about it.'

Sergeant Wilson made a growling sound, deep in her throat.

'The Major Investigation Team were over here like flies on...well, Brodie. How do flies even get on a corpse in March? You never see them until summer, but there they were. The man was crawling with them. And the maggots. Big, fat, juicy things. He must have been there for days before the kids found him.'

Sergeant Wilson's grim musings were interrupted by the polite cough of the waitress, who had arrived with two sausage sandwiches and a macaroni pie.

The Sergeant tucked a napkin into the neck of her body armour and picked up her cutlery.

'Well, what are you waiting for, Wank Boy. Eat,' she instructed, lifting a piece of creamy macaroni to her lips.

Unable to shake off the notion of fat, juicy maggots, Jim shuddered.

'Suddenly, I'm not hungry anymore,' he muttered.

'All the better for me,' said the Sergeant, leaning over to snatch the sausage sandwich off his plate. 'I wasn't sure whether to ask for a pie, a sausage bap or both. Problem solved. Is Weasley coming out or shall I have his as well?'

Gordon's head appeared above the table, like a hungry meerkat.

'You're not having mine,' he squeaked, scrambling onto his chair and pulling his sandwich towards him. 'Anyway, how did you get a pie? They're not serving them until midday.'

'It's a simple three-step process,' said the Sergeant, pointing her laden fork at Gordon. 'First, you find Mr Singh's mum when she's gone for a wee midnight wander in her birthday suit. Second, you threaten to use your entire taser collection on the care home manager unless he gives her a place. Third, you accept free macaroni pies for life from Mr Singh. You should try it.'

Jim could tell that Gordon had follow-up questions, but he

was in no mood to discuss how a civilian could amass a taser collection without getting arrested. Or sit outside the chipper every night with a pair of binoculars just in case Margaret's mother decided to shed her winceyette and take a stroll down the harbour. Gordon was very fond of the chip shop's deep-fried haggis. No, it was time to divert Sergeant Wilson back to the point.

'You were saying the MIT's here,' he reminded her.

Sergeant Wilson's brow furrowed into a deep scowl, and through a mouthful of pastry, she grumbled, 'Aye. Rumour has it that DCI Fudmuppet's for the chop after turning down the Juniper Key case, so he hates me, hates Dunderheid and is determined to impress the Superintendent by solving this one himself. I've been sent to knock on doors and ask if anybody knows anything.'

'Fudmuppet?' asked Gordon.

'It says Fred Moffat on his warrant card, but that's only because they got the spelling wrong.'

'If you're supposed to be knocking on doors, what are you doing here eating a macaroni pie?' asked Jim.

Sergeant Wilson rolled her eyes and said, 'Community policing. Obviously. Listen, I'm going to solve the Beacon Brodie murder just to spite Fudmuppet, and...it fucking hurts to say this but...I might need some...what's the word when you don't have the womanpower to do something yourself, so you get other people to do it for you?'

'Help?' Jim suggested.

'No, no. I know that one. Easy uses it when we do taser practice in the church hall on Monday nights. Minions! That's the word. I need some minions. I'm commandeering Losers Club, but not you two. You're the weakest links. You carry on with the vigilante macbuggery, and the rest of us will do the proper investigating.'

'But we'll need Penny,' said Gordon. 'She's always in charge of this stuff.'

Sergeant Wilson gave him her sternest police scowl and

said, 'No way, Weasley. Fanny Features is mine. You can have Fred to be in charge. I also bagsy Space Cadet, Curtain Twitcher and Thatcher.'

'But I wanted to bagsy Space Ca…Eileen,' said Gordon. 'And anyway, you hate Thatcher. What do you want her for?'

'You're right. You can have Thatcher,' said the Sergeant.

'What did you have to go and say that for?' asked Jim, glaring at Gordon. 'Now we're stuck with Sandra Next Door for at least a week.'

'Nae takesie backsies,' Sergeant Wilson said with a grin. 'I am the A team, and you are the Z team.'

Jim was about to object to this characterisation of himself and Gordon, but Harminder Singh chose that moment to appear. He was a short man, sporting a greying beard and blue turban. His eyes twinkled with good humour as he set down macaroni pies in front of the two men.

'I heard you wanted these. Any friend of Martisha Wilson's is a friend of mine,' he told them in a beautiful Welsh lilt.

'Loose acquaintances,' the Sergeant protested. 'I never say the fucking eff word.'

'Thanks, and ignore her,' said Jim. 'She hasn't had her morning arrest.'

'Yet,' growled the police officer, glaring at him meaningfully. 'Pull up a chair, Mr Singh, and tell me what you know about the murder of Beacon Brodie.'

'Nothing,' said Harminder, taking a seat beside her. 'I heard that Hector and Edith Moon found him. Is that true? They must be in an awful state. If that happened to my Alisa, she would need so much therapy.'

Sergeant Wilson raised an eyebrow and wondered whether she should remind Mr Singh that his precious daughter had been down on the beach at the time, drinking a bottle of vodka that she'd shoplifted from the supermarket. Only the thought of no more free pies stayed her tongue, so instead she grunted, 'Teenagers.'

'I hear you're thinking of moving back to Wales,' Jim commented, moving the conversation on before Mr Singh could ask him how the twins were coping.

The truth was that they were coping well. Both were delighted. There had been an initial moment of shock, but by the next morning the tale had grown legs, and they were enjoying their fifteen minutes of fame. The notoriety of their father, Alex, meant that the story had been picked up nationally, and by the time Penny returned from the mainland, there was a reporter from the Sun sitting in Mary's living room, drinking tea and trying to be polite about the freshly baked cheese and chocolate chip cookies she'd pressed upon him.

'You saw that in the Gazette, did you? About me going back home?' asked Mr Singh. 'Don't believe everything you read in the papers. True, I was in shock. I mean, who would poison my tea with hallucinogenic drugs?'

Sergeant Wilson was about to suggest his own daughter, when Gordon chimed in, asking, 'What exactly happened?'

'I was having my tea as usual. I always have a cuppa first thing when I come to work. It's a special herbal blend that Mrs Hubbard gets in for me.'

'From India?' asked Gordon.

Mr Singh eyed him curiously and said, 'From Wales, of course. Why would you assume India?'

'Sorry, it's just that she has a pen pal in India. Some lad from a call centre in Mumbai. He was only trying to sell her a mobile phone deal but somehow found himself agreeing to a monthly subscription to her buttery delivery service. What with India being where tea comes from, I wondered if she was getting him to post her tea when she posts his butteries.'

Mr Singh looked relieved.

'That makes perfect sense. For a moment, I thought you were going to say something racist.'

'I've nothing against the Welsh,' Gordon assured him. 'Although, I am curious about the sheep sha–'

'Glad we've cleared that up,' Jim interjected firmly. 'Carry on with your story, Mr Singh.'

'There isn't much more to it. I drank my tea and the next thing I know, Alan Titchmarsh is there, refusing to put on his underpants. Then I woke up in the hospital and PC Piecey said he'd found a letter under the kettle. Which reminds me, Sergeant Wilson, when can I get my kettle and shortbread back? PC Piecey said they were sent off for forensic testing.'

Sergeant Wilson shifted uncomfortably in her seat and muttered, 'Aye, erm, they'll have taken the kettle to bits so you might have to manage with the spare one.'

She'd be having words with Easy when she got back. If she'd known the wee sod had eaten all the biscuits, she'd never have given him a commendation for sourcing a new police kettle.

'What exactly did the letter say?' asked Jim.

Mr Singh dug into his pocket and produced a piece of paper and a pair of spectacles. He slid the spectacles on and ceremoniously unfolded the paper. With great aplomb, he read, 'Did you enjoy your high tea? Wrong righted. The Vik Vigilante.'

He held the note out to Jim and said, 'Keep it. I made nine copies, I did.'

Jim was intrigued. The note was typed, so there were no clues about the author. He and Gordon quizzed Mr Singh as to any enemies or whether he'd upset someone recently, but the man shrugged and pleaded ignorance.

'It sounds as though whoever did it must have been familiar with your routine. What about the garden centre?' asked Jim. Any disgruntled staff or customers?'

'Oh, there are always those. Mrs Next Door is the worst, I tell you. She bought leaf shine for her yucca and wanted to sue me because the leaves weren't shiny enough. Then there was the time she broke into my kitchen during the night and cleaned it because she'd found a mark on her teacup. It was a manufacturing fault! Still, she always comes back for begonias. Apparently, a terrible cat keeps killing them off with,' Mr Singh lowered his voice to a whisper, 'faeces.'

'We know it wasn't Sandra because she was with us at the time,' Jim grudgingly admitted. 'What about high tea? Does that have any significance?'

He noted that Mr Singh avoided eye contact when icily assuring them, 'My garden centre high teas are of the finest quality.'

So that was it. Something to do with the high teas. People were quite particular about their high tea. One didn't want to confuse it with afternoon tea. The Scottish high tea came with toast or bread and a proper main course, followed by cakes. Afternoon tea was just sandwiches and cakes - wishy-washy girl food. Jim would have called afternoon tea an English thing, except that it had taken over to the point where you couldn't get proper Scottish fish and chips and toast anymore. He thought back to childhood days out on the mainland. A visit to Auntie Maud, followed by a poke around Huntly castle and a go on the trampolines at the park, then high tea at the Gordon Arms. You couldn't beat it.

'Have any customers complained about your high teas?' he asked.

Mr Singh visibly stiffened and repeated, 'My garden centre high teas are of the finest quality.'

Definitely the high tea, then. Jim made a mental note to check them out. Maybe he and Gordon should come back and sample one, just to be sure, ye ken.

When Mr Singh had gone, Sergeant Wilson lazily stirred her coffee and said, 'That'll be the last free macaroni pie you get from him, turdnuggets. There's a knack to questioning witnesses and you two don't have it.'

'Oh aye, what's that then?' Jim retorted. 'Sit on them until they tell you everything you need to know?'

'That as well,' the Sergeant conceded, 'But for the more obliging witness, you need proper people skills, like they teach you at police school. Encourage them gently. Tease the facts out. Watch and learn, fartspangles, watch and learn.'

With that, she abruptly marched off in the direction of the garden centre exit, her large bottom narrowly missing displays of trowels, candles and china knick-knacks. She disappeared around a corner, scattering a shelf of Wellington boots in her wake, and a moment later, her voice issued stridently forth from the PA system that the cashier normally used for crowd control on Half Price Cake for Pensioners Tuesdays.

'Hi-de-hi. If any bastard here knows anything about the murder of Beacon Brodie or the Vik Vigilante, come and see me in the café, or your life will not be worth living.'

There was a pause then…

'Police Scotland thanks you for your cooperation.'

There was a general scraping of chair legs against hardwood flooring, and Jim watched in astonishment as a queue formed next to the table at which the Sergeant had been sitting.

'See,' said Wilson, suddenly appearing beside him and sending Gordon scooting backwards in fright. 'Gentle persuasion.'

She regarded the queue, which was now snaking between the tables and out into the main body of the garden centre.

'I reckon I've got most of South Street here. Saves knocking on a few doors and gives me time for another coffee. Off you pop, Weasley. And I'll have a slice of Dundee cake while you're at it.'

While Gordon scuttled off to order another round of teas and coffees, Jim listened in to Sergeant Wilson's interviews. Who knew that the power of persuasion involved so many swear words, he thought, as she sent Mrs Mortimer sobbing back to her table.

Gordon returned bearing mugs, and both men sat through the interminable questioning of people who knew little beyond what they'd heard at the pub or bingo. Some of them were quite surprised to be asked anything at all. They were only here because they'd seen a queue and joined it. All in all, Jim and Gordon agreed, this interview business was quite dull. Sergeant Wilson's job wasn't as glamorous as it seemed. Oh no, it wasn't all free pies and making Easy dance to the tune of a thousand volts. In fact, Jim and Gordon were starting to think they could go home and simply get the highlights from Sergeant Wilson later.

Sergeant Wilson, her internal police radar finely tuned to the intentions of potential troublemakers, handcuffed them both to their chairs.

'You two decided to stick your fingers in my investigative pie, so they'll remain firmly stuck until I'm done.'

With a sigh, both men yielded to the inevitable and miserably wondered how a morning that promised all the breakfasty delights had been brought so low.

Then came the interview with Pat Hughes from the Post Office, and that's when things got interesting.

CHAPTER 4

Penny hadn't gone back to her own house yet. Exhausted from seemingly needless worries about the twins and feeling ground down by the pain in her kidneys, she'd slept in her old bedroom in her parents' bungalow, taking comfort from the familiar dip in the mattress and the warmth of her border collie, Timmy, who had nosed his way under the duvet and was now snoring gently next to her, sending wafts of dog breath directly into her face. With a grunt, she turned over, only to be greeted by a shaft of mid-morning sunlight streaming through the gap in the curtains.

'The gods are telling us it's time to get up,' she grumbled, giving Timmy a nudge with her elbow.

Startled awake, Timmy turned and attempted to scramble off the bed, taking the duvet with him as he did so and leaving Penny, suddenly cold and exposed, to lever herself into a sitting position.

'The question is,' she told him, 'which one of us gets to go for a pee first?'

Timmy's ears pricked up at the mention of going for a pee, and he danced his most delirious pee dance by the bedroom door, just in case his human was in any doubt as to the order of priority.

Penny grabbed her phone and pulled on an old jumper over her pyjamas before releasing the hound. She smiled as Timmy bolted down the hall, claws clattering against the wooden floor, a furry bottom taking out the coat stand when he lost control on the corner in his haste to reach the kitchen. In bare feet, she stumbled after him, righting the coat stand and pushing him away while she fumbled the key into the back door lock. With a low woof, he sprang joyfully into the garden, leaving Penny to take care of her own morning needs.

A missed call and six texts, she noted as she sat on the loo.

The first text was from Jim:

```
Just to warn you that SW has bagsied you,
Eileen and Mrs H.
```

The next four were from Sergeant Wilson:

```
Welcome to the a team fanny features
briefing 1 pm lighthoose dont tell easy
because he is a ducking grass
```

```
ducking
```

```
no ducking ducking for ducks sake
```

```
ducking phone
```

. . .

What was that all about? And had the woman never heard of punctuation and capital letters? You'd think she'd have learned her lesson after the Horse, Cock and Bush incident of 2019, when the judge had misunderstood her description of Stevie Mains as never being away from the village pub and sentenced the poacher to an extra six months for lewd behaviour.

The last text was from Minky Wallace:

```
Can you pop by the café? Need a favour
```

Ooh, very mysterious, thought Penny. Today is shaping up to be quite interesting.

By the time she had showered and dressed, the twins were in the kitchen happily ruining their grandparents' pans. She turned down Edith's burnt offering of bacon, beans and eggs in favour of coffee and the Vik Gazette crossword.

'It's too late for breakfast and too early for lunch,' she declared. 'I'll grab a sandwich while I'm out.'

'Where are you going?' asked Hector. 'Can we come?'

Definitely not, thought Penny. A return visit to the lighthouse won't be on the cards for a long while.

'Yes, of course,' she said. 'I'm meeting Sergeant Wilson.'

'What? Voluntarily?' asked Edith, her tone one of disbelief.

'Something like that. Still want to come?'

Hector and Edith exchanged glances and said in unison, 'No way.'

Penny felt a stab of guilt. Her wee darlings were obviously desperate to spend time with her. She'd barely seen them in a week, and even though they seemed fine, there must be some lingering trauma after their discovery of the lighthouse keeper.

'How about I cancel and do something with you both instead?' she offered.

'Nah, it's okay, Mother,' Hector told her, nonchalantly biting into a charred slice of bacon. 'We only wanted to come because we thought you were going shopping and might buy us something. Edith has to work this afternoon, and I promised to take Granny to her over-60s Burlesque class in the church hall.'

'He's making a boob tube video of us,' said Mary, strolling into the kitchen, her six-foot frame bedecked in a purple feather boa, sequinned corset and green lounge pants. 'We're going to go virus, become boob tube famous and influence all the social medias. Has anyone seen Len? I've had an idea for an over-60s male stripper group called Hingin' Mince, but he refuses to discuss it. Mm, I'll have some of that bacon.'

'Have you checked the shed?' Penny asked.

'Of course,' her mother snorted. 'I'm not daft. It's locked.'

'From the inside or the outside?'

Mary halted in her attempt to pick a piece of bacon from the pan without burning her fingers.

'Oh. Good point, Chunky. I'll check.'

She wedged her feet into Len's slippers, which were two sizes too small, and trundled out the back door, muttering, 'Such a shame we don't have pound notes anymore. I wonder where the Magic Mike boys keep all that loose change...'

Penny turned to the twins, adopted her sternest expression and said, 'Whatever you do, don't let her watch The Full Monty.'

They seemed about to object, so she held up a warning hand.

'No, I don't want to hear about how you're not responsible for Granny. Every one of us is responsible for Granny, except Granny. Subject closed. Now, help me with the crossword. Three down. Eleven letters. Chair stud.'

She didn't finish the crossword, instead taking it with her to Cuppachino, much to the chagrin of Len who, having been enticed out of the shed by a plate of freshly baked scones, had been quite looking forward to some quality Len time in the loo with his newspaper. Penny knew this because he'd texted her:

```
Your mother used the power of scones on me.
Where is my poospaper?
```

Peering over her shoulder, Minky Wallace, the café owner, said, 'Aye, your mother does a nice scone, when she sticks to the recipe. I'm nae a fan of the ham and pineapple ones.'

'I was hoping the weird cooking phase would wear off,' said Penny, 'but since they announced the village coronation street-party, she's been worse than ever. Although at first she thought it was a Coronation Street themed party, and all the actors would be there. She spent days trying to persuade Dad they should have one of those lists. You know, the list of people you get a free pass to sleep with if you ever meet them? Ken Barlow is at number three.'

'He'd be a fair age now,' said Minky.

'She says she likes the older man. Let's just pray that Sirs Ian McKellen and Michael Gambon never visit the island.'

With a lascivious wink, Minky snickered, 'Aye, your mother in a threesome with Gandalf and Dumbledore. That would be magic. What about your dad? Who did he have?'

'Felicity Kendal, obviously, and all the men mum picked. I think he felt sorry for them and wanted to offer a more reasonable alternative.'

'That's our Len. One ring to rule them all,' Minky grinned. 'Now, you didn't just come here to blether about your parents. I want to run something past you.'

Penny was intensely curious, but her stomach was also sending urgent signals about the sandwich it had been promised.

'Is there any chance of something to eat while we talk?'

she asked. 'I'm meeting Sergeant Wilson shortly, so I should probably line my stomach.'

Minky reached for her apron, which hung limply on a hook behind the kitchen door, and sighed.

'Officially, I don't open until twelve, but seeing as you've got an ordeal ahead of you, I'll make you a pity panini.'

The café was small, and the kitchen was only a few feet away, behind a low counter bedecked in cakes under glass domes. Turning her framed health and safety certificate to face the wall, Minky propped the kitchen door open with a fire extinguisher so that they could continue their conversation.

As she sprinkled layers of onion, chicken and mozzarella onto the bread, she asked, 'Have you seen the headlines in your dad's poospaper today?'

Penny hadn't. She'd been expecting yet another few pages of speculation about the Beacon Brodie murder, so had turned straight to the crossword. Now, however, the concerned note in Minky's voice made her flip the newspaper over.

'Vik Vigilante claims fifth victim,' she read aloud. 'The Gazette has received a letter from the Vik Vigilante, complaining that we have neglected to mention his or her fifth victim.'

Penny looked up at Minky, who was standing in the doorway, heavily tattooed hands on hips.

'They haven't said who the fifth victim is. I'm guessing you know.'

Minky nodded disconsolately, her eyes studying the slate floor tiles as if the solution to her problems could be found in the cracks between them.

'It's my Zack,' she admitted. 'Look, I've no right to ask you for any favours after what he did, but we all know he's thicker than a bowl of second-day broth. I hoped that bringing him up away from my dad and sisters might make a difference. Turns out the Wallace genes are strong buggers.

Anyway, even though he's in jail, the Vik Vigilante still got to him.'

'What? Like, *shanked* him or something?'

The word sounded very odd coming from Penny, and Minky's lips twitched in amusement.

'No, nothing like that. They took it out on his girlfriend.'

'Zack has a girlfriend?' gasped Penny, then instantly regretted the tone of disbelief. 'Sorry, that didn't come out right. I meant, what's happened to his girlfriend.'

'Hang on. I'll finish your panini, then I'll explain.'

A few minutes later, Minky slid the hot sandwich and a latte onto the table and sat down opposite Penny.

'He's been seeing Dirty Dolores,' she said. 'That lass with the beauty salon on North Street.'

'The one who always smells like feet?'

'That's the one. Zack doesn't seem to mind the smell. He says you get used to it after a while. She's nice enough, I suppose, although a good bit older than Zack. Offered to do my lips for free, but I said no. Look at me. What would I want wi' lip fillers? If I needed to look like I'd been punched in the mouth, I'd start a fight in the pub on a Friday night.'

Penny regarded Minky's muscular, tattoed arms and her spiky, green hair. She knew that beneath the frilly apron, there were enough body piercings to bring airport security to its knees. Minky's self-esteem did not require an Instagram pout.

'Fair enough,' said Penny. 'What happened to Dirty Dolores?'

'She's been offering them tanning injections on the side, even though it's illegal. She says somebody roofied her vodka and injected her. We don't know how much they used, but she's a right bonnie shade of teak. Here, I took a photo to send to the furniture shop in Aberdeen. I've been after a new wardrobe.'

Minky scrolled through her phone and stopped on a photograph of a startled woman standing in a bedroom.

'You see?' said Minky, zooming in on the image. 'You

wouldn't think teak would go with the sage walls, but it does.'

'How do you know it was the vigilante?' asked Penny. 'Could it maybe have been a prank by some of her pals?'

'No, there was a note.'

Minky scrolled through her photos again and brought up an image of a typed note. The words were printed at the top of what appeared to be an ordinary sheet of white paper. Again, she touched two nail-bitten fingers to the screen and zoomed in so that Penny could read the text:

"Have a taste of your own medicine. Wrong righted. The Vik Vigilante."

'I don't understand,' said Penny. 'This sounds more like someone getting back at Dolores for a treatment that went badly. What has it got to do with Zack?'

Minky shifted uncomfortably in her chair and looked down at the table.

'Just before he went to prison, he had an argument with one of his mates and locked him in Dirty Dolores' sunbed. It was an hour before anyone found the lad and he couldn't sit down for a month. Turns out that the sweat pools around your bum cheeks and his arse was fried. I was so ashamed. I had to have a serious word with my son. I've told him to use one of the standy-up sunbeds next time. Anyway, I think they went after Dolores because they couldn't get to Zack.'

'I suppose it could be aimed at either of them,' said Penny. 'Have you ever thought that Zack's a bit...erm...maybe he should see someone?'

Minky sat up straight and glowered at Penny.

'What are you trying to say about my boy?' she snapped.

'Jjjjust that, well, mmmaybe there are some issues?' Penny stuttered. Minky may be the nicest Wallace, but she was still a Wallace.

Her relief was almost palpable when the woman grinned and said, 'Ha! You should have seen your face there. Me doing the mama bear act. Aye, he's been barred from every child psychologist in Scotland. Oppositional defiance disorder, apparently. In our day, they just called it being a wee shite. Och well, now that he's technically an adult, there's not much I can do, other than hope he comes out of the jail with his lesson learned.'

'So, what do you want me to do about it?' asked Penny. 'The vigilante, not the oppositional thingy.'

Minky had clearly given this some thought because her lips immediately tightened and she leaned forward, stabbing the table to hammer home her point.

'Obviously, whatever you do, I don't want my Zack to get arrested again. Dolores too, although that's mainly because she'll stay teak for the next six months and I'll need her to come to the other furniture shop so I can colour match her against some bedside tables. I mean, it would be really annoying if I took them all the way home only to find they don't go with the new wardrobe.

'Sorry, I'm blethering on about furniture when I should be making sure that Losers Club will take my case. Do a bit of investigating. I can pay if you like. I've improved Hector's chocolate cake recipe, and I've got a whole one out the back.'

'You do know that we're a weight loss and healthy lifestyle group?' Penny reminded her.

'Aye. A crime-fighting weight loss and healthy lifestyle group,' said Minky. 'I can't see why you wouldn't take the case. Or is it just murders that you do?'

'We don't murder–' Penny started to say, then sighed. 'What I mean is, we're not supposed to eat cake. Jim's already looking into the vigilante, so I'll pass the details to him. No payment required, and if Jim comes to you and even hints that he'd like a slice of cake, you're to refuse. He survived on sausages and chips while we were away, so he's back on the healthy eating plan. I think you should tell the police, though. There might be some important evidence in the note.'

Minky regarded her pleadingly and laid a hand on her arm.

'Maybe you could tell Sergeant Wilson for me and ask her to be discreet. Cut Zack some slack about the sunbed thing. She listens to you.'

Penny doubted that very much. The only person that Sergeant Wilson listened to was Sergeant Wilson. The woman ploughed her own furrow through life. Nevertheless, underneath all the bluster and sitting on folk was a kind heart. Penny knew first-hand from their recent trip to Inverurie that the Sergeant was the person you'd want on your side in a crisis. Most people had a good Wilson tale to tell, which was likely why the islanders tolerated all the other nonsense. Well, that and she was quite scary.

'I'll ask Mrs Hubbard,' said Penny. 'She seems to have some control over the woman.'

'Thanks,' said Minky. 'Just one final thing.'

She reached into her apron pocket and produced a sealed plastic sandwich bag.

'Dirty Dolores' knickers,' she explained. 'The vigilante injected her in the bum, so I thought there might be some DNA on them. Although, you'll want to wear a mask when you open it. Turns out it's nae her feet that smell of feet.'

CHAPTER 5

Humming happily to herself, Sergeant Wilson headed through the garden centre car park. She had a strange feeling that she'd forgotten something but couldn't think what. Och, it would come back to her later.

She poked her car key into the armhole of her stab vest and gave her right breast a satisfying scratch. If everything that Pat Hughes had said was true, then she'd better round up the turdnuggets and get investigating.

Grimacing, she slid her other hand down the neck of her stab vest and rooted around, deciding that perhaps she should keep her phone in a pocket rather than her bra because it probably looked like she was attacking her boob from all sides. Maybe she'd ditch the police notebook to free up some space. It only ever got used for shopping lists anyway.

Hampered by the stiff body armour, she twisted her hand to dig deeper, then with a bark of triumph, she extracted the phone and quickly typed a text to Penny. Then followed it up with a few clarifications. Ducking autocorrect.

She looked at the key in her hand. Something was there, poking out of the filing cabinet at the back of her brain. Something to do with a key. What was it? Had she forgotten to put the padlock on the police biscuit tin? That Fudmuppet was a greedy bugger when it came to the KitKats. Aye, that must be it. It was all Easy's fault. He was supposed to remind her about these things.

Getting into her vehicle, she began to compose a text to Easy, telling him to stop interviewing people and get himself down to the biscuit shop for six KitKats and a packet of the cheap custard creams. 'Leave the custard creams out as a diversion so they dont go looking for the good biscuits,' she instructed. Then, job done, she turned the key in the ignition and drove off to do some very important interviewing of her own. At the chip shop.

In the garden centre café, Jim was also texting Penny, although his typing was much slower due to it being executed one-handed.

'I can't believe she went away and left you two handcuffed to your chairs,' said Pat Hughes, plonking herself onto a seat next to him. 'What's she going to use if she needs to arrest folk? As if there weren't enough problems on this island already.'

'And we're stuck,' Jim pointed out.

'Well, there's that, of course. But, really, with everything that's been going on, you'd think the woman would be more organised. We're counting on her. Here's me, just back from my holidays, and the island has gone to the dogs without me.'

Jim sighed, unsurprised at Pat's lack of interest in his predicament. He liked the Post Office shop owner. She was the Port Vik equivalent of Mrs Hubbard, only shorter, darker-skinned and about twenty years younger, with a penchant for brightly coloured cardigans and tall men. Being a six-footer himself, he'd been on the receiving end of her flirtation more than once. A couple of times, in the days before Penny, he'd considered taking her up on it. She was an attractive woman and had the sort of soft Glaswegian accent that made him feel warm and fuzzy inside, like being tucked in at night by Lorraine Kelly. Not in a sexy way! More as if Lorraine was reading him a bedtime story and folding the blanket beneath his chin. And then she'd give him a kiss on the forehead and…oh bugger, he'd just sullied Goddess Lorraine Kelly. He was officially a pervert. Penny must not find out about this. He'd never hear the end of it.

He dragged his filthy mind back to safer ground. Pat. It was the gossiping which had put him off. Pat did like, as she put it, "a guid blether." Jim wasn't sure whether it was a shop owner thing, but between them, Pat and Mrs Hubbard possessed an encyclopaedic knowledge of every skeleton in Vik's cupboard. Although perhaps this wasn't such a bad thing when he thought about it. He could use that to his advantage.

'How did you know about Brodie being a thief?' he asked.

'I never reveal my sources,' Pat sniffed. 'But let's just say that I have a friend on the mainland called Diane Turner, who knew him in his younger days. She recognised him when the Press and Journal did that feature on Britain's last lighthouse keepers. He was in the background in one of the photos. If you ask me, he was in Vik hiding his sordid past.'

'If my real name was Richard Less, I'd probably run away and change it,' said Gordon. 'I wouldn't need a sordid past as an excuse.'

'Do you think he could have stolen something, and the Vik Vigilante killed him for it?' asked Jim.

'Randy Mair doesn't think so,' said Pat. 'He told Moira Bell, who told me that he'd heard from Carly French who got it from Doc Harris that Brodie was drugged with something that paralysed him and would have killed him if the heart attack hadn't got him first. Everybody agrees that the vigilante's a nuisance, not a killer. Obviously, my sources are confidential, so keep it under your bonnet.'

'What about the identity of the vigilante?' asked Gordon. 'Have you heard anything about him…or her…or them?'

Pat's eyes widened, and she leaned across the table, asking in a stage whisper, 'Are you saying it could be a they?'

'I dunno,' whispered Gordon, moving forwards so that his head was almost touching hers. 'What's a they?'

'I'm not sure. It's got something to do with identifying as… What I mean is, you maybe feel different on the inside from how you look on the outside. I think.' Pat shrugged. 'I'm struggling to keep up with it all. Even computers, and I was always very good at them. I'm only forty-eight and it already feels like the modern world is slipping away from me.'

'I thought you were fifty-five,' said Jim.

'I identify as forty-eight,' snapped Pat.

'I was only thinking that the vigilante could even be two people,' said Gordon glumly, slumping back in his chair. 'What do you think, Jim?'

'Aye, you make an interesting point.'

Gordon perked up at this. He didn't think he'd ever made an interesting point before. Maybe he should ask Jim to repeat that in front of Fiona, just so she would know that he said interesting things.

'We need a starting place for our vigilante investigation,' he declared, determined to capitalise on his being interesting. 'I suggest that we make a list.'

'A list of what?' asked Jim, immediately regretting the question because whatever came out of his friend's mouth next was practically guaranteed to be something along the lines of a list of the stingiest wasps.

Gordon regarded him blankly for a moment, letting the old brain cogs whir. A list definitely sounded like a good idea; something important and official. Maybe they could make one of them bucket lists. They could start here in the garden centre and then move to Hardy's Nails, the ironmongers in town. That's where you could find all the best buckets. He had just opened his mouth to suggest this when he was beaten to the punch by Pat.

'How about we make a list of the victims and I tell you what I know about them,' she suggested. 'Shall I order three macaroni pies to see us through? It's officially lunchtime now. Do you want chips as well?'

'God, you're even better than Mrs Hubbard,' gasped Gordon, all thoughts of buckets forgotten. 'I do like a woman who appreciates a pie and chips.'

Pat's cheeks flushed, and she beamed at Gordon.

'Thank you. How tall are you?'

'About the same height as his *wife*,' said Jim sharply, giving her a warning look.

She scraped back her chair, winked at Gordon and said, 'Pity. The dungarees give you an alluring air of mystery.' Then, without a backward glance, she headed to the café counter to place their order.

'Do you hear that, Jim?' said Gordon. 'I'm telling you, it's these new dungers. I'm giving off pure animal magnetism.'

'Aye, pal, Brad Pitt's shaking in his designer jeans at the prospect o' the competition. Stop flirting with Pat and listen. We need a plan that goes beyond an excuse to come in here for macaroni pies every day. We'll get the gossip from her on each of the victims then visit everybody one by one. We can do this. We can solve this. Sergeant Wilson thinks we're the Z team. Let's prove her wrong.'

'Go the Z team!' shouted Gordon, his attempt to offer a high five stymied by the fact that one hand was clutching a cappuccino with All The Sprinklings (he'd been quite specific about that) and the other was handcuffed to the chair.

Jim frowned, suddenly realising that making any list at all would be challenging while they were still attached to their chairs. However, his concerns were soon put to bed when Pat returned with three macaroni pies and a set of bolt cutters.

'That'll be thirty quid please,' she said. 'Mr Singh told me he couldn't sell them if they got damaged, so I had to buy them.'

'Most expensive macaroni pie I've ever had,' Jim grumbled, but allowed her to wrestle his wallet from his jeans pocket and extract the required funds. He couldn't swear to it, but the wrestling did seem to take a while and her fingers came dangerously close to little Jim, who was nestling quietly like a wee traitor in his underpants, ready to poke his head up next time big Jim told Sergeant Wilson a lie. He knew she was talking rubbish, but now she'd said it, the thought was firmly lodged in his brain and the outcome was inevitable.

Oblivious to Jim's discomfort, Pat pulled the wallet free, helped herself to the money and kneeled behind the two nervous men, who were suddenly very conscious that a sharp tool was about to be wielded at their wrists. Deftly, she severed the handcuffs and popped the bolt cutters in her handbag, claiming that they might come in handy for personal use. Nobody wanted to ask.

An hour, several cups of tea and eight toilet trips by Gordon later, Jim sat back and reviewed the notes he'd made in the back pages of Edith's old science jotter, a dogeared thing which had been given to him by Penny when she'd caught him on Wikipedia doing what he claimed was important vet research. He had actually disappeared down an internet rabbit hole when he'd asked Google what a chair would look like if your legs bent the other way, but she didn't need to know that.

Pat Hughes had gone, presumably to meddle in someone else's business, and the lunchtime rush had died down, leaving the two men alone in the café to chew over what they had learned.

The notes on Harminder Singh were fairly scant. Pat knew little about the man, other than that he was happily married and blissfully unaware that his teenage daughter was the scourge of the island. There was no love lost between Mr Singh and Jenny Balfour, the manager of the other garden centre. Nobody knew why. Pat had heard from Mrs Hubbard who got it from Ernie on the Other Side that Mr Singh recently replaced Jenny's potting compost with ericaceous compost after she filled his water feature with liquid sulphur. However, in Pat's opinion, Mr Singh's most heinous crime was to serve cucumber sandwiches instead of toast for high tea. It was the talk of the island. Someone in the kitchen had ordered a hundred cucumbers instead of ten and, as Mr Singh had frantically explained to his angry customers, there was only so much you could do with a cucumber.

'The consensus was that he'd missed off shoving them up his own, well, you know,' Pat had explained. 'So, he decided to give them away at the door. I took one, but it didn't agree with my arthritis.'

'Is your condition affected by diet, then?' Jim had asked.

'No,' came the reply. 'I carried it to the car, but my fingers are so stiff that sometimes once they get into a position, they're impossible to move. I waved at Gary Bield when I was driving past the loch and he road raged me for calling him a wanker.'

Ignoring the odd looks from the other customers, she'd waggled a half-closed fist under Gordon's nose.

Jim's eyes moved down to the next victim, Alec Carmichael. The notes covered three pages. The man was, as Sergeant Wilson would say, a prolific twatbadger. There didn't seem to be a person on the island with whom he hadn't quarrelled. To Jim's mind, the main items on the list were:

1. **Parks his Range Rover in disabled space at supermarket. Does not have badge. Also uses ten items or less till when has full trolley. Enemies – everyone on the island.**
2. **Never puts his phone on silent in church. Reverend Green finding it increasingly difficult to turn the other cheek.**

3. Sends his neighbours (Mei and Keith Hee-Hawes) reminders to mow their lawn. Once mowed their lawn himself and tried to charge them a fee.
4. Put his own hair in his soup at Cuppachino and refused to pay. Gordon Finch saw him do it and says Minky went mental.
5. Banned Geoff Next Door from the golf club after Sandra Next Door put bleach in all the holes to make them more hygienic during Covid.
6. Pat doesn't know much about the wife-swapping but heard that Geoff Next Door asked if they could take Sandra for a couple of hours so he could get peace to watch the football.
7. As Grand Wizard of the Freemasons refused to let Iona Cameltoe, local drag artist and pig farmer, join the society on the grounds that "only real men wear the aprons around here." Numpty.

Moving on, thought Jim, Glossop the Gossip had been made to eat his own words, which could relate to something he'd written. The man had a history of misogyny and creative reporting that had proved too much even for the worst of the tabloids and had been relegated to reporting from the sleepy backwater of Vik following the Photoshop scandal last year, when it emerged that he'd been adding cellulite to the pictures of bikini-clad reality TV stars for the past decade.

Since arriving on Vik a few months ago, he had done a centre page spread on Mrs Hay and Ernie on the Other Side (Older Woman Seduces Vulnerable Man With Peppermint Slice), a feature on the Vik Hotel being a den of iniquity (Three in a Bed Romps at Honeypot Hotel) and an unflattering article on the partners of the five-a-side football team (WAGs or Hags?). As Jim was the goalie, Penny's name came up in the article, where she was described as a curvy babe with the thighs of a premiership midfielder. It was just as well that Penny had been away at the time of the assault on Glossop because she'd threatened to remove his testicles with a spoon. Still, the man hadn't been on the island long enough for Pat to find out any gossip about him, so the vigilante was quite possibly someone in those articles or, of course, the latest one about Ben and Marjorie McCulloch. Nevertheless, a sizeable suspect pool.

Finally, there was Brian Miller. The taxi driver shamelessly used his vehicle to conduct affairs and had been known to accept…alternative means of payment. The guy was a sleazeball, but to Pat's knowledge, he hadn't done anything that he hadn't been doing for years anyway. They needed to talk to him to find out more.

'We can't visit Carmichael because he's taken off,' Jim concluded. 'But we can visit the people he's upset recently. Then we'll speak to Glossop and Brian Miller.'

Gordon nodded enthusiastically and said, 'I've been thinking about Barry Glossop. If we're going to visit the people he's upset, we can probably rule out Mrs Hay and Ernie on the Other Side because they're both about a hundred and fifty years old. You can speak to your five-a-side mates. Which only leaves Rachel and Martin MacDonald at the hotel and the McCullochs.'

'Good thinking,' said Jim.

He scribbled something on Edith's old jotter and passed it over for Gordon's approval:

List of folk to speak to

Reverend Green
    The Hee-Hawes
    Minky
    Geoff Next Door

Rachel and Martin MacDonald
Five-a-side team
The McCullochs
Barry Glossop
Brian Miller

Gordon quickly scanned it and was just about to remind Jim to add Iona Cameltoe when they were interrupted by a burst of "I'm too sexy for my shirt, too sexy for my shirt, so sexy it hurts."

'Bloody Penny. She thinks she's funny changing my ringtone,' Jim spluttered, lifting the phone to his ear. 'I'm going to put her right in her place,'

'Hello. Aye, aye, aye. No! No. Aye. Well, just…aye, okay. Aye, dear. Love you too, dear.'

'Glad you put her in her place,' Gordon smirked. 'How many macaroni pies did you confess to?'

'Two and I didn't tell her about the chips. Turns out we have a fifth victim. We need to add Dirty Dolores to the list. Somebody injected her with tanning stuff and she's like a smelly Oompa Loompa.'

Jim put his phone away, then looked up and noticed that Gordon was staring at him in horror.

'What's up, pal?' he asked.

'Dirty Dolores,' Gordon squeaked. 'There's something you need to know about me and Dirty Dolores.'

CHAPTER 6

The two men were in Jim's old Land Rover, rattling over potholes on their way to Port Vik. Following his revelation, Gordon was so full of anxiety that he hadn't uttered a sound, even when his head ricocheted off the window as the wheels hit a particularly deep trough.

His voice grim, Jim asked, 'What makes you think that you're the father of her child?'

'She said I am. I only found out after he was born. I've been secretly paying maintenance for two years and fiddling the books at the farm so that Fiona doesn't find out. She'll kill me if she finds out. Then, once she's killed me, she'll never let me see Ellie-Minty again.'

'But how would you make a baby with her?' asked Jim.

Gordon looked at him in disbelief.

'Well, when the daddy seed meets the mummy seed, a special miracle happens.'

'No, I mean how did your daddy seed even get in her in the first place.'

Gordon rolled his eyes and patiently explained, 'The daddy seed lives in the daddy's willy, and the mummy has a special tunnel in her hoo-ha that goes up to the mummy seed in her tummy. Have a wee think about it. I'm sure you can work the rest out for yourself, pal. Did Penny not tell you all this stuff when you started dating? Fiona had me brought up to speed immediately. There's this wee button that's really important to find, but it's like one of those floaters you get in your eye. The minute you think you've got it in your sights, poof, it's darted off somewhere else. Which is annoying because you know how much I like pressing buttons.'

'For ffff....' Jim shook his head and spoke through gritted teeth. 'I don't mean the birds and the bees. How did you end up with Dirty Dolores?'

Gordon sat in silence for a moment, casting his mind back to that fateful night, not long after he and Fiona had arrived on the island. They'd had a huge row because, well, probably because of something stupid that didn't matter in the grand scheme of things. He'd stormed out and gone to the pub.

'The last thing I remember,' he told Jim, 'was drinking vodka with some of the younger ones. Zack Wallace was there, even though he was underage at the time. I think Bertie the barman was scared to refuse to serve him. I got mortal drunk, someone suggested a party and I woke up the next morning in Dirty Dolores' bed. I just scarpered. I couldn't find my trainers and it took me two hours to walk home barefoot. Fiona said I stank, so I told her I'd slept in a barn and an animal had made off with my shoes.'

'And you've kept it to yourself ever since,' said Jim. 'Did you get a paternity test done?'

'No. I asked, but she said that if I was going to be difficult about it, she'd tell Fiona. And now, even if he turns out not to be my son, I've made everything worse by lying for two years.'

'Aye. It's a fine mess for sure.'

'You won't say anything to Dolores when we see her?' Gordon asked, a small quiver in his voice.

'None of my business, pal.'

'Aye.'

They didn't talk for some time. Jim drove on, wincing as

each pothole tested the suspension, and Gordon gazed out of the window, watching the first lambs of the year gambol in the fields. He wished he could be new again. Eventually, Jim broke the silence.

'We're going to see Dirty Dolores first. Kill one bird with two stones.'

'Is it nae two birds with one stone?' Gordon asked.

'I was playing with my idioms.'

'Aye, I did that once and my mam said if I didn't stop, they'd fall off.'

Jim couldn't help flashing Gordon a wry grin.

'Pity they didn't. You'd have saved yourself a lot of bother.'

They were entering Port Vik now, and Jim steered the car through the narrow streets to a housing estate on the western edge of the town. Dirty Dolores lived in the centre of a short row of identical, white, pebble-dashed houses behind the main street that ran through the estate. On either side of the property, neat gardens and freshly painted doors told of proud homeowners and young families. Dolores' home, however, had something different to say about its main occupant.

Jim bent to open the iron gate. It was fixed between two low pillars that guarded the entrance to a litter-strewn, patch of bare earth and grass that was intersected by a line of cheap paving slabs. Instead of swinging open, however, the gate fell onto the path with a metallic clang. Startled, Jim stood still for a beat, then stepped over it, bent down and propped it against the low wall that separated the garden from the public footpath. Gordon hadn't bothered with the gate. The garden wall came to below his knees, so he'd simply hopped over it and was now making his way across the patchy lawn, dodging empty cider cans and dog mess as he went.

'Tell you what, mate,' he groaned, rubbing his belly as they stood on the doorstep. 'I might have eaten too much. It feels like I've got a big sausage baby in here. Have you got a big sausage baby?'

'Aye, a bloody enormous one, honey,' Jim snickered.

Gordon was too anxious to snicker back. Instead, he shuffled his feet awkwardly and said, 'Remember, you're not to interfere.'

'Are we still talking about your big sausage, baby?' asked Jim, hoping to coax a smile.

Gordon obliged, offering him a weak grin.

'No, we're talking about whether I'm Mason's dad, sweetheart.'

'Mum's the word, darling.'

Raising a fist to knock on the peeling front door, Jim was surprised when it swung open. Behind him, Gordon let out a small yelp. It seemed that Dolores had spotted their arrival and was now standing on her threshold, urging them to hurry inside before the neighbours saw her.

She was a thin woman, with short blonde hair and large teeth. Her face was almost skeletal, and although she was only in her mid-twenties, the deep shadows beneath her eyes made her appear older. The fact that she almost blended with the peeling brown paint on her front door didn't help.

Given the state of the exterior and the woman's personal hygiene, Jim had expected the inside of the house to be filthy, yet it was neat and smelled of lavender. Dolores didn't have much, but the little she did have was vacuumed, dusted and polished. Bare floorboards led down the hall to a bright kitchen, and to the left, the living room door stood open revealing a cream leather sofa and matching chairs, a small television and a glass coffee table. The magnolia paint on the wall by the stairs bore the scuff marks of the bags and shoes that filled a tall rack behind the door, and the hall radiator sported a line of tiny, damp t-shirts and trousers. In other words, Jim thought, a basic yet surprisingly ordinary home.

From the kitchen, there came a low growl, and he backed up warily as a large, black dog of indeterminate lineage came barrelling down the hall towards them, its meaty paws rising at the last moment to land on Gordon's chest. The creature's tongue delivered a joyful lick on the chin before its mistress pulled it back and dragged it away, shutting the kitchen door firmly on the slavering beast.

'Smoochy,' Gordon told Jim, gesturing towards the door, from behind which issued a series of impassioned whimpers. 'He's big, but he's just a daft galoot.'

'You're a bit early for your weekly visit,' Dolores snapped, eyeing Gordon with suspicion.

'I'm nae here to see the bairn,' he said. 'No, that came out wrong. I'd like to see him, but there's another reason we came.'

'Mason's out. My sister's got him for the day.'

'Ah, right, uh,' Gordon mumbled lamely, ignoring the dig in the ribs from Jim that was meant to prompt further explanation.

Dolores, however, had never been backwards at coming forwards.

'Why are you here?'

'Minky said you'd had some trouble with the Vik Vigilante and asked us to help,' Jim explained. 'Do you think we could sit down rather than stand here in the hall?'

With a reluctant sigh, Dolores showed the men into the living room.

'Take your shoes off first,' she instructed. 'It's the only carpet in the house and I'll not have it ruined. And your feet better not stink either.'

Jim's barely suppressed laugh turned into a strangled snort, and she looked at him sharply before evidently deciding to pay him no heed. Instead, she waved the men to the sofa, with an admonishment that they shouldn't expect tea and biscuits. She pushed the coffee table back and flopped into the chair opposite, tucking her legs beneath her.

'As you can see,' she said, pointing at her dark orange

face, 'I'm not taking visitors at the moment, so say your piece and bugger off.'

Jim related what he'd been told by Penny and asked Dolores for her views on why she had been targeted.

'Minky thinks it's somebody getting at her Zack,' she said. 'But that's impossible. He wouldn't hurt a fly.'

Jim recalled the fight he'd had with the spotty youth in the old distillery houses a while back and silently disagreed. Zack was a dangerous combination of fearless and stupid.

He cleared his throat and said, 'Minky thought it might have been the sunbed thing. Do you know of anyone else who might have a grudge against Zack?'

'Och, no. The sunbed thing was ages ago, and Malcolm's fine now that they've given him the gel cushion. He and Zack Glasgow kissed and made up. I'm telling you, everybody loves Zack. It's me the vigilante was after, which means it could be half the women on the island. Last week, I did Elaine Fallon's eyelash extensions and accidentally glued her eyes open. The week before that, Sophie Hendry ended up with stitches when I got careless during her bikini wax. I told her, that's why God gave us two of everything, so that if one gets mangled…well, let's be honest, I'm an absolute disaster as a beautician, but I'm the only one on the island so….'

Dolores shrugged nonchalantly as if the lack of competition was entirely to blame for these disasters.

'I don't think it's Elaine or Sophie, though,' she continued. 'I offered them both compensation, although Sophie will have to wait until the stitches are out before she can sit long enough for her free pedicure.'

'Has anyone seemed particularly upset when things have gone wrong recently?' asked Jim. 'Do you have any enemies?'

Dolores tapped a ridiculously long gel nail on her thigh while she mentally catalogued her recent work cockups and all the people with whom she'd argued in the pub.

Eventually, she reluctantly admitted, 'Edna Mains. You know, Stevie Mains' mum. The one with no eyebrows. I told her they'd grow back, but it's been three months now. Anyway, she blames me for him splitting up with his girlfriend.'

'Why?' asked Gordon.

'I don't know,' Dolores snapped, yet the guilty hunch to her shoulders suggested that she knew perfectly well.

Unwilling to accept her answer, Gordon said, 'Aye, you do. You may as well tell us because we'll be speaking to Edna. Come on, Dolores, get your side of the story in first.'

Dolores' gaze remained fixed on the coffee table and her tone was muted when she replied, 'I didn't do it. She said I slept with Stevie then told Sergeant Wilson he was poaching again when he wouldn't lend me money to pay the rent on the salon. It's true that I asked him for a loan. He sold his story to the papers, remember, and got all that cash. But he said he'd spent it ages ago getting a place of his own, away from the old witch. I didn't grass him up for the poaching.'

'Did you sleep with him?' asked Gordon.

Dolores looked up sharply and protested, 'That was three years ago! Don't tell Minky or Zack. He thinks he was my first.'

'But you've got a child,' Jim pointed out, feeling a sense of outrage begin to swell in his chest. 'How can Zack think you were a…that he was your first? He must know about Gordon.'

Jim sensed Gordon stiffen beside him and mumbled, 'Sorry, mate.'

Dolores smiled weakly, her eyes straying around the room, looking anywhere but at Gordon.

The long fingernail twitched nervously against her thigh as she said, 'He doesn't know about Gordon. I told him I was blind drunk on a night out on the mainland and we agreed that it doesn't count if you can't remember it.'

'Sounds suspiciously like what happened to Gordon,' Jim commented, his expression stern. 'Maybe he should say it doesn't count because he can't remember. Maybe we should be asking for a DNA test because if you were sleeping with Stevie Mains three years ago, how do we even know that Gordon is Mason's dad?'

Gordon let out a cry and sprang to his feet.

'I think this has gone far enough,' he gabbled. 'I knew it wasn't a good idea to come here. She'll tell Fiona and I'll be toast and I'll never see Ellie-Minty again, and even though she hardly lets me see Mason and won't tell him I'm his dad, I wanted to see him grow up and things.'

Jim ignored him and pressed on.

'Judging by the photo on the wall behind you, Mason has more in common with Stevie than Gordon. For a start, he's not even ginger.'

Dolores rose from the chair and flung out an arm, gesturing towards the door. When she spoke, it was through clenched teeth.

'Get out. I will not be insulted in my own home.'

Jim stood, towering over her. He could feel his ears becoming hot as anger got the better of him.

'And where would you like to be insulted?' he growled. 'Gordon will not be paying you a penny more until he gets a DNA test.'

'Ignore him,' Gordon squeaked, pulling on Jim's fleece in a vain effort to move him towards the door.

'His wife will be pleased to hear all about it. All about how I was drunk, and he took advantage of me,' roared Dolores.

Jim shook Gordon off and eyeballed the woman.

'Fiona's going to find out eventually,' he told her, 'and nobody is going to believe that Gordon took advantage of you.'

'I didn't,' squeaked Gordon.

'Let's see how this goes when he takes you to court and forces a DNA test. Because that's what he's going to do. You'll have to pay back every penny he's given you over the years.'

'I won't take you to court,' Gordon howled. 'Stop it, both of you.'

He firmly grabbed Jim's arm and dragged him towards the door.

'Get the fuck out of my house,' Dolores spat, then pointed a single long nail at Gordon. 'And you! Ginger nuts! Don't come back here. If you ever see Mason again, it will be over my dead body.'

Gordon's eyes were wild, and beads of sweat prickled his temple as he pulled a red-faced, raging Jim from the house. Behind them, Dolores slammed the front door.

'There will be no more money until you produce a DNA test,' Jim shouted at the peeling, brown paint. 'Do you hear that? Not a fucking penny.'

He turned on his heel and stomped down the path, kicking the broken gate as he went and sending it clattering to the ground.

By the time Jim reached the car, he had calmed down and the first tendrils of regret were beginning to curl around his stomach. He leaned against the vehicle, pressing his hot forehead onto the cool metal and breathing hard.

'I'm sorry, pal. She just got to me. I was trying to stick up for you.'

There was a long pause then Gordon said flatly, 'You told me you wouldn't interfere. I was dealing with it. I didn't need you wading in with your size twelves.'

Jim slowly raised his head and turned to face his friend.

'*You* should have told Fiona and had this sorted out years ago.'

Seeing the hurt expression on his friend's face, he immediately wished he hadn't said that, but his temper was still simmering and his tongue was sharp with it.

Gordon crossed his arms, hissing irritably as his sleeve caught on the button of his dungarees. He glared at Jim defiantly.

In an icy tone, he said, 'It was none of your business and it will remain none of your business. Just...just stay out of things in future. I'll make my own way back to the farm, and I don't want to hear from you again.'

Jim watched, his shoulders sagging in defeat, as Gordon marched off in the direction of town. He could feel tears pricking the corners of his eyes and took a deep breath to steady himself before unlocking the car and slumping into the driver's seat.

Should he go after his friend or let the man stew awhile? He didn't think he could persuade Gordon to get in the car. If it were him, he'd want to walk it off. Jim threw his head back against the headrest. Buggering hell, Gordon would be well within his rights if he never spoke to him again. What had come over him in there? He was mild-mannered Jim. He worried about whether chips counted as one of your five a day and how many Jaffa Cakes he could fit in his mouth in one go. He wasn't the sort to get angry and start accusing people of ripping off his friend. Even though she was. And now Dolores was going to claim that Gordon had done something terrible, and Gordon wasn't speaking to him. Quite rightly so. He'd made matters far, far worse. Maybe he should go back and apologise to Dolores. Persuade her to say nothing. No, that would just make things far, far worser.

Feeling the tendrils of regret wrap themselves around a large boulder of guilt in the pit of his stomach, he sought solace in the one person whom he knew had the capacity to forgive even the most enormous of mistakes. He got out his phone and rang Penny. The call went immediately to the dreaded voicemail, so he texted her instead.

```
Need to talk. Have ducked up.
```

CHAPTER 7

Eileen and Mrs Hubbard were already waiting at the lighthouse when Penny arrived. Mrs Hubbard was resplendent in a pink and yellow "Mrs Hubbard's Cupboard" tracksuit that she'd had made in the hope that it would, as she told Penny, "...become all trendy with the young folk, like the Greggs ones that Primark are doing." Penny wasn't sure that this was one of Mrs H's better business ideas, not least because she was wearing the thing with her usual low-heeled court shoes and had popped a luminous orange shower cap over her rollers. Still, she was a welcome splash of colour on a dreich day.

Eileen, who had been sitting on the doorstep reading her horoscope in that day's Vik Gazette, looked up and said, 'Alright there, Rubber Duck? I'd stand up to say hello, but my hair's stuck to the police tape.'

Suppressing a grin, Penny stepped closer and gently tugged a hank of blonde hair free from the Police Scotland crime scene tape which had been liberally plastered across the lighthouse door.

'There, you're free now, Winnie the Pooh. I see Easy was put in charge of taping things off again,' she observed, holding out a hand to pull Eileen upright. 'I hope Sergeant Wilson brings her police scissors.'

At Eileen's sharp glance, she clarified, 'For the police tape, not your hair. What does your horoscope say?'

Her friend squinted at the newspaper and intoned, 'Saturn is your friend today as the stamina planet helps you through a *sticky* situation. Ha! And you told me horoscopes are a load of old rubbish. Oh, ye of little faith, Rubber Duck.'

She grinned and waggled a knowing finger towards Penny. 'Or should I call you Saturn? Hmm?'

Penny put an arm around Eileen's shoulders and gave them a fond squeeze.

'Just as long as you don't call me Uranus,' she said, returning Eileen's grin. 'That might just tip Jim over the edge.'

'What does my horoscope say, dearie?' asked Mrs Hubbard, a hand straying to the back of her neck to tuck in a roller which had sprung free of the shower cap.

Eileen scanned down the columns until she came to Sagittarius. Her lips slowly formed a tight O and her eyebrows crept towards her hairline as she read the entry.

She looked up at Mrs Hubbard and said, 'Things may seem uncertain, but Mars brings passion and determination to put your best foot forward. Ooh, that's the dancing, Mrs H. Do you think you'll be declared the winners now that the McCullochs are probably going to be disqualified.'

'I'm up to high doh with the whole thing,' said Mrs Hubbard, her false teeth shifting slightly as they plucked her lower lip. She pointed to the shower cap. 'That's why I have the curlers in. There's a meeting tonight where they'll announce what's happening. I need full battle paint and my curly helmet to face the news. If the committee decide that the McCullochs can stay in the competition, Douglas and I might leave. We refuse to share a dancefloor with cheats. But that'll make me cry, hence the battle paint. You can't cry with mascara on.'

The older woman's voice caught on that last sentence, and Penny and Eileen rushed to her side, holding her hands and rubbing her back. Penny felt a wave of fierce loyalty towards the shopkeeper.

'Dad and Elsie used to supply half the committee with the special medicine he grew in the shed. We could threaten to tell Sergeant Wilson,' she offered.

'No, dearie. That would make us just as bad as the McCullochs.'

'You're right,' said Penny glumly. Then she brightened. 'But we can put public pressure on them. That's fair.'

'What do you mean?' asked Mrs Hubbard.

Eileen, whose eyes had been darting rapidly between the two women during this exchange, suddenly smiled and nodded knowingly.

'Our mothers,' she said. 'We harness the power of Mary Hopper and Jeannie Campbell.'

Mrs Hubbard's eyes regained some of their sparkle and, with a delighted giggle, she enveloped both women in a hug.

'Is this a kinky threesome?' said a voice behind them. 'Because if it is, can I do the video? I need to make some extra cash to buy a new set of arrest bracelets. I can't find mine anywhere, and I'm not telling Dunderheid that I've lost another pair.'

The three women turned to find Sergeant Wilson bearing down on them, her solid figure striding along the path with surprising speed. She stopped beside the group, panting a little and pulling on the armpits of her body armour to let the air circulate.

'We're talking about the dancing competition,' Penny told her. 'There's a committee meeting tonight, and Mrs Hubbard was worried that they'll let the McCullochs stay in.'

The Sergeant stared at her companions in disbelief.

'What is the point of having a Mary Hopper on the island if you don't deploy her? And while you're at it, can you ask her to give me back my good taser?'

71

Penny's brain did a double-take. Her mother couldn't be trusted around anything sharp, pointy, shooty, hurty or flammable. Sergeant Wilson knew this, yet she'd ignored all common sense and given the woman a lethal weapon.

'Why?' Penny asked, shaking her head in exasperation. 'Why would you lend Mum your taser?'

Sergeant Wilson looked at her like she'd just dropped fifty IQ points.

'To see what would happen, of course. It was during that power cut last month. Len fancied a nice pork chop and they'd run out of gas for the camping stove.'

Penny inhaled sharply through her nose then asked, 'She didn't...? Not a pig?'

'Och, no, dearie,' Mrs Hubbard interrupted. 'Not even a slice of bacon in the end. Although she managed an egg, and Sandra Next Door did them some soldiers with the crème brûlée torch.'

'Right,' said the Sergeant, rubbing her hands together. 'Now that we've solved Vikly Come Dancing and established that you can't cook a pork chop with a taser, can I get on with my briefing? Because I've just eaten...,' she quickly counted on her fingers, '...far too many macaroni pies, and with my IBS, well, let's just say you don't want to be the one behind me when we go up the stairs.'

She paused briefly to take some satisfaction from the horrified looks on the faces of her companions, then continued, 'Our mission, ladies and Fanny Features, is to solve the murder of Beacon Brodie. The reason for this is that Fudmuppet is a biscuit-thieving skidmark on the underpants of life. Okay, what else do you need to know? We've fully covered information and intention. Oh aye, method, administration, risk assessment, communications and human rights. Scratch that last one. It's nae relevant.

'Lugs pinned back? Just be your usual pain in the arse selves and we'll be fine. We're on a deadline here. We have to find the murderer before Fudmuppet cons Easy into giving him a chocolate finger. Phone me if you find anything interesting, and don't breathe a word to Easy because he's a big clype who'll grass me up for the price of a custard cream. Now, raise your right hands and repeat after me...'

Baffled into dumb compliance, the three women raised their right hands.

'I promise that I will do my best and do my duty to all, to serve Sergeant Wilson, and kick other people, and nail their balls to the wall.'

The women exchanged confused glances and mumbled the oath, although Penny crossed her fingers behind her back at the kicking bit. Having taken a hard blow to the kidneys recently, she preferred to steer clear of violence. In fact, she probably shouldn't even be attempting the lighthouse stairs. Despite feeling much better, painkillers were still her friends, and she hesitated at the thought of doing anything too strenuous.

Oath complete, Sergeant Wilson made the sign of a cross and pronounced the women deputised. Holding up a hand to ward off their questions, she took a penknife from her utility belt, sliced through the police tape and instructed Penny to pick the lock on the lighthouse door.

Penny was fairly sure they shouldn't be doing this. She tried to suggest they find a legitimate method of entry but found herself merely a piece of driftwood in the face of a Wilson tsunami.

'Fudmuppet is guarding that key as if it's the password to his personal porn collection. It's like he thinks I'd break in or something, which is just fucking insulting when I think about it. How else does he expect me to get in? Or maybe that's exactly what he wants. Maybe he's testing my problem-solving skills. That's what it must be. It's my appraisal next week, and he's desperate to find a chink in the Wilson armour that he can report to Dunderheid, the wee arsegoblin.'

The Sergeant stopped for a moment to consider the logic of this, then gave herself a pat on the shoulder.

'Aye, Martisha. You're right, Martisha. It all makes perfect sense. By confiscating the key, he's actually giving us permission to break in. Get your kit out, Fanny Features, we have the blessing of Fudmuppet.'

Reluctantly, Penny fished her set of lockpicks from her handbag and got to work. The lock was old and heavy, so the task took some time and was made harder by Sergeant Wilson, who hovered over her, hands on hips and swearing under her breath. Penny caught something about bastarding arrest bracelets.

'And there was me thinking I'd forgotten to lock the biscuit tin, when all the time it was Wank Boy and Weasley,' the officer eventually announced, looking around expectantly at her companions as if they knew exactly what she was talking about and should be offering a congratulatory attagirl.

The lock chose this moment to spring open, so they were all saved from having to request further clarification.

The inside of the lighthouse smelled of old wood and damp mould. What meagre light penetrated the narrow windows did little to dispel the chilly gloom, and Penny couldn't help but imagine the lighthouse keepers who had lived here before the cottage was built in the late nineteenth century, trudging up and down the stairs with oil lamps, keeping the flame at the top alive while the sea raged below and thick walls kept the daylight at bay. She'd spent enough time in Vik Museum to know that life was harsh for all islanders in the old days, but this must have been a particularly strange and lonely place to work. With a small shiver, Penny eyed the stairs spiralling above her and suggested that the others go ahead; she'd do this climb at her own pace.

Sergeant Wilson immediately declared her intention to lead the way and began to march upwards, a tiny yet perfectly audible parp accompanying each step. After a short scuffle, Mrs Hubbard managed to push Eileen ahead of her into second place then slowly followed, heels clicking and a toot of her own resounding with every second step as the trio slowly ascended, leaving Penny to bring up the rear.

From around the bend, Sergeant Wilson's cheerful voice drifted back.

'Pick up the pace, Curtain Twitcher, and between us, we'll have the William Tell Overture nailed by the time we get to the top.'

What felt like an hour later, all four women stood panting in the lantern room. Every surface bore traces of the dust used by the fingerprint technicians and several floorboards had been removed. The wind whistled through boarded-up gaps in the glass panes, and the marks in the wood where Brodie had been winched to his death were still visible. In short, Forensics had clearly been through the place with a fine-tooth comb, and Penny doubted that there was anything left to find. She gazed around the desecrated carcass of the room and felt a shiver run down her spine.

'Why did you bring us here?' she asked. 'It's creepy.'

The Sergeant's face was serious and her voice low as she said, 'You lot are flies on a festering turd, and here we are at bum central. If there's some tasty shit in here, you'll be the ones doing the eating.'

She looked at the blank faces of her companions and sighed dramatically.

'Because you're a bunch of nosy bastards with a talent for seeing what other folk have missed.

'Brodie was injected with something that paralysed him and was probably going to kill him, then he was covered in glue, hoisted up and stuck to the glass so that the shadow of his body was projected onto the sky like a Batman signal.

'We're still waiting for toxicology, but the pathologist thinks the killer used tetro…hetero…tetris…the puffer fish poison. He had a heart attack and died before it could do its job, poor bugger. You can see that the Scene Examiners have been through the place like dysentery through an arsehole. And I don't think I'm overdoing the metaphor when I say I want you flies to land on their shite and dig your tongues in deep. So, get licking, Losers.'

'You always manage to bring it to the lowest level,' Penny observed.

'Thank you, Fanny Features. It's my special talent,' said the Sergeant proudly.

'We could do a séance,' Eileen suggested. 'Can you feel his presence? I can feel his presence.'

'The only presence you'll feel is the toe of my police boot up your hoop if you carry on like that,' Sergeant Wilson told her.

Looking hurt, Eileen scuttled off to examine the lantern, leaving Mrs Hubbard to admonish the Sergeant for her sharp words. However, she too was soon sent scurrying when Wilson casually removed her second-best taser and offered to experiment on how long it took to cook a human liver.

'It seems a very elaborate crime, dearie' said Mrs Hubbard as she poked around under the lantern. 'The killer brought poison, glue and a rope all the way up here.'

'You're right. They must have known that Beacon Brodie would be here,' said Penny, who was on her hands and knees examining the floorboards. 'Perhaps it was someone he knew.'

'Or someone that likes making a scene,' Eileen suggested. 'Maybe the Batman symbol was a reference to something. Have there been any other similar murders, Sergeant Wilson? Anything to do with movies or superheroes?'

'Sometimes I suspect you're nae as thick as you look, Space Cadet,' said the Sergeant. 'Then I remember that time you shut yourself in a freezer because you wanted to know what being an ice cream felt like. I suggested the Batman thing to Fudmuppet, but he told me to go away and do the door-to-doors because the real police were here now, and they'd handle the grown-up stuff.'

For a moment, the Sergeant's usually defiant nature receded, and she looked so defeated that Penny almost reached out a hand to comfort her. Almost. Because even a rabid dog could look vulnerable, yet you wouldn't stick your hand in the cage. She contented herself with a muttered, 'Shocking,' and got on with the task at hand.

After an hour of peering, poking and prodding, the women concluded that there was nothing more to be found, and a disappointed Sergeant Wilson led them back downstairs.

This time, there were no inappropriate jokes or curse words. The police officer seemed to be deep in thought. Her mouth was a grim line as she ordered Penny to lock the lighthouse door, then led the trio to Keeper's Cottage.

As they waited for Penny to pick her second lock of the day, Sergeant Wilson explained, 'The superhero connection is definitely a line of enquiry we should follow up. The other thing is whether it's somebody he knew. I was at the garden centre doing the door-to-doors and macaroni pies just before I came here and–'

'Door-to-doors and macaroni pies?' Penny interjected.

'It's called multi-tasking. Like washing your bum and your face at the same time in the shower.' The Sergeant waggled an admonishing finger. 'But never change hands halfway through.'

Eileen stifled a giggle and wrinkled her nose.

'You were saying something about the garden centre,' she prompted.

'Pat Hughes from the Post Office was in for…actually, I don't know why she was there. Probably a mortality check ahead of pension day. All the old buggers go there for their breakfasts on a Sunday. She told me that according to her highly confidential source, Dawn who has the Post Office in Rothienorman, Brodie was Richard Less, a former thief from Aberdeenshire. Maybe somebody he upset back in the day decided to settle an old score. Have a dig around the house and see what you can find out about the man.'

'Won't Fudmuppet already have that covered?' asked Penny.

She was squatting by the ancient, green door, the tip of her tongue poking between her lips as she manoeuvred the lock picks inside a large keyhole.

'Aye, but there's stuff that people will tell the polis, then there's the stuff they'll tell you,' said the Sergeant. 'And then there's convincing Fudmuppet to listen to anything I have to say.'

'Have you checked the police records, dearie?' asked Mrs Hubbard.

The Sergeant reached into her bra, extracted her phone and held it out to the elderly shopkeeper.

'Mabel from Mensa's on the line. She says don't bother renewing your membership this year. Did I not mention that I came here from the garden centre? Maybe Harminder keeps the police national computer under a rosebush. Aye, right you are Harminder, I'll take six marigolds and a pair of secateurs, and while you're at it, can you do me a quick PNC check? Och, you're just annoying me now. I'm going back to the station to be ignored by Fudmuppet. At least there I'll have the satisfaction of slowly eating a KitKat in front of him.'

'I thought you were breaking in here with us,' said Eileen.

'Nope. Let the record state that Curtain Twitcher has a point. I'm more useful back at the station doing the checks. And I have some ideas of my own. What is it that Fanny Features always says in the Losers Club meetings?'

'Play to your strengths?' Penny suggested.

'No, that's not it.'

'Read the food labels,' said Eileen.

'What the fuck has that got to do with anything?' Sergeant Wilson jeered.

'Teamwork is dreamwork,' declared Mrs Hubbard.

'Don't be stupid. We all know that I'm a very supportive person. No, it's either "Learn when to leave the table" or

78

"Always go for a shit before weigh-in." I can't remember which. Wise words, Fanny Features.'

'I didn't say–' Penny started to protest, but the Sergeant held up a hand to stop her.

'No need for false modesty. I'm getting that last one made into a sign for my desk and your name will be at the end of the quote.'

CHAPTER 8

The three women watched Sergeant Wilson go. Although she appeared to march through the gap in the wall with her usual brio, something was missing.

Penny couldn't put her finger on it but said, 'I think Fudmuppet might be getting to her.'

'You're right, dearie,' Mrs Hubbard replied. 'This is about more than him eating her biscuits. Normally she'd be raging, but she just seems…'

'Wounded and quietly determined?' suggested Eileen.

'Well, I wouldn't go quite as far as quietly,' said Mrs Hubbard.

'Less shouty,' said Penny. 'And far more informative. She's dead set on sending Fudmuppet back to Aberdeen with his tail between his legs. Ah! Got it at last.'

There was a scrape and a click as the old lock finally sprang free. Yet the door was not about to give up. Years of wind and rain had lashed this rocky outcrop, warping and swelling the wood so that it sat at a slight angle in its frame. Together, she and Eileen pushed their shoulders against the thick timber until it grudgingly gave way.

A moment later, they found themselves in a dusty living room, gazing at piles of old newspapers, an ancient television and a leather wingback chair. The fireplace was a soot-blackened thing, a tiled monstrosity that had been added in the nineteen-fifties, and the large rug in front of it bore a worn path between chair and TV. Beside the chair, a mug sat on a small side table, as if its owner would return at any moment to pick it up and settle in for an hour of Coronation Street. Penny wondered whether Brodie even watched the soaps. He was a grumpy old bugger so probably spent his time shouting at the bloke on Newsnight. Still, the man had lived a life here, and despite the dishevelment and the gaps left behind by the police, it felt like he had simply popped out.

She gestured to the stairs on her right, which she assumed ran up to an attic bedroom.

'Eileen, would you mind taking the upstairs? We'll have a poke around in here. We're looking for any trace of friends or family.'

'I feel like an intruder,' Eileen whispered.

'Technically, you are,' Penny pointed out.

'Yes, but you know I'm psychotic. His presence is strong here. There's something of him left behind.'

'Psychic, dearie. You're psychic,' said Mrs Hubbard.

'No, she's not,' Penny scoffed. Then seeing the hurt look on her friend's face, she added, 'Sorry, I shouldn't have said that. I'm a bit freaked out too. Do you want one of us to go up with you?'

'I'll do the upstairs,' Mrs Hubbard offered. 'You girls stay down here.'

She looked up at the wooden stairs, which were little more than a glorified ladder in the corner of the room, and gingerly placed a foot on the first step. There was an ominous groan, but the wood held. Clinging to the thick length of rope that served as a banister, she pulled herself up the stairs, wincing at each creak.

Once they heard her feet on the floorboards above, Penny and Eileen turned to their own tasks.

Originally, the cottage had probably consisted of two

rooms and an outside toilet, with the cooking done on a range in the main living area. At some point, a small extension had been added to house a tiny kitchen and bathroom. Eileen agreed to check these, while Penny rifled through the drawers of the tall oak cabinets which stood on either side of the chimney breast. A void in the dust on a table near the door indicated that the police had removed a computer. And any other devices, Penny supposed. This was going to be a very low-tech investigation.

She found what she was looking for immediately, which was slightly disappointing because, despite feeling guilty about going through a dead man's things, she'd been looking forward to a good rummage. Yet here it was, right at the front, ticking all the boxes for getting to know Brodie and his family.

The photograph album was old and, judging by the marks on the edges of the pages, well-thumbed. Four photographs were displayed on each page, most being happy family snaps of a man, a woman and two children. A few contained other people in party hats or Sunday best, their faces smiling across the decades as fashions changed from mini-skirts and flared trousers to batwing jumpers and bomber jackets. Someone, most likely Brodie himself, had written the dates, places and names on the back of each photograph. She carefully removed the picture of a red-faced man in a brown suit and kipper tie, an unlit cigar clutched between his teeth. He was standing next to a sullen teenager in an Alice Cooper t-shirt who was clutching a skateboard to his chest as if it were a shield with which to fend off the attentions of the photographer. The legend on the rear said "Boxing Day 1972 Me and Uncle Charlie."

Penny set the album aside and continued her search. Among an assortment of ancient bills and invoices, she found a few old birthday cards which Brodie must have kept for the memories. The names and messages on them meant nothing to her, but she tucked them into the photograph album in the vague hope that she could match them to faces later.

She'd expected to find bank statements and personal items, such as a birth certificate and passport, but assumed that the police had taken these. Never mind, she thought, there's plenty here to start building a picture of the man.

The floorboards beneath the rug protested as she moved to the chair and dug her fingers down the sides of the cushions. Everything here was old and grotty, she thought, extracting a yellowing receipt and a ha'penny coin. The ink had long since faded on the receipt, but someone had scrawled an address on it. The ink was sharp and bright, leading Penny to wonder if the note was recent. She quickly typed a text to Sergeant Wilson:

```
Please check who lives at 14 Walker Lane
Fraserburgh
```

She pressed the send button, but the signal was so poor in this godforsaken spot that she didn't expect it to work. She was not disappointed. A message popped onto the screen advising her of the failure to send and inviting her to try again.

'I'm just going outside to get a signal,' she shouted.

Above the clattering of pots and pans in the kitchen, she heard Eileen shout back something that sounded like, 'Don't leave me on my own.'

'I'll only be a minute,' she said.

It would be a relief to get away from the smell of damp, even if only for a short while. In the short time that the cottage had stood empty, the cold had seeped into the very bones of it, and with a small shudder, she imagined decay already beginning to slide through the cracks in the window frames and between the floorboards, like a silent, taphonomic parasite looking for a host.

Stop it, she told herself. Eileen has you in a right fettle with all her talk of presences.

Taking a deep breath, she reached out a hand to grasp the doorknob, feeling her fingers slip slightly as she began to turn the iron sphere, the grooves in the metal worn almost smooth by a century of palms twisting against its cool surface.

For a second, she felt resistance. Then the knob began to turn, seemingly by itself. Her brain screamed "Poltergeist!" and before the rest of her body could react, she snatched her hand back from the knob. Catching up to the idea that something unexpected was happening, her heart kicked in, making its presence in her chest loudly known. She took an involuntary step back, clamping her lips shut to stifle the scream that rose in her throat. Above the rapid doomf doomf doomf of her heart, she could hear…see?…sense the rattle of someone trying to open the door.

The world narrowed to fight or flight. Penny's focus zeroed in on the door. Whoever was on the other side was struggling with the swollen wood. Thump, thump, thump. A shoulder? Even as her conscious mind spotted the small bolt at the top of the door, Penny's subconscious was roaring, "Choose flight. Run!"'

Her fingers felt like they belonged to someone else; thick, trembling stubs that seemed incapable of closing over the bolt to slide it home. Using the heel of her hand, she managed to push the thing into place then, yielding to instinct, she ran to the kitchen.

Without explanation, Penny pulled Eileen into a crouch, pressing them both against the oven door.

'What the–' Eileen began to object, but Penny put a finger to her lips.

There was little she could do to prevent Mrs Hubbard from coming down to find out what all the fuss was about, but she could at least keep herself and Eileen out of sight.

Because Penny knew that if it were her out there, unable to get in, her next step would be to peer through all the windows. She could only pray that whomever it was, they hadn't heard her close the bolt and they'd assume the place was locked up and empty.

There was a sound of feet on gravel outside, and Penny felt Eileen stiffen beside her. She slid an arm around her friend's shoulder, pulling her in closer, holding her there until they heard the footsteps fade.

The two women stayed where they were for a full minute until Penny loosened her grip on Eileen and crawled forward into the living room. Slowly, she raised her head to peek through one of the grimy windows. In the haze of the mizzle that had descended since they'd entered the cottage, she could just make out a tall figure in a long, dark overcoat disappearing through the gap in the wall.

There was a small rustle behind her.

'Stay there,' Penny hissed, waving Eileen back towards the kitchen. 'I'm going to follow them.'

'Don't!' Eileen squeaked, 'It's too risqué. Wait for me and Mrs Hubbard.'

But it was too late. Penny had already shot back the bolt, heaved the door open and was gone.

CHAPTER 9

Jim drove around aimlessly, trying to think how he could patch things up with Gordon. He'd tried calling Penny, but there was no signal. He'd considered going to his dad's. Ivor Space was a kind and decent soul who always offered a slab of shortbread with his fatherly advice, but today was moving day. Dad had finally bitten the bullet and declared himself ready to live in sin with Eileen's mum. Now that Jeanie Campbell and her sharp tongue were permanently in the mix, Jim felt hesitant about confiding in his dad. If Ivor let anything slip to Jeanie, it would go straight to Penny's mum, which pretty much guaranteed that Penny would get the unabridged version with bells on.

Should he phone Fiona? His brain reared up in horror at the thought and delivered a very firm 'No, you big twat.'

Thus it was that he found himself in the one place he least expected. The one place where he would probably find no sympathy at all, yet there might be some common-sense advice once the earbashing was over. He'd been going to come here at some point about the investigation anyway. Eventually.

He rang the bell and watched as the outline of a figure approached the frosted glass door. He heard the key turn, the chain being removed and then the click of a latch. The door opened a couple of inches and a pair of steel-grey eyes glared at him.

'Bugger me with a cordless nibbler,' he said. 'Why would you put all that protection on a glass door?'

'Did you just come here to make smart remarks about my home security?' asked Sandra Next Door.

She made to close the door but stopped when Jim hurriedly said, 'No! I need your help.'

The crack widened again, and the rest of Sandra's face came into view. Her thin lips had widened into a satisfied smile, which would have annoyed Jim had he not been mesmerised by the white, foamy line above them.

'Eh, you've got a wee something just there,' he said, pointing to his top lip.

'It's bleach, you cheeky lump.'

'That's a relief. I thought you'd been snogging Mrs Humphries' chihuahua. She made an emergency appointment for it the other day because she thought it had rabies. Turns out it had eaten half a packet of indigestion tablets.'

This story would have amused Penny, but Sandra Next Door merely rolled her eyes and told Jim to leave his trainers on the doormat. Curling his toes to hide the holes in his socks, he padded down the hall to her impeccably dusted living room.

Nothing had changed in the months since his last visit; the floral sofa and chairs still bore their clear plastic coverings and eight coasters were neatly stacked on the coffee table. A small television stood on a wall unit, surrounded by ornaments, whisky glasses and Geoff's golfing trophies. Otherwise, the room was a sterile environment.

Sandra Next Door saw him eyeing the trophies and said, 'I've been trying to make Geoff get rid of that cabinet for years. It's just a dust magnet. He says there are two of us living in this house, so I have to compromise.'

She said that last word with a hint of venom. Jim

supposed that Geoff Next Door must see something in his wife that had passed the rest of humanity by. It was the only explanation for how he'd managed to live with her for all these years.

'As you're here,' she added, 'you may as well make yourself useful. Get yourself through to the kitchen and put the kettle on while I wash off this bleach. Warm the teapot before you fill it, mind.'

Jim had never been so scared of making a pot of tea in his life. One spill, just one tiny grain of sugar on the worktop, and he was a dead man walking. Sandra Next Door was the only woman he knew who packed a handheld vacuum in her holiday suitcase.

He cast around for something to lay over the work surface to catch any mess and to his relief, spotted a box on the kitchen table marked discreet hygiene pads.

'Ah, that's the ticket,' he said, quickly unwrapping the contents and covering the worktop.

The kettle rumbled and steamed before clicking off, and he did as instructed, pouring some water into the teapot to warm it before the main event. A small spill was immediately absorbed by one of the pads, and Jim gave himself an inner high five. Carefully, he made the tea and placed the pot on a tray. He had just begun a search for mugs when the doorbell rang.

Sandra Next Door's muffled voice came from the bathroom. 'Can you get that? I have to leave the bleach on for another couple of minutes.'

Oho, thought Jim, this might be the perfect opportunity to get revenge for the parking ticket you gave me a few weeks ago. Sandra Next Door took her part-time job as a traffic warden almost as seriously as her cleaning, and she was about as forgiving as a Brillo pad when it came to pleas for mercy, so Jim did not feel in the least ashamed about the plan which had just sprung to mind.

Smiling to himself, he ambled down the hall to the front

door, where he fumbled through the key, chain and latch process, loudly assuring the visitor that he'd only be a second, a few seconds, well maybe a minute until, sweating profusely, he managed to fling open the door.

'Oh,' said the man on the doorstep, looking nervously up. 'You're not Geoff.'

Jim grinned broadly at the short, bespectacled figure in the overly long coat.

'Nope, I'm Sandra's red-hot lover who takes care of all her womanly needs when Geoff's not around. I hope you're nae here for a threesome because I've told the saucy wee minx that I'm nae into the kinky stuff.'

The man's eyes widened, and he shuffled backwards, almost tripping as his heel met the edge of the step.

'Um, oh, ah, yes, no, oh no. I'm Reverend Green. I...I came to see if Sandra would help with the coffee morning next week.'

There was a very long, very awkward silence until, eventually, Jim cleared his throat and said, 'Aye, well, sorry about that. I don't know what came over me, talking about kinky sex. Maybe the devil, eh? You'd know all about that. The devil, I mean, nae the kinky sex. Although you probably know more about God, and we all know what He has to say about kinky sex.'

He stopped, took a deep breath and held out his hand.

'Jim Space. Local vet, total idiot and just a friend of Sandra's. Sorry. I was just joking about the...other thing. Bad joke. Please come in. Sandra's in the loo bleaching her moustache, but she'll be out shortly. Oops, leave your shoes by the door. Just curl your toes and nobody will see the holes in your socks.'

Jim wasn't sure if his second waffle was any better than his first, but Reverend Green seemed happy to follow him into the living room.

'I've just made tea if you'd like a cup,' Jim offered once the minister had settled into an armchair.

Without waiting for a reply, he scuttled off to the kitchen, whispering, 'Fuck-a-doodle-do' all the way. If Reverend Green mentioned any of this to Sandra Next Door, she'd shove his balls in that teapot and slam down the lid. Also, the Rev was on his list. He was supposed to charm the man into giving answers about the vigilante, not scare him half to death with lewd suggestions.

'Aw Jim, man,' he groaned. 'You're going straight to hell. You can't get anything right today.'

He added mugs, teaspoons, a sugar bowl and a jug of milk to the tray and was about to carry them through to the living room when he had an idea. Everyone likes a handy life hack, he thought. This might just put me back in the good books with the big man upstairs.

Thirty seconds later, he breezed through the living room door and laid the tray on the coffee table.

'Would you like to be mother or shall I?' he asked the Reverend.

'Go ahead,' the man nodded. 'Two sugars and just a dash of milk please.'

'Coming right up, sir,' said Jim. 'But first, the coasters. And these aren't your run-of-the-mill coasters. Prepare to be amazed.'

A few minutes later, Sandra Next Door stood in the living room, her mouth open and two pink spots glowing right in the centre of her cheeks. Her voice, usually sharp and disapproving, appeared to have deserted her.

'Ah, Mrs Next Door, said Reverend Green. 'How clever of you to find these super-absorbent disposable coasters. The perfect size for a cup of tea and a biscuit, and the sticky strip on the back is simply genius.'

'Absolutely brilliant,' Jim agreed. 'Although you might want to get bigger ones for the worktop. I had to use eight there.'

Sandra Next Door's mouth opened and closed. Nothing emerged.

'I hope you don't mind,' said the Reverend. 'I've taken a few to show the social activities sub-committee. Linda Robertson who runs the church hall rota was going to pop by to ask you to help with the coffee morning next week, but I said I'd ask you myself. I was going to Len and Mary's anyway. Len's had a great idea about repurposing the shed behind the manse. Are you okay? You seem very quiet.'

Sandra sank into the chair behind her and slowly breathed in through her nose, then out through her mouth. She was clearly struggling with something, and Jim felt a momentary pang of guilt for the doorstep prank, although the minister had promised never to mention it. Perhaps he should say something to cheer her up.

'Your moustache has turned out lovely. You can hardly see it now.'

The pink spots on Sandra Next Door's cheeks grew even brighter, and Jim began to have a sneaking suspicion that he might have said the wrong thing. He tried again.

'If you do your beard the same, it'll be ace.'

Nope. If anything, she looked like she was going to have a stroke. The bit above her top lip, which had been a bonnie pink colour when she came in, was now a hard, white line, punctuated by deep wrinkles, and her mouth was puckered so tightly that he thought she might have to drink her tea through a straw. Maybe this was a normal reaction to moustache bleach, he didn't know. Or maybe now would be a good time to stop talking.

'The coffee morning?' prompted Reverend Green.

'Yes,' whispered Sandra Next Door.

She cleared her throat and said more loudly, 'Yes, I'll help. Ask Linda to email me the details. And I'd prefer it if we could keep the disposable coasters between ourselves. They're at an, erm, experimental stage. Still being tested.'

'I understand,' said the Reverend, digging around in his pocket and then handing her three individually wrapped pads. He tapped the side of his nose. 'You don't want any leaks.'

'We'll keep it under wraps,' Jim assured her.

Quietly, Sandra Next Door moved the mugs onto regular coasters and peeled the pads from the table.

'I'll just get rid of these,' she said. 'I'll be back in a minute.'

As he watched her march, straight-backed, from the room, Jim couldn't shake the feeling that he'd done something wrong, yet for the life of him, he couldn't think what. With a small shrug, he set the thought aside and decided to take advantage of the Reverend's presence to cross someone off his list of folk to be interviewed.

'I was going to come and see you, sir,' he said.

'Gregor,' the Reverend corrected him. 'Call me Gregor. I don't stand on ceremony, except when it's a church one. Ha ha.'

'Aye, ha ha,' said Jim, giving the man a weak smile. 'I wanted to ask you about Alec Carmichael. Sergeant Wilson's snowed under with the murder at the lighthouse, so I said I'd ask around about the Vik Vigilante. Carmichael was one of the victims, I believe. What's your impression of the man?'

The Reverend bit his lip and ran a hand over his balding pate, knocking his glasses to the floor. Jim swiftly leaned across the coffee table, plucked them from the thick pile of the carpet and handed them back. He stayed there, hunched forwards and gazing intently at the minister, trying to figure out why the man looked so worried.

'Gregor,' he prompted, judging that the silence had gone on a little too long.

'Sorry,' said Reverend Green. 'I was trying to think how to say…we're not supposed to speak ill of people.'

'As we're all keeping secrets today, I promise that I won't quote you to anyone.'

Jim sat back and waited as the Reverend took a sip of his tea.

'Alright,' the man said. 'I'll be blunt. He's an absolute scunner. There. I've said it. The man's a scunner.'

'Aye, I've heard he can be a nuisance,' said Jim.

'It's more than that.' Reverend Green was leaning forward now, seemingly eager to get whatever was bothering him off his chest. 'He'd take calls during services, argued with many of the Elders and seemed determined to exert some authority over the congregation. I was at the point of taking the matter upwards.'

Jim leaned forward, his eyes wide, and whispered, 'What? To the big man upstairs?'

'No, of course not, although I did say a few prayers. To my, for want of a better word, superiors.'

Jim relaxed. 'You didn't think about taking matters into your own hands?'

'Of course not. You don't think I'm the vigilante, do you?'

'Well, it's hard to find anybody the man hasn't pissed off, but your name came up as someone who was becoming particularly exasperated.'

'That's fair. I have had some very unchristian thoughts about him. That's as far as it went, though. Anyway, I can't be the vigilante. For a start, I wasn't aware of the wife-swapping rumours and secondly, I was on a Church of Scotland retreat when it happened.'

'When what happened?'

'The parish newsletter being hacked. Linda Robertson writes it, and she'll confirm that the hack happened on publication day. I was at the retreat where there's no access to the internet and no phone signal. It's all about quiet meditation. The newsletter had gone out, the Carmichaels had disappeared and Linda had disinfected the collection bowl by the time I got back.'

'Then I am pleased to inform you that your name is off my suspect list.'

Reverend Green closed his eyes for a moment before opening them and saying, 'Just a wee thank you to the big man. Sandra Next Door's been gone a while. Should we check on her?'

'Och, she's probably in the garage with Geoff's strimmer doing her bikini line. You know what these wimmen are like.'

'Aye, wimmen,' said the Reverend, as if he had great experience with the opposite sex.

Thanks to Pat Hughes, Jim knew that the man lived alone and had been valiantly resisting Pat's charms for the past few years. She'd made an exception for his height because, as she'd confided, 'God made him a little one, and who am I to argue?'

Sandra Next Door emerged only once Reverend Green had left. Jim closed the front door, turned and nearly choked on his own tongue when he found her standing directly beside him. Just a few centimetres separated them, and she was breathing through her nose like a bull about to charge. He looked down, just to check she wasn't pawing the laminate flooring with a hoof.

'How could you humiliate me like that?' she rasped, anger tight in her throat. 'We have had our differences, but I never thought you'd stoop so low. It's just as well he didn't know what they were.'

Jim was baffled. She appeared to be waiting for him to say something, perhaps offer an excuse, before she launched her next salvo.

'I think he does know what a threesome is,' he said. 'But I told him I was just joking.'

It was Sandra's turn to look confused.

'Why were you talking to him about threesomes?'

'It was when I said I was your lover. I told him I wasn't into anything kinky, like, just in case he was here for a threesome. Then I said it was a joke and you and me are purely friends.'

Sandra Next Door's blonde helmet of hair quivered ominously as the rest of her body prepared to explode with rage. The pink cheeks were now mauve, and she'd clenched her fists so hard that a false nail went skittering across the floor. The kinky sex thing was clearly news to her.

'I thought you must have overheard us talking,' Jim said, backing away from her and feeling behind him for the key in the lock. 'If it wasn't that, what were you on about?'

'Get out,' hissed Sandra Next Door. 'Get out before I do something I probably won't regret.'

She pushed past him and swiftly unlocked the door. Then, powered by pure wrath, she shoved him outside, threw his trainers at him and yelled, 'Don't ever come back, you filthy animal.'

Stunned, Jim stood on the drive watching her through the window as she stomped into the living room and lifted the tea tray. If he didn't know she was hard as nails, he'd swear she was crying. She looked up and caught him watching her. Laying the tray down again, she strode to the window and drew the curtains, leaving Jim no choice but to put on his trainers and slope to his car.

Tears stinging his eyes for the second time that day, he sat in the driver's seat and texted Penny.

```
Please call me soon. Another major duck up.
Having a ducking ducker of a day.
```

CHAPTER 10

Penny dashed through the opening in the wall, silently cursing herself for leaving her coat in Brodie's cottage. A fine dusting of tiny droplets had settled on her sweatshirt and would soon begin to soak through the material. Worse, it was bloomin' freezing. You could always count on Scotland to offer four seasons in a day: wet, monsoon, hurricane and skiing.

Ahead of her, she could just make out the figure striding towards the small car park that was normally crammed during the summer monsoon but now stood empty save for three cars and a dog poo bin. Staying low, she scurried forwards and crouched behind the bin, breathing through her mouth and trying not to step on any of the squelchy bags carelessly tossed in the general direction of the bin by dog owners who seemed to have the aim of a lager lout in a train toilet.

She wasn't quite close enough to identify the person through the mist, but she could see that they wore a baseball cap pulled low. The long coat disguised their build such that it was impossible to tell whether it was a man or a woman.

Shivering, Penny watched as the figure stopped by one of the cars and peered in. That was Eileen's car! She hoped that

Eileen had removed the Tourist Office parking pass that came with her part-time job. She wasn't supposed to use it unless she was at work, but she had been known to "accidentally" forget when there was a shopping emergency, such as urgent shoes or crisis chocolate. The last thing Eileen needed was Shady McDoorbasher over there figuring out who she was and coming for her.

The figure moved on to the next car, Penny's. Oh, flippin' Lordy. What had she left lying around that could identify her? Penny began a mental inventory of the inside of her car but gave up when she encountered the six empty crisp packets of shame from last month's period binge. All she could do was hope that anything with her name on it was obscured by the approximately forty tons of rubbish, emergency comfy shoes and the coats she'd bought in three different colours because she liked them so much. As Jim often said, you can't beat a good coat. He should know. He hadn't thrown out a coat in twenty years.

Realising that anxiety was making her brain gremlins run amok, Penny ceased the internal wibble about coats and focused on the third vehicle, which she assumed must belong to Shady McDoorbasher. Carefully peeping around the edge of the bin, she waited for Shady to get into the silver hatchback before making her move. A simple squatting run, using the other vehicles for cover should do it.

With a silent prayer to Workout Wendy, the ridiculously lithe woman on YouTube who liked to "get those thighs workin' baby," Penny emerged from her hiding place and, deploying something just short of a toddler's bum shuffle, she began a low, fast waddle towards the cars. She had travelled about five metres and was already regretting not paying more attention to Workout Wendy, when a blur of pink and yellow swept by, heels clicking on the tarmac.

She caught a muttered, 'I am not cowering in that cottage waiting to be murdered. Bring it on, dearies, bring it on.'

Penny watched in astonishment as Mrs Hubbard marched

up to Shady McDoorbasher's car and rapped loudly on the window.

'There's no point in hiding in your car, dearie,' the elderly shopkeeper boomed. 'I have your number and I'll get the dark interweb hackers to run your plates. Oh, I don't need them. I forgot. Sergeant Wilson's on *our* side now. Righty-ho. I'll get Sergeant Wilson to put out a BOLO and alert the Feds. Come out with your hands up, you big DUI.'

Penny, who had abandoned her squat in favour of a short sprint, drew to a halt behind the older woman and said, 'Have you been watching American cop shows again, Mrs H?'

'Yes, I have,' bellowed Mrs Hubbard. 'Throw your weapons out of the car. Licence and registration ma'am.'

'Is it a ma'am?' asked Penny, bending to take a closer look at the figure sitting rigidly in the driver's seat, no doubt hoping that Mrs Hubbard would give up and go away.

'I have no idea, dearie! It's a John Doe!'

'You can stop shouting now, Mrs H,' said Penny. 'I think they've got the message.'

Mrs Hubbard put a hand on the roof of the vehicle and leaned down, making a winding motion with her other hand.

The figure paused for a moment then pressed a button and the rear window slowly slid downwards.

'Bugger. I keep doing that. Sorry, wrong button,' said a female voice.

The rear window went back up then the driver's window slid down. The woman removed her baseball cap, letting her long brown hair tumble around her shoulders, and stuck her head through the gap, coming almost nose to nose with Mrs Hubbard.

'Lisa Jennings, Ecclefechan Express. Who are you?'

'Deputy Mrs Hubbard, assistant to Sergeant Wilson. Although I crossed my fingers at the bit about kicking folk and nailing their dangly bits to a dyke, so I might only be half a deputy. Still, as I always say to my Douglas, it's not where you start that counts - it's where you finish. Or was it the other way around? I think it was that time the little blue pill wore off before he got to the good bit, so it was probably the other way around. Gail Forsyth at the chemists said it was because they were out of date, but they give you so many in a packet, is it any wonder you're still using the same ones ten years later?'

Mrs Hubbard looked expectantly at the journalist as if anticipating wholehearted agreement that this was ridiculous. Penny decided to intervene before the shopkeeper moved on to all the marvellous things you could do with a pair of washing-up gloves and an ice cream scoop. She'd sat through that particular brain dump before, and quite frankly, she was surprised that Douglas was still able to rhumba.

'I know who you are,' she told the reporter. 'You're the Mata Hari. The one who tried to cosy up to Stevie Mains for information last year. Which murder was that?'

'The distillery murder,' said Lisa. 'Although you get so many of them for such a small island, I can barely keep up.'

Penny had been thinking the same. It would be nice if they could have a normal crime for once. Perhaps a gentle spate of car thefts or a wee insurance fraud. She wondered how Jim's vigilante investigation was coming along. Hopefully, he hadn't done anything stupid like arguing with Sandra Next Door. She glanced down at her phone. Still no signal.

'I take it you're here about Beacon Brodie's murder?' she asked.

Lisa nodded but otherwise stayed tight-lipped.

'All the way from the big smoke of Ecclefechan,' said Mrs Hubbard, impressed. Then she remembered something, and her face fell. 'You reported on Elsie's death as well.'

'The librarian lady?' Lisa asked.

Mrs Hubbard shook her head glumly.

'Poor Elsie. Mind, I'll give you your due. It was a good article. You did right by her.'

'She'd had an interesting life,' said Lisa. 'It's not every day that half of Hollywood turns out for your funeral.'

'Och, they're all knitting mad, dearie. And that Al Cuppachino took a right huff when yon laddie beat him at the miniature golf in the afternoon. What was his name? Bradie something. Bradie Pitt. What his mother was thinking when she named him after a Scottish pie, Lord only knows. I like a bradie, though. What time does the supermarket close on a Sunday? I might stop and get one on the way home.'

'Mrs Hubbard, maybe you could go back and check on Eileen,' Penny suggested, interrupting the older woman's stream of consciousness. Mrs Hubbard tended to gabble when she was worried.

'Goodness, I forgot about poor Eileen. I told her to stay and make sure nobody came into the house. I mean, you can't have strangers going through the man's things, can you? Although, I suppose we're strangers. I mean other strangers. Uncertified strangers. We're okay, I think. We should be certified.'

'In your case, I completely agree,' muttered Lisa, earning herself a sharp look from Penny.

'Mrs H. Eileen?' Penny prompted.

With a hurried apology, Mrs Hubbard made off in the direction of the cottage, leaving Penny alone with Lisa. Her first order of business was to find out why the reporter had been trying to break into Brodie's cottage.

'I have an arrangement with DCI Moffat,' Lisa explained. 'He gives me the story, and I give him the glory. He lent me the keys to the cottage and the lighthouse so I could have a poke around on my own, but even though the cottage was already unlocked, I couldn't get in. I guess you were already in there, barring the door.'

This was not good news. Sergeant Wilson would be extra sweary when she found out that Fudmuppet had plans to take all the credit. In fact, it was better for all concerned if Sergeant Wilson didn't find out. Moreover, under no circumstances could it get back to Fudmuppet that the Sergeant was planning his downfall. Penny quickly ran through the problem in her mind and concluded that all she had to do was get the reporter on Sergeant Wilson's side without either of them realising it and discreetly undermine Fudmuppet. She could do that. Couldn't she?

'Yes, we were in there,' Penny admitted. 'I'd be grateful if you didn't tell Fud…erm DCI Moffat. The police tend to get a bit sniffy about Losers Club sticking its nose in. Fiona told you about us last time, didn't she? We're a weight-loss and healthy lifestyle group that solves crimes. Do you think that would be a good story for your newspaper?'

Lisa didn't hesitate.

'Yes, that's an excellent idea. I sold the scoop Fiona gave me last time to the nationals and there were a few enquiries about Losers Club's involvement. I do some freelancing, you see. The Ecclefechan Express is great, but it hardly covers the bills.'

'I thought you were at one of the bigger newspapers,' said Penny.

'I was, but let's not talk about that. Why were you in Brodie's cottage?'

Penny chose her words carefully.

'Curiosity, mainly. Sometimes we can find out things that the police can't. We simply wanted to find out more about the man. Where he came from, his family, why he came to the island. We heard a rumour that he had a shady past on the mainland.'

'Did you tell Moffat?' Lisa asked.

Penny shook her head. Her denial was technically true. She didn't know whether the MIT were aware, but she'd lay odds on Sergeant Wilson not telling Fudmuppet anything unless she absolutely had to. Lisa didn't need to know that.

'And what was Mrs Hubbard talking about when she said that Sergeant Wilson was on your side?' Lisa continued.

'Something about her deputising the woman. Does the Sergeant know about your enquiries?'

Penny tried to keep her face as blank as possible. Darnit, she'd forgotten about Deputy Mrs Hubbard chuntering on about BOLOs and the Feds.

Feeling like a traitor, she scoffed, 'Mrs Hubbard also said something about kicking folk and nailing their dangly bits to a dyke, went on at length about her husband's blue pills and told you that Al Cuppachino and Bradie Pitt were playing mini-golf. Between you and I, she's still living at home with Douglas, but he's finding it increasingly difficult to cope with her. And if she tries to tell you anything about washing up gloves and an ice cream scoop, walk away.'

Lisa gave a soft snort and flashed her a complicit smirk.

'Not a reliable source, then.'

'She's a font of local knowledge with a tendency to go off on a wee ramble of her own sometimes. We mostly take her with a pinch of salt, and it's probably not a good idea to leave her and Eileen alone in the cottage, so I better get back. Are you coming?'

Lisa looked up at her, surprised.

'I thought you wouldn't want me around. I'm a journalist. I'm not used to people wanting me around.'

'Better the devil you know,' Penny grinned. 'And if you're going to make your fortune by writing an article about us, would it not be better to stick with us?'

'You're right,' said Lisa, pressing a button and getting out of the car.

The two women watched as the window slowly moved back up then, with a salutary thunk, the locks were engaged, and Lisa followed Penny to the cottage.

Silently congratulating herself for achieving part one of Mission Get the Journo On Our Side, Penny failed to notice the other woman's calculating glance. In her hubris, it didn't occur to her that the journalist might have her own agenda.

CHAPTER 11

Eileen had Mrs Hubbard backed up against the wall, a soup ladle at her throat, and was yelling, 'What costume did I wear to Mary and Len's Hogmanay fancy dress party?'

Entering the cottage just in time to see Mrs Hubbard raise her hands to soundly box Eileen's ears, Penny rushed forward and inserted herself between the two women.

'What's going on?' she screeched.

'She says that I told her not to let strangers in and that I might not be me,' Mrs Hubbard explained.

'I saw a documentary about it!' Eileen roared. 'All these people turned into other people.'

Penny thought for a moment, then…

'Was there a lad called Harry in it?'

'Yes!'

'And a girl called Hermione?'

'Yes!'

'It wasn't a documentary. It was the movie you're not allowed to watch because you'll believe it's real.'

'Oh. Right. So, are you saying it wasn't real?'

'It's just a story, nothing else.'

'Alright, if I agree that it wasn't real, does that mean I can watch Ghostbusters now?'

'No, because I can see you have your fingers crossed behind your back.'

'Cordon bleu. There was a man in the documentary who did that. He had a magic false eye.'

Eileen leaned in to peer closely at Penny's eyes, and Mrs Hubbard took the opportunity to squirm away from her. With a small whoop of delight, the older woman spotted Lisa, who was hovering, bemused, in the doorway, and scurried across the creaking floorboards to take her hand and drag her into the room.

'Come in, dearie,' she said. 'Ignore Eileen. She has a different view of the world, which comes in handy sometimes. She's perfectly harmless. Mostly. And very good if you ever need someone to help you liberate things from trollies in hotels.'

Mrs Hubbard rummaged in her handbag and produced a foil-wrapped object.

'Teacake?' she offered.

'No thanks.'

'How about a wee bottle of conditioner? You've lovely hair, mind you. All long and shiny. I don't suppose you have much need of wee bottles of shampoo and conditioner. How about a knife and fork? We were at a hotel on the mainland for nearly a week, and they just kept leaving them out on the tables, unattended, so I have the full set and some spares. Where are you staying?'

'I managed to get a room at the Vik Hotel,' Lisa told her.

'Oh, they do a lovely napkin. I don't suppose you could…'

'No.'

Throughout this exchange, they had watched Penny calm her friend down, and it was a much more subdued Eileen who apologised to Mrs Hubbard.

'Jimmy Choos and days holy, Mrs H. I got a bit carried away there.'

Mrs Hubbard's brow furrowed in confusion and her eyes darted to Penny, who was gathering up the items she'd set aside to look at later.

Clutching the photograph album to her chest, Penny clarified, 'Je m'excuse and désolée. She means sorry. Now we've cleared that up, Eileen meet Lisa. She's a reporter with the Ecclefechan Express. The one who helped Jim and I pose as journalists when we went to the distillery, remember?'

'The one that tried to get Stevie Mains to sleep with her?' asked Eileen, wide-eyed.

'I didn't exactly–' Lisa began, but Eileen cut her off and raised the ladle, shaking it threateningly.

'You better not come after my Kenny, you big tiger.'

'Cougar,' Penny corrected.

'I'm not a cougar,' Lisa protested.

Eileen brandished the ladle again.

'I don't care what species of big cat you are, all I'm saying is that you better not go after my Kenny. Because he's not a cheetah.'

'Cheater,' said Penny automatically.

'That as well.'

'I like a nice leopard,' said Mrs Hubbard. 'Although they're a right tooter when you go for a pee.'

'Leotard,' said Penny automatically.

Lisa crossed her arms and sighed impatiently, tilting her head as she regarded the three women. The stern look she shot them seemed to presage a lecture, but then she sighed again, and this one sounded more resigned.

'Look, I'm not going to steal anyone's husband, boyfriend or napkins. I just want to take a gander around the cottage and lighthouse and then get back to the hotel to write my story.'

Eileen and Mrs Hubbard opened their mouths to argue, but Lisa did a neat pivot, distracting them with the matter at hand.

'Is that a photograph album, Penny? Do you think it might be important?'

Penny felt some sympathy. Corralling Mrs H and Eileen could be both exasperating and exhausting. She was aware that she and her friends may not have made the best first impression. Looking at it from Lisa's point of view, they were an odd bunch; an eclectic mix of blithering blonde with a ladle, bossy dark one with tired eyes and a stout kleptomaniac in a shower cap. Yep. If this woman wrote an article about them, they were going to look like they were actual losers. Something had to be done about this. She must demonstrate to Lisa that despite their quirks, they were good at this investigating business.

She lowered herself into Brodie's armchair and opened the album to show her companions what she'd found. They crowded round, stooping to look more closely at the faded, tiny figures in their kipper ties and paper crowns. Lisa leaned across her to switch on the small table lamp, and Penny caught a whiff of Chanel Coco Mademoiselle. She made a mental note to start dropping hints to Jim for next Christmas. It was over eight months away, so there was a reasonable chance that the message might sink in by then.

Flipping one of the photos, Penny ran a finger over the handwritten names and explained that she thought it was worth tracing some of the people to find out more about Brodie.

'It's going to take a wee while to sort through everything,' she cautioned in response to the excited murmurings of her companions. 'I'll take it home for a proper look, then I'll let you all know what I find.'

'Wait,' said Eileen. 'You're going to let Lisa know? Is Lisa part of our team?'

Penny had been praying that neither Eileen nor Mrs Hubbard would let the cat out of the bag about them assisting Sergeant Wilson in the downfall of Fudmuppet, and she could feel Eileen coming perilously close.'

'She's been working on a story about DCI Moffat's investigation, but she thinks that what we do would make an interesting story. And she's not going to tell DCI Moffat what we're up to, are you, Lisa?'

Lisa's gaze remained steadfastly neutral as she replied, 'Not unless I think you've discovered something material to the investigation. Then we're all obliged to hand the information over.'

'But Fudmuppet—' said Eileen, and Penny hurried to stem the flow of incriminating Sergeant Wilson-related facts that were about to come gushing from her lips.

'I'll tell you about it later. Lisa, carry on and do your thing. We'll share what we find with you if you do the same. In the meantime, let's exchange phone numbers so we can keep in touch. I'm going to treat these two to a well-deserved cup of tea and some cake. Even though we're supposed to be back on our diets, I don't suppose one slice of cake will do much harm.'

She'd said the magic words. Eileen and Mrs Hubbard gathered up their things and followed her from the cottage without a word of protest, leaving behind them only a good-natured warning to Lisa about the sticky door.

'You don't want to get trapped in here on your own, dearie. It's creepy and smells far too much like my Douglas' bowling socks for my liking.'

Outside, the mizzle had turned to light rain and the three women hurriedly donned their coats for the short walk to their cars.

'Did either of you find anything interesting in the kitchen or upstairs?' Penny asked as she unlocked her rubbish bin on wheels.

Eileen and Mrs Hubbard shook their heads.

Pointing to the album, Eileen said, 'It looks like you struck gold, though. Do you think Lisa really will share anything she finds with us? There's something about her that I don't trust.'

'We have to work with her,' said Penny.

She explained that Lisa had a cosy relationship with Fudmuppet and that they couldn't let Lisa know that they were working with Sergeant Wilson because then it would get back to Fudmuppet that the Sergeant was running her own investigation on the side, and she would get into trouble. Which meant that Sergeant Wilson would be very angry.

'And none of us wants to be on the receiving end of her taser collection, do we?' she concluded.

'Wow, said Eileen, pushing back a hank of wet hair that had plastered itself to her nose. 'That seems very complicated. I kind of get it, but I'm not sure I could explain it to someone else.'

'All you have to remember is that Lisa must not find out about Sergeant Wilson, and Sergeant Wilson must not find out about Lisa. Capiche?'

The others looked uncertain, but they capiched and it was agreed that they'd avoid Sergeant Wilson as much as possible and try to keep her away from their investigation.

Penny was just about to suggest that they go to the café by the loch for cake when her phone beeped. It had finally caught a weak signal, and she glanced down at it to see that her earlier text had been sent. Bugger. If they were to keep the Sergeant out of things, she should have deleted that message and got Eileen to ask the hackers to check on the address. Never mind. What was done was done. Oh, goodness. There were more texts and missed calls, most of them from Jim.

She opened the most recent message and read it. Eh? Her brow furrowed in confusion. She scrolled to the previous message. Her face fell. This sounded serious. Oh lordy, what the duck had he done now?

CHAPTER 12

A mile inland from the coast, the mist had cleared, and the day appeared to have settled for cloudy with showers. Yet it was still bitterly cold, and Penny's hands were deep in her coat pockets as she gently pressed a shoulder to the loch café door.

The building had been constructed using Scots pine from Laird Hamish's estate and resembled a giant log cabin. The glass doors which spanned the rear wall gave visitors a panoramic view of Loch Vik and the small jetty from which the tourist boat ran in the summer. Dougal, the new owner of both café and boat, had put considerable effort into convincing his guests that an ancient monster lived in the waters, to the extent that even the tablecloths depicted a giant two-headed fish with legs that he'd dubbed The Terror of the Loch, or Terry for short. He'd wanted to call it the Loch Vik Monster but there had been a meeting about it in the church hall and the islanders agreed that the competition from around Inverness was just too big. They couldn't risk getting sued by the Nessie brigade, so Terry it was.

Normally, the Losers would congregate at the big table by the window but today, Eileen and Mrs Hubbard were huddled by the log fire. Penny hung her wet coat over the back of her chair and angled it so that the garment could gently steam dry in the crackling warmth.

'I've asked Jim to meet us here,' she said. 'He's had some sort of falling out with Gordon and Sandra Next Door. That's pretty much all I could make out. There was a lot of talk about feelings and not liking having feelings, and if this was what feelings felt like, then he wanted them to go away. Have you ordered?'

Eileen and Mrs Hubbard confirmed that they were waiting for the lassie behind the counter to get off the phone and shift her backside in their direction.

'I think she might be breaking up with her boyfriend,' Mrs Hubbard said in a low voice, her eyes darting to the girl to check she hadn't been overheard. 'He went with Melanie in the wheelie bins round the back of the pub, and now he's given the lassie an LCD.'

'STD?' Penny suggested.

'Does that mean the same? Because once when me and my Douglas went camping, there were communal showers and–'

Eileen was leaning forward, eager to hear more, but Penny raised a hand.

'TMI, Mrs H. Please don't put me off my cake. Shall I go up and order for all three...four of us? I'll get Jim a sausage sandwich. That worked a treat the last time he had feelings. A sandwich filled with both savoury deliciousness and potential innuendo. He likes things like that. Although he can become quite unbearable around pulled pork.'

As she wandered off to place their order, she heard the older woman ask, 'TMI? Can you get cream for that?'

By the time Penny had interrupted the hissed remonstrations that "Melanie is a cow, Melanie is ugly, Melanie has a weird mole in her lip, and I hope you catch big hairy moles" ... the cursing took a while...and a while longer...by the time Penny had successfully interrupted the remonstrations and placed their order, Jim was thawing out by the fire.

'I ordered you a sausage sandwich,' she told him.

Jim's eyes momentarily lit up, then his shoulders slumped, and he stared disconsolately at the slightly rumpled Terry on the tablecloth.

'Gordon's got a big sausage baby.'

'Don't worry about it, sweetie,' said Penny, putting an arm around him and pulling him close. 'Yours is perfectly acceptable.'

Despite his dolour, Jim gave a little snicker at this, as she knew he would.

Once their food and drinks had arrived, Penny got to work on coaxing Jim to reveal how he had ended up on non-speaking terms with both Sandra Next Door and Gordon, and by extension Fiona, on the same day.

'I'm not supposed to tell anyone about Gordon,' he murmured, with a knowing glance at Mrs Hubbard.

'Oh, don't you worry about me, dearie. I am the soul of discretion,' said the village gossip and current holder of the island award for offending the most people in one day when she accidentally leaned on the dentist's keyboard and emailed a halitosis help sheet to his entire patient list.

Taking a sip of his coffee, Jim gathered his thoughts and began recounting how he had confronted Dolores about her deception regarding Gordon's alleged paternity, believing he was doing the right thing by helping his friend. However, Gordon had seen it as meddling in his personal affairs.

'And now he's going to have to tell Fiona. I just made everything turn to shit,' he moaned.

Penny and Eileen sat frozen in shock at the news, cups raised halfway to their lips. It was left to Mrs Hubbard to lean across the table to pat his hand reassuringly.

'He should have told Fiona a long time ago. But that doesn't excuse what you did. I don't think I've ever told anyone this, but years ago, back when Penny was a baby, Mary and I had a spectacular falling out. It was my fault. She told me a secret about Len. I told Elsie, not realising that it impacted on her, and the whole thing turned into a huge stramash.'

'What did you do about it?' asked Jim.

'I went to Mary on my hands and knees and begged forgiveness. What else could I do? Oh yes, and I promised never to gossip again.'

'And how's that working out for you, Mrs H?' Eileen asked.

Coming from anyone else, it would have sounded sarcastic, but with Eileen, it was impossible to tell. Mrs Hubbard chose to take it as curiosity.

'She forgave me, and we'll leave it at that. The point is, Jim, that you have a lot of apologising to do. But not today. Give things a day or two to calm down. He's a decent man, even if he does hide Mars Bars around the house and Fiona can't work out why he's put so much weight on. Oh. Did I just say that? I was not supposed to say that.'

With an unrepentant grin, Mrs Hubbard took a hefty bite of her carrot cake and sat back, her best advice delivered.

'What about Sandra Next Door?' Jim asked. 'I don't even know what I've done wrong there, so how can I apologise to her?'

At Penny's urging, he related the events at Sandra's house, concluding with, 'And me and Reverend Green thought the disposable coasters were a grand idea!'

Mrs Hubbard, Eileen and Penny exchanged glances, each wondering how to break it to him.

Eventually, Penny suggested, he do an internet search for discreet hygiene pads for older women. With much spluttering about having to give his personal information to strangers, he logged onto the café Wi-Fi, and the three women watched as his cheeks went from fireside pink to roaring crimson.

'Oh.'

'Aye, oh,' said Penny.

'Will you come with me while I apologise?'

'Alright, but we have our hands full with Beacon Brodie,' Penny sighed. 'I have to go through this photo album we found and identify the people in the pictures. And stop sneaking bits of cake off my plate. It might seem as if I'm not looking, yet I can see.'

'It's true,' said Eileen. 'You can't tell it's a magic eye unless you get in really close. Do you want me to make a start on the photo album, Penny? I could get the hackers to help me. They adapted their facial recognition software to use AI so they can compare images with what's on the internet. It uses a powerful algorithm to narrow down the possibilities so that you get ninety percent accurate results. I didn't offer before because I didn't think you'd want me to mention the hackers in front of Lisa.'

'Who are you and what have you done with Eileen?' asked Penny, absent-mindedly smacking Jim's sneaky cake hand, which was once more encroaching on her Victoria sponge. 'You used to think that Al Gorithm was an American former politician who bangs on about climate change and dances to the beat. Also, that's a brilliant idea, asking the hackers. Thank you.'

'Hang on a minute,' said Jim, who had deployed new tactics and was now talking through a mouthful of Eileen's lemon drizzle cake. 'Rewind. Who's Lisa?'

The three women explained about the reporter and how they'd agreed to keep Sergeant Wilson out of the investigation as much as possible.

'But she's the one who invited you into the investigation,' said Jim. 'Oh, this does not bode well. She'll go ballistic when she finds out. I think you should tell her.'

'We're not telling her, and neither will you,' said Penny firmly. 'Not unless you want me to tell her about the disposable coasters. She'll never let you live that down. Agreed? Right, how are you coming along with the vigilante investigation?'

Jim glumly explained that things were moving slowly, and

now that Gordon was no longer helping, they were likely to go even slower. He showed the women his notes and his suspect list.

'You can cross the McCullochs off,' said Mrs Hubbard. 'I heard this morning that they were off doing Ballroom Boot Camp in Mintlaw all last week. And the Hee-Hawes have been visiting her family in Hong Kong for the past month.'

'And it's unlikely to be Minky,' Penny pointed out. 'She was the one who told us about Dirty Dolores in the first place.'

She muttered a hasty apology as Jim winced at the mention of Dolores.

Eileen pointed to Stevie Mains' mum's name and Jim told her about the eyebrow disaster.

'Is Edna Mains the one who crashed the mobility scooter into Randy Mair's pond?' asked Eileen.

'No,' said Mrs Hubbard. 'That was drunk Keith, the plumber. Watch out for him when you're driving past the farm. My Douglas has nearly run him over five times. Edna's the one who ran out of battery halfway up Windy Brae, rolled through an electric fence and blew up a goat.'

'I remember now,' said Eileen. 'It attacked her, and she fended it off with her oxygen tank. So, we can rule out Edna Mains. Terrible COPD, poor woman.'

Penny slid her plate from Jim's place back to hers and poked him in the arm with her cake fork. With her other hand, she picked up his list and scanned the names.

'That whittles it down to Geoff Next Door, Rachael and Martin from the hotel, the five-a-side team, Barry Glossop, Brian Miller and Iona Cameltoe. We can probably cross Geoff off when we speak to Sandra, and you can speak to the football team. Leaving you with the hotel, Barry, Brian and Iona to visit. Does that seem more manageable to do on your own?'

Penny wasn't sure if it was the group support or the illicit sugar rush, but Jim seemed to have perked up. His usual twinkle was back as he flung an arm around her shoulders, pointed at the menu and asked if she'd like a cream muffin.

The rain had eased off by the time they paid the bill and headed off to the car park. Penny handed over the photo album to Eileen, showing her the cards inside which might be helpful. She offered to take Mrs Hubbard home, then meet Jim at Sandra Next Door's house. A slight sense of dread settled over her when she thought about Jim's upcoming apology. Sandra Next Door was not renowned for her forgiving nature, and she and Jim had a history of minor skirmishes. Penny was quite glad that Mrs Hubbard snoozed for the short drive to the village as it gave her time to mull over the best approach.

Jim had parked in her parents' drive rather than inflame things further by waiting in the car outside Sandra's living room window. A wise yet cowardly decision thought Penny as she did the same.

They spent a few minutes rehearsing what Jim was going to say, and then together, they walked out of Len and Mary's drive and immediately turned right into Sandra's. Her bungalow was of a similar ilk to Penny's parents', with its once white pebble-dashed walls now slightly grey with age and its bland boxiness relieved only by a bay window. Here, the wooden window frames that her father stained and varnished every few years had been replaced with white uPVC, and instead of an expanse of gravel, a neat length of tarmac led to the small garage where Geoff Next Door stored his Honda Civic and his golf clubs.

Taking a deep breath, Penny knocked on the front door. It was immediately answered by a rather harassed-looking Geoff.

'Thank goodness you're here,' he said, gesturing with a beringed hand for them both to come in. 'She's being impossible. Has there been some sort of falling out? I came home to find her scrubbing the contents of the tins cupboard with a toothbrush. She only does that when she's really angry, and now I can't tell tomato soup from beans. All the labels are gone.'

He brandished a shiny tin and asked, 'Sweetcorn or carrots? Anyway, I'll let her know you're here.'

He left them standing awkwardly in the hall, straining to hear whether a small explosion would follow the news that Sandra Next Door had visitors. No such explosion occurred. Instead, Sandra emerged from the kitchen and stood a few metres away, her arms folded and her lips compressed into a tight, forbidding line.

'Yes?' she snapped.

'Jim explained what happened and I've explained to him why you were so angry,' said Penny. 'He has something to say to you.'

She nudged Jim with her elbow, and he started nervously, realising that it was his turn to speak.

'Aye well, I'm really sorry. I didn't realise what they were. I thought it was something to do with cleaning because you like cleaning and this place is always so clean and I thought maybe they were special cloths or something and they were really good for mopping up the spills so I just thought I'd save your coasters for good.' Jim stopped to draw a deep breath then continued, 'Penny told me what they were, well, she made me google them, and bugger me with a Spontex scourer, they were for a different kind of spill altogether. So, what I'm saying is, I'm sorry. You must have felt so embarrassed, and even though I didn't mean for it to happen, it was my fault. Your moustache is looking brilliant, by the way.'

Penny watched Sandra Next Door closely, scrutinising her for some relaxation of the body language, some sign that might indicate she was willing to forgive.

After a long pause, the woman uncrossed her arms and said, 'A sponge scourer or a stainless steel one?'

'I'll take the stainless steel one,' said Jim contritely.

'Good. It's more scratchy. How do you feel about beavers?'

'Aye, well, eh, aye,' Jim said, putting his hands in his jeans pockets and taking a step backwards.

Then he clocked the look on Sandra Next Door's face and hastened to assure her, 'I love beavers, me. Can't get enough of them. I was just saying to Penny the other day that you don't see many beavers these days, and I'd like to see a lot more.'

Sandra Next Door curled her lip and gave a small shake of her head.

'You can wipe that smirk off your face. I'm doing a talk on road safety at the school, and I need someone to be Barney the Road Safety Beaver. You're it. Turn up at the primary school a week on Monday at eleven. The costume will be provided.'

Jim started to object, but she fixed him with a steely glare and said, 'I hear Sergeant Wilson's doing stranger danger with the Brownies next week and is looking for a Stuart the Squirrel. Aye? No. I thought so. See yourselves through to the living room. I'll put the kettle on.'

CHAPTER 13

Sandra Next Door took little persuading to work with Jim on the vigilante investigation. With her lollipop lady duties on hold until the school children returned after Easter break and only her part-time job as a traffic warden to fill her time, she had been looking for a project.

From the other room, they heard Geoff Next Door mutter, 'Thank goodness for that.'

'I thought that Gordon would be your first choice for a partner,' said Sandra, carefully pouring the tea into four identical, floral-patterned mugs.

'Erm, we're not speaking at the moment,' Jim told her. 'That's why I came round earlier. I was going to ask for your advice about him. I was going to ask you to help with the investigation as well, of course. But I couldn't get hold of Penny, and I needed someone to talk to. It's okay, though. Penny's sorted me out now.'

'I don't know whether to be flattered that you wanted my advice or offended that I'm your last resort,' sniffed Sandra, then yelled, 'Geoff Next Door! Leave your golf things alone. Your tea's getting cold.'

Geoff sloped into the living room, grumbling about how the polish she'd used on his clubs was affecting his swing because the handles were too slippery. He sat down heavily then leaned forward in his chair to ladle three spoonfuls of sugar into his cup.

'It would help if you just accepted that golf's a muddy game and not everything has to be scrubbed to within an inch of its life.'

He lifted his mug and, stirring the tea vigorously, asked Jim, 'How would you like it if you had a woman washing your balls every five minutes?'

There was a short hiatus while Penny thumped Jim's back and Sandra Next Door sprinted to the kitchen to fetch a cloth to mop up the mouthful of tea he had just sprayed across her coffee table.

Once the kerfuffle had died down, Geoff continued, 'You know she went out and cleaned the holes during lockdown. She said she was going for a walk, and I thought it was strange that she was taking a bottle of bleach and a bucket of hot water with her, but I just assumed it was to sterilise the lampposts as usual.'

'Dog wee,' Sandra Next Door interjected. 'You have no idea how many times I have complained to the council about people letting their dogs lift their legs on the lampposts in the village.'

Geoff Next Door ignored her, well used to this particular diatribe.

'She killed the grass around the holes, and I thought Alec Carmichael was going to have a fit. I had to pay to repair the damage, which I didn't mind, but I could have done without the strife.'

'Were you upset with Alec?' asked Jim. 'I hear he can be a right pompous…'

'Twat,' said Geoff. 'No, he was well within his rights as chairman to be annoyed. He was fine once I added in a wee sweetener. The machine was broken, so now everyone comes to Sandra Next Door to get their balls cleaned. They're happy and she's happy. Are you okay?'

Jim had managed to swallow his mouthful of tea this time, along with an uncomfortable bubble of air.

He burped loudly and said, 'Sorry. Glad you sorted it out. Can you think of anyone who'd have a grudge against Carmichael or any of the other vigilante victims?'

Geoff Next Door settled back in his armchair and mulled this over for a few moments.

'Most of the island would happily see Carmichael brought down a peg or two,' he said. 'There were rumours about the wife-swapping, but I think that was down to Pat Hughes. You know what a claik she is. An even bigger claik than Mrs Hubbard, and that's going some.'

Jim laughed and said, 'Pat Hughes denied all...well, most knowledge of the wife-swapping ring. She said that you–'

He stopped abruptly at a sharp dig in the ribs from Penny's elbow. The move was executed so quickly that, for a second, Jim wondered if he'd ruptured something when he swallowed that air bubble. Then he realised that perhaps repeating the rumour about Geoff trying to persuade a wife-swapping ring to babysit Sandra Next Door might be offensive. Instead, he decided to change the subject to something more neutral.

'You've a lovely beard there, Geoff Next Door. Tell me, do you and Sandra Next Door share a razor?'

Penny breathed a sigh of relief when her phone rang. Honestly, what was going on with Jim today? The man's foot was so firmly wedged in his mouth that she was surprised he wasn't shitting trainers. She glanced down at her phone screen, preparing to send the call to voicemail if it was her mother. Mary had a meeting with the Island Warriors, Vik's reenactment group, this afternoon, and Penny would rather sit through a thousand awkward conversations with Sandra and Geoff Next Door than endure another monologue from her mother about how Lorna Murray said she was too old for a short, leather skirt and, anyway, it wasn't her fault she forgot to wear knickers that time. Instead, Penny felt a small stab of excitement when she saw Lisa's name on the screen. With a warning glance at Jim, which she hoped he would interpret as "don't say anything daft while I'm gone," she excused herself and went into the hallway to take the call.

'Hello, Lisa. Is everything okay?'

She hadn't expected to hear from the woman so soon and had a sudden notion that Lisa might be trapped in the cottage. That front door needed a good carpenter. Goodness knows how Brodie managed on his own. She could only think that there must be a knack to it.

'I'm fine, but there's something here that you need to see,' said Lisa.

'What have you found?'

'I don't quite know yet. Come to the cottage and I'll show you.'

'Alright. I'll be fifteen minutes or so.'

'See you then.'

Penny went back into the living room, where Jim was holding forth on the many times she had blunted his good razor by using it to shave her legs, and how he had once blunted it himself when he'd shaved his own legs. Just for fun, like. Just to see what the crack was. Obviously, he hadn't gone that far up so he hadn't actually seen his–

'Stop talking,' said Penny. 'You've got a spade for a tongue today. You keep digging yourself into deeper and deeper holes. Sandra and Geoff Next Door don't want to hear about leg shaving.'

'It's all the feelings,' Jim protested. 'If I'm talking then I don't have to think about them. I think I might be channelling my inner Mrs Hubbard.'

'Actually, it was quite interesting,' said Geoff Next Door. 'I was going to ask for tips because I shave my legs when I play the panto dame every year, and it's a bugger to do. Although Iona's taking over this year, and I'm playing Buttons.'

Penny had forgotten that Geoff Next Door and Iona Cameltoe were friends. They had argued over a pair of stilettos in Linda Loves Laces a couple of years ago and Linda, the shoe shop owner, had resolved the issue by refusing to sell them the shoes, so they'd bonded over their temporary hatred of Linda and taken themselves off to the driving range to hit balls at things. This friendship might come in useful when Jim and Sandra went to interview Iona about her argument with Alec Carmichael.

'Look, I have to go,' she told Jim and Sandra Next Door. 'Are you two okay to follow up the vigilante leads without killing each other?'

'No problem,' said Jim.

'I can't guarantee anything,' said Sandra Next Door.

'Och, you love me really,' said Jim.

'I tolerate you,' said Sandra Next Door.

'Great,' said Penny, shrugging on her coat. 'If you need me, I'll be on the end of a phone or at my mum's. I'm going to stay there tonight. Hector texted to ask for an extra night because Granny's going to teach him to twerk.'

With that, she made a quick exit and strode back to her car, all the while turning things over in her mind.

Both investigations didn't seem to be leading anywhere. Jim needed to find a common thread in his vigilante case, and there was very little to go on with Brodie.

As she turned the key in the ignition, two thoughts jostled for headroom. The first was a short prayer that Eileen would turn up something on Beacon Brodie. The second, what on earth had Lisa found?

CHAPTER 14

Sergeant Wilson didn't even like KitKats very much but she'd be buggered if she was going to let that stop her from licking one very, very slowly, all the while engaging in steady eye contact with Fudmuppet, who was sitting at *her* desk by the window.

They weren't bad, as biscuits went. It's just that she was going through a chocolate Hobnob phase. Now, Oreos. In her humble opinion, which to be fair, was not very humble at all, Oreos were the biscuit equivalent of a badly spelt text saying click this link for a tax refund. They should be arrested for impersonating real chocolate biscuits.

Her thoughts were interrupted by a voice from behind her left shoulder.

'I've done that check you wanted, and DC Khan says the forensics results are back.'

'Can you not see I'm engaged in important police business here?'

'I just thought you were sucking a KitKat and trying to seduce DCI Moffat.'

The Sergeant broke off eye contact with Fudmuppet and swung her chair around to face Easy.

'Seduce...what makes you think I'd go anywhere near that

twatbadger's underpants? They're probably crispier than your duvet on a Wank Holiday Weekend. Now, stop trying to distract me with all the sexy talk, and tell me what we've got.'

She clicked her fingers impatiently and Easy gulped.

'Fourteen Walker Lane, Fraserburgh. It belongs to a Martia Mathers.'

'Eminem?' the Sergeant asked.

Easy's eyes darted left and then right, as if the correct response was pinned to either the murder board or the door of the men's toilets. She tried again.

'Marshall Mathers. Eminem. Two trailer park girls go round the ootside.'

'Round the ootside?'

'Round the ootside.'

'I dunno. I can check if you like, but I don't think they have trailer parks in the Broch.'

'Och, you've gone and spoilt it now. And we were just getting into the rhythm. Who, pray tell, is Martia Mathers?'

Easy was on firmer ground with this one.

He slipped a printout onto the desk and explained, 'Mathers, Martia. Thirty-six years old. Born in the tins aisle in Asda, Dyce. Former drug addict. Can you be a former addict? Never mind, that's what it says here. Previous convictions for theft and assault but has been quiet for the past four years. Inherited the property from her mother, who died...oh, four years ago. Maybe being a property owner has made her clean up her act.'

Sergeant Wilson looked at the photograph on the paper in front of her. A gaunt woman with a prematurely lined forehead and tired eyes stared back at her. There was something familiar about the woman, but she couldn't put her finger on it.

'Maybe we just haven't caught her yet,' said the Sergeant. 'Enough with the Wikipedia entry. Give me the real dirt. Any known associates?'

'Intel says she was buddies with a few of the local dealers, but because she hasn't come across the police radar for a few years, there's nothing up to date.'

Sergeant Wilson mulled this over. There was no way that a drug addict in Fraserburgh suddenly went quiet unless they were dead or up to no good. And Easy hadn't mentioned a death date. She should pass the information to Fudmuppet, yet it had to be done in a way that meant she could later claim "I told him, and he wouldn't listen." Hmm.

In an ideal world, she would also pay Martia a visit, but this wasn't an ideal world. This was a world where Fudmuppet was deaf to any views but his own. A world where nice, friendly Sergeant Wilsons were expected to be seen and not heard. There was only one thing for it.

'I have terrible period pain. It's like my womb is trying to batter its way out of my arsehole. And the flow! It's like that time the river Don burst its banks and all the lumpy bits got tangled up under the bridge at Inverurie.'

This announcement was made loudly and clearly. Heads shot up from behind computer monitors, and DC Khan gave Sergeant Wilson a sympathetic look. From across the room, Fudmuppet frowned at her, his lip curled in disgust. Sergeant Wilson pushed off with her legs and let her chair wheel across the room, coming to a halt beside his desk.

'That's me finished for the day,' she told him. 'But I'd like to take a personal day tomorrow if that's alright. It's like a serial killer's doing an internship in a butcher's shop down there. I'm happy to talk more about it, but I'd ask you to respect my privacy as a woman. Obviously, I don't want the whole office to know.'

Fudmuppet regarded her in the same way as she would regard Easy when he came back from the shop with bourbons instead of Jaffa Cakes.

'This is a murder investigation, Sergeant. We don't have the manpower to spare.'

'Did I not do your door-to-doors in record time? I saved you at least a day. I also passed on the gossip from Pat

Hughes, and I've had an anonymous tip if you'd like to hear it. I think it's worth following up. In my opinion–'

She was counting on the man's arrogance and disgust. She was not disappointed. Fudmuppet laid his pen on the desk and stared at her down his long nose.

'We don't work on the basis of rumours. Facts, Sergeant, we need facts,' he intoned, his plummy Edinburgh twang setting her teeth on edge. For God's sake, it was like a pissed-off Dame Maggie Smith had her hand up his backside and was throwing her voice.

Sergeant Wilson's brain ran through a number of ways to steer this conversation and settled on the one most likely to make him shit a brick.

'I completely agree, sir,' said the Sergeant. 'Facts are very important. About this anonymous tip. I think–'

'I've said it before and I'll say it again. You're not paid to think, Sergeant. That's what my team are for. You're paid to do as I say. There is no I in team, other than me…I…you know what I mean. I expect you here in the morning, ready to do more canvassing.'

'I'm sorry, sir, I shouldn't have bothered you. I'll let Acting Chief Inspector Deed know that I raised it with you. As my immediate superior, I should have asked him first. I just thought that as you were here, I'd do you the courtesy. I think he's chairing the Chief Constable's Misogyny in Police Scotland meeting at nine, so I'll get to it first thing.'

The new Chief Constable's recent and very public acknowledgement of internal sexism, racism and misogyny had rocked the force, effectively putting many of Sergeant Wilson's male colleagues on notice that their days were numbered. The culture was rapidly shifting from one of victim-blaming to one where whistleblowers were being encouraged to speak out. Fudmuppet had been in the job for a very long time, and Sergeant Wilson would bet that there were more than a few skeletons in his closet. She was not above giving them a wee rattle.

There was also the fact that Fudmuppet saw Deed as a threat. The younger man's star was in the ascendency, whereas if the police grapevine was reliable, Fudmuppet's was rapidly shooting earthward. She almost felt sorry for the DCI. No, she didn't. The sneery flaprocket was sitting there at *her* desk, with his back to *her* window, the pubic fuzz of his hair plugs casting a sparse halo atop his big, beaky face, while his wet lips pissed a stream of condescension on her parade. If ever there was a chain that deserved a good yank, it was Fudmuppet's.

The DCI's face went from crowing confidence to...what was it?...oh, right, the face that Easy had when the men's toilets were broken and she wouldn't let him use the ladies' for his regular morning appointment with the porcelain and a copy of the Vik Gazette. Aye, that face.

For a moment, he said nothing, and the Sergeant was tempted to break the silence by telling him her theory that the Chief Constable was a secret Satanist. However, she was glad that she had waited because the result was the sudden rearrangement of his features into...what was it?...oh, right, the one that Penny made her do when they had their photo taken at the Bravery Awards. A smile, that was it.

'I have carefully reconsidered your request, and on this occasion, I'm prepared to grant it,' the DCI told her. 'Nevertheless, and notwithstanding...'

Sergeant Wilson didn't hear the rest. She was too busy wondering what sort of pube-twiddling cockmonkey used the phrase "nevertheless and notwithstanding" in conversation.

She allowed him to finish before she pushed her office chair into a fast reverse towards her desk, nearly taking out Easy and his tray of mugs and biscuits. Her hand shot out and grabbed a custard cream on the way past. They were the pale, bland cousins of the Oreo, but why indulge the MIT more than was necessary?

She stashed the biscuit in her desk drawer. Because she

wasn't actually going to eat the thing. As she did so, she wondered whom she would take with her to visit Martia Mathers tomorrow. She couldn't take Easy. There wasn't enough time between now and the morning ferry to dislodge his nose from Fudmuppet's arse. It would have to be one of the Losers. A vaguely sensible one. Normally, that would be Fanny Features, but they'd miss out on a whole day's worth of her being a nosy bastard. Ah, fuck it, it would have to be a Weasley. The woman one, nae the daftie. Fred. Aye. She'd phone Fred, and if there was any nonsense about not having a babysitter, she'd threaten to arrest her for being knowingly ginger in a public place.

That settled, the Sergeant wasted no time in snapping her laptop closed, gathering her things and making for the door. Just as she was about to exit, she met Easy, who was returning to the kitchen, mumbling something about being a custard cream short.

'I forgot to ask you about the forensics,' she said. 'Was there anything interesting?'

'That's the weird thing,' Easy told her. 'You wouldn't expect it of a man like him. He was a bit of a loner, and fierce with it. But I suppose it makes sense when you think about how he warned people off and barked at intruders. I took three calls from him about miscreant youths last month.'

'Miscreant youths,' the Sergeant scoffed. 'You're only about fourteen yourself. That's why you spend so much time in bed, with your laptop in one hand and your…I don't have time to waste. Get to the point.'

The young Constable's Adam's apple bobbed nervously in his throat, and he replied, 'Well, first there was the poison. His palms were sweaty.'

'Knees weak, arms heavy?'

'There was vomit on his sweater.'

'Already. Mom's spaghetti?'

'Eh, no.' Easy took a sheet of paper from his pocket and checked it. 'It says here it was stovies.'

The Sergeant sighed the sigh of the long-suffering and the put-upon.

'What wi' you being fourteen, I suppose I shouldn't be surprised that you don't appreciate the genius of Eminem. You're probably into boy bands and yon Barry Styles. Never mind. What else did they find?'

Easy's didn't beat around the bush this time. He briefly glanced down at the paper and then back up at his boss.

'Traces of heroin on his clothes. Brodie had recently come into contact with high-grade, uncut heroin.'

Well, this was interesting. Connections to Fraserburgh, a town known, perhaps unfairly, for its association with the drug trade. Traces of heroin on yer man Brodie. You could almost put two and two together and come up with four. Add to that the rumour that Donald Wallace, the ugly ball of scrotum cheese who was Minky's father and Aberdeen's answer to Pablo Escobar, had arrived on the island yesterday. Yep, add that, and five was Sergeant Wilson's lucky number.

The Sergeant resolved not to wait until the morning. There was still time to make the afternoon ferry. She scrolled through her contacts, her finger alighting on Weasley's name. They were going to get some answers from this Martia Mathers and break the case wide open.

CHAPTER 15

Penny put a shoulder to Brodie's cottage door, turned the handle and rammed hard. To her utter amazement, the door flew open, and she found herself stumbling into the living room, wheeling forwards, hands outstretched to clutch the nearest solid object.

Which happened to be Lisa.

Once they had untangled themselves and got up from the floor, Penny straightened her coat and said, 'Sorry about that. I didn't expect it to open.'

'I found a tub marked "Door Grease" in the kitchen cupboard,' Lisa explained. 'I figured that if Brodie lived here alone, he must have some way of getting in and out.'

Penny silently cursed Eileen for not mentioning the tub. She must have seen it when she was searching the kitchen.

However, it would be disloyal to moan about her friend to an outsider, so instead she asked, 'What was the emergency? What else have you found?'

Lisa smoothed down her hair and grinned knowingly.

'I went through his papers, but I figure you must have already taken the good stuff, then I sat down to think about my article. And that's when it occurred to me that there might be one place where nobody had looked. Have you noticed how creaky the floorboards are?'

'Yes,' said Penny. 'Everything about the place is creaky and creepy. I'm surprised you stayed this long. I looked at the floorboards, but I didn't see any that were loose. Mind you, it was just a quick look. I didn't get down on my hands and knees or anything.'

'It wouldn't have mattered,' Lisa assured her. 'You'd only have ended up with dirty knees. No, this is something else. First, bolt the front door, please. I don't want anyone walking in on this.'

Penny did as she was told.

'Cheers. Now, go and sit in the chair.'

Penny sat in Brodie's armchair.

'Get up and walk to the telly,' Lisa instructed.

Again, Penny obeyed, walking across the rug, all the while conscious of the noises beneath her feet.

'Stop,' said Lisa when she was a couple of feet shy of the TV. 'Jump up and down.'

Penny did as she was bidden, putting an arm across her breasts and vigorously leaping from foot to foot, hoping that the ancient floorboards didn't give beneath her weight. However, instead of the anticipated protests from the wood below, there was a faint clatter. She jumped again. Creak-clatter.

'What is it?' she asked.

Without a word, Lisa gently put her hands on Penny's shoulders and moved her aside. Then she got down on her knees, wincing as they hit the hard floor, and whisked the corner of the rug back to reveal. Nothing. The corner merely sprang straight back into position, so Penny moved the chair and the side table, then helped her slide the rug into the centre of the room.

This time, it was clear what Lisa had intended to show her. Beneath the rug was a trapdoor, its circular, iron handle sunk into the wood so that it was impossible to detect when walking across it. No lumps or bumps. Simply a wooden hatch that seamlessly blended into the surrounding floorboards.

Penny sensed the hairs on her arms rise, and a small flutter of excitement rippled within her belly. The moment felt at once auspicious and scary.

'Wow,' she breathed. 'A secret trapdoor. Have you looked inside yet?'

'No,' Lisa murmured. 'I was too scared to do it on my own.'

Penny acknowledged that she would have felt the same and thanked the reporter for sharing her find. She had half-expected that the woman wouldn't keep her word yet was happy to admit that she'd been wrong.

'Oh, ye of little faith,' said Lisa sardonically. 'I know I'm a journalist, but we're not all bad. Let's open it together.'

Shoulder to shoulder, they bent over the trapdoor and hooked their fingers into the handle. To Penny's surprise, the door lifted easily. Given that it had probably been here for as long as the cottage, she'd anticipated having to struggle with heavy wood and rusted hinges. As soon as they raised it, however, the reason became clear. Someone, presumably Brodie, had added modern spring hinges. Penny realised with a sense of relief that these also prevented the door from clattering down on their heads as they peered into the dark rectangle below.

'We could do with a couple of torches,' she said.

In response, Lisa hunted through her pockets, eventually producing her phone. She tapped the screen a few times. Then there was light, and Penny could see a set of ancient stone steps leading down to what appeared to be a room below. She cast her eyes around the edge of the trapdoor and spotted another modern innovation.

'Lordy, the man may have lived a simple life on the surface, but he was all mod cons underneath,' she said, flicking the small switch embedded in the frame of the hatch.

Then there was more light. A row of lightbulbs affixed to the rock wall, stretching down into the far reaches of the stairwell.

'Are you game?' asked Penny, her eyes sparkling with excitement.

'I'm game,' said Lisa, standing up to take the first tentative step into the unknown. 'Let's see what secrets Brodie was keeping.'

With a last look around the living room, Penny followed her, their feet clattering on the stone. The temperature immediately dropped, and she could see the steam of their breath as they huffed and puffed their way down the damp, narrow stairway. She looked up. The hatch was already receding, a rectangle of dim afternoon light obscured by the artificial brightness of the lightbulbs.

She faced forward again, taking a few quick steps to catch up with Lisa. The dampness had made the stone slippery, and her heart beat a loud tattoo in her chest as she felt her foot skid forwards. Lisa put a hand out to steady her.

'Careful,' the journalist whispered. 'We don't want you coming a cropper before we've even found out what's down here.'

'Sorry,' Penny whispered back. 'I wasn't paying proper attention. Are we nearly at the bottom?'

Lisa put a hand to her forehead, shielding her eyes against the glare of the bulbs, and nodded.

'Just a few more steps to go, I think.'

Some seconds later, their feet hit the rock floor of what they now realised was a tunnel. There was no choice as to which way to turn. To their left, Penny could see the string of lightbulbs snaking its way towards what she presumed was the sea. To their right was a fissure from which a slow, steady stream of water issued, twinkling in the warm glow as it trickled its way down the path.

'I don't have a great sense of direction, but I think this is leading us into the cliff below the lighthouse,' she hissed.

'I think you're right,' said Lisa, grasping her arm.

'Why are we whispering?' asked Penny.

Both women giggled nervously and exchanged glances.

'Because we're a pair of idiots,' said Lisa. Then she shouted, 'Look out ghosties! There's a screw loose aboot this hoose!'

Laughing, they followed the gentle downward slope of the tunnel. The moment's levity had broken the spell, but still they clutched each other, their eyes straining to make out the way ahead. A flickering lightbulb cast eerie shadows along rough-hewn walls slick with algae, and the women squealed when a creature appeared to loom towards them, only to reveal itself as a cricket when it hopped from a small ledge.

Above them, some sections of the ceiling appeared to have been carved from the rock, while others were undulating expanses of brick supported by withered beams sunk into hollows carved in the stone. Penny gave an involuntary shudder as she imagined the weight of the cliff overhead. Despite her best efforts to ignore it, an insistent little voice in her mind whispered, 'There are thousands of tonnes right above your head. What if the tunnel collapses?'

'Then I hope it's a quick end,' she muttered defiantly.

'What?' asked Lisa.

'Nothing,' Penny replied, trying to suppress the anxiety plucking at her vocal cords. 'Just my imagination going rogue. Sandra Next Door is claustrophobic, and I'm starting to know how she feels.'

She winced as her toe caught on something. Beneath their feet, the way was wet and uneven, littered as it was with slimy boulders that had probably once formed a flat surface but were now twisted and skewed into angles which seemed designed to discourage the unwary traveller. Yet oddly, this was an advantage. If she concentrated very hard on what her poor feet were doing, Penny could almost forget the stifling fear of being crushed to death by a cliff.

The tunnel went on and on. They were quiet now, only the

scraping of feet and the urgent exhalations of breath audible as both women slipped and stumbled down the channel. The ceiling was lower here, and they had to crouch slightly to avoid the beams overhead, an awkward stoop on leaden thighs. Despite the cold, Penny felt a sheen of sweat prickle her upper lip.

On and on they crept, through musty air and leering shadows, heads down, each locked in their own world of stone, foot, stone, foot. Until Penny called a halt. She breathed in deeply and the welcome scent of saltwater and brine filled her nostrils.

'We're nearly at the end,' she said. 'I can smell the sea. Do you think this was a smugglers' tunnel?'

Lisa was leaning against the wall, a hand pressed to her aching back, the other massaging a leg. She blew a stray strand of hair from her eyes and nodded.

'I'd hazard a guess that it was. Have you noticed all the recesses in the wall? I read somewhere that they'd hide contraband in the tunnels while they waited for it to be collected. Chuck a dark cloth over a barrel of brandy and it would be practically invisible to prying eyes.'

'You know a lot about smuggling. Are you sure you're a journalist?'

Lisa pushed a toe into a protruding rock, neatly flipping it so that it lay flat, and said, 'There was an article in the Scotsman a few years ago. They'd take in brandy from the Netherlands as well as using the tunnels for illicit whisky stills. Smuggling was rife from about the seventeenth century onwards.'

'I don't suppose the excise man was the most popular person in town,' Penny remarked, vigorously rubbing her burning thigh. 'I'd say that this tunnel has been here a lot longer than Brodie's cottage. I wouldn't be surprised if the cottage was deliberately built over it. A lighthouse keeper would be well-placed to keep the boats safe and see the contraband safely ashore.'

'I wondered why Brodie was here,' said Lisa. 'You don't get many lighthouse keepers these days.'

'I think it was something to do with the island being so remote that it was cheaper to pay someone part-time to keep an eye on things than to send engineers out every time something small went wrong. He also did the tours in the summer, although he was quite a bad-tempered host.'

'Bad-tempered? How?' asked Lisa.

'Och, shouting at the kids if they dropped an ice cream, that sort of thing. He wasn't the friendliest of men and pretty much kept himself to himself. I'm not aware of him having any friends on the island.'

Lisa squeezed Penny's arm.

'He obviously had a side hustle that meant maintaining this tunnel. Look, I think I can see the end.'

Ahead of them, Penny could just make out a difference in the quality of light; a grey where until now there had only been darkness and yellow. The tunnel had twisted a few times, so she wasn't sure exactly where they would come out, but the smart money was on a cave.

Sure enough, they stumbled over the last of the higgledy-piggledy stones and found themselves high on a ledge at the back of a large cavern. Where the tunnel had been narrow and oppressive, the cave was tall and wide. Looking below her, Penny could see niches carved into the rock and realised that these were hand and footholds. Jeeze, they must have been lithe little beggars in the olden days, she thought.

They only had to scramble down a couple of metres before they reached a slab that formed a natural slope, and then it was a short slide and jump to the floor. Looking back, Penny wondered how they would make it up again.

Beyond the mouth of the cave, a shingle beach ran down to the roiling grey of the North Sea. The afternoon ferry was just visible through the mist, lurching through the waves to discharge one set of passengers and pick up the next.

Penny wandered across the sandy gravel to peer through

the opening. The cave was nestled deep in a small bay surrounded by cliffs, and her only view was that of the ocean. She turned her head to the left and spotted a depression in the rough grass that ran down the slope, forming a seam with the gravel of the beach. The beginnings of a path, perhaps?

She could see why the smugglers had chosen this spot. The stream must once have been more powerful, its steady force eroding the rock to carve out a channel to the sea. Behind her, she could barely make out the tunnel opening, but she could see where the water had laid its path, running down the side of the cave to meet its Neptunian master. The endless supply of fresh water would have made this an excellent spot for an illicit still. Penny couldn't help but feel a sense of admiration. Those enterprising vagabonds had merely taken what was already there and adapted it to their own purposes.

'Look at this,' shouted Lisa.

She was pointing to a stack of crates piled on top of a long, flat slab that was raised a few feet off the ground. Penny made her way back inside the cave and let her gaze wander, taking in the craggy blocks hewn by millennia of wild rollers and whitecaps.

'And this,' she said, her eyes alighting on a giant crate atop a similar slab at the other side of the cave.

She grasped the edge of the platform and tried to push herself up, but it was too high, and her arms simply didn't have the power to propel her weight. Perhaps it was time to stop making little exceptions for just another wee slice of cake, she decided. More gym, fewer carbs, bum like a Kardashian.

Abandoning the attempt, she cast around for an alternative route, and her eyes rested on a rock formation that created some natural steps. Probably should have looked before I leapt in the first place, she thought, hauling herself up the steps and onto the slab.

The crate seemed even more enormous close up. It

dwarfed its surroundings, stretching almost to the ceiling. Hinges at the top indicated that pulling from the bottom would allow one side to open, somewhat akin to the hatch they'd gone through earlier.

Penny reached down and slipped her hand under the lower edge and tugged. Nothing happened. She looked more closely and realised that a crude lock had been affixed to the frame. The keyhole implied a simple latch, something that was well within her means to defeat. She knelt, pulled her set of lock picks from her pocket and got to work.

In the meantime, on the other side of the cave, Lisa was keeping up a steady monologue as she tried to open the smaller crates.

'They're screwed shut. I need a wrench or something to get them open. I don't suppose you routinely carry a crowbar? Damn, I've broken a nail. I'm going to have to get it replaced now. Do you know anyone that does nails? Not the hardware type, the hand type. Sorry. Didn't want to confuse you with all the talk of tools and nails. If I can find it, maybe a drop of glue will do the trick. Do you know where I can buy some glue?'

'Dirty Dolores. Hardy's Nails,' said Penny, fighting the urge to tell the other woman to shut up and let her concentrate.

'That makes no sense. Are you saying that Dirty Dolores is hard as nails? Or is there a nail bar called Hard As Nails?'

Penny sighed, put down her tools and looked across the cave to where Lisa was clutching a finger.

'Hardy's Nails for glue. Dirty Dolores for nails. She's quite good if you can hold your breath for long enough. I'm not sure why, but she smells like a used tampon that's been left in for too long. Don't look at me like that. We've all done it!'

'Not me,' said Lisa smugly. 'Where do I find this Dirty Dolores?'

'She has a salon in Port Vik, but she'll be closed today.

Martin and Rachael at the hotel will probably have one of her leaflets. Now, if you don't mind?'

Penny gestured towards the lock, and Lisa mumbled a hasty thanks before turning back to her own challenge.

They worked on in a companionable silence, punctuated only by a failed attempt by Lisa to bash the lid off a box using a rock. The woman was certainly resourceful, Penny mused. She quite liked her. She could envision the two of them staying in touch after this. Now, all she needed to do was lift the left pick just a fraction of a millimetre and...ah, that was it.

There was a satisfying click and Penny rocked back on her heels, glancing over her shoulder to see how Lisa was getting on.

She registered that the other woman had switched to trying a different crate, then turned back to look at her own. Then froze. Something. Something was wrong. She wanted to turn her head, look again, but her inner voice told her to keep staring ahead. Maybe it would go away. Maybe she'd imagined it.

Or maybe she hadn't.

From the entrance to the cave, a voice said, 'Well done, ladies. Now, take a step back and tell me, how much do you value your lives?'

CHAPTER 16

'Aye, aye. No? Aye. Well, aye. Aye? No. Aye, cheers mate.'

Jim laid his phone on Sandra Next Door's coffee table and shook his head.

'It wasn't anyone on the football team. I'm sure of that. Three of them had never even heard of Glossop's article, and the rest are either injured or their wives were delighted to have been called WAGs. Pat Hughes told Ally Morrison who told Sandy Dewar that Sophie Hendry got a free bikini wax from Dirty Dolores off the back of it. Although Sandy says Dolores made a right mess of things. Apparently, Sophie refused to talk about it. Said her lips were sealed. Maybe she's the vigilante, or it could be one of the hags. I suppose they could have read the article and taken matters into their own hands without telling their other halves.'

Sandra Next Door deftly slipped a coaster under his phone and said, 'If Penny had been called a hag, do you think she'd have been able to restrain herself?'

'You make a fair point. If she hadn't been with us on the mainland at the time, Penny would probably be my number one suspect. She doesn't suffer fools gladly. Although, when you think about it, who does? You never hear someone coming out with utter shite and everyone saying how glad they are, do you?'

Sandra Next Door's expression indicated that she was not very glad with him at all.

'God, I miss Gordon,' he said glumly.

'Och, pick up your lip before you trip over it,' said Sandra Next Door. 'Who's next on the list? Rachael and Martin at the Vik Hotel. Then we'll go and see that Glossop.'

Sandra Next Door spat the name and pursed her lips in disapproval, then her expression brightened.

'I wonder if Rachael and Martin would like another unannounced room inspection. I'll get my things.'

She bustled off, and Jim heard the sound of cupboard doors banging and what he suspected was the vacuum cleaner being dismantled, before she returned pulling a large suitcase.

'I couldn't get the Hoover in. It would have meant sacrificing the UV lamp, and I couldn't bring myself to do that. It's a vital piece of equipment.'

Seeing Jim's confusion, she added, 'I got the box set of Hotel Inspector for Christmas. That Alex Policey is a wonderful woman. Absolute angel with a UV light and a set of stained bedsheets.'

She trundled off in the direction of the front door, and Jim had no choice but to follow her.

He thought his back was a goner when he tried to lift the suitcase into the boot of his car.

'What else have you got in there? Fifty gold bars and the contents of your secret lair in the basement?'

'Don't be silly. Where would I get fifty gold bars from?'

He eyed her suspiciously, making a mental note that she hadn't denied the secret lair. What did they really know about Sandra Next Door? He had lied earlier when he'd said that Penny would be his number one vigilante suspect. Sandra Next Door had a vengeful streak that Penny lacked, and he could well picture the woman sitting in her secret lair, cooking up nefarious plans. She was a mask short of a super-villain, that one.

'I suppose I should just be thankful you left the coffin at home,' he said, giving the suitcase a final shove.'

'Coffin?' asked Sandra Next Door.

'Aye, the one you sleep in.'

This set the tone for the journey. Insults were traded all the way to Port Vik, where a startled Mrs Innes witnessed a furious bottle blonde slam the door of the Land Rover with an enraged cry of, 'And I'm going to make balloon animals from your intestines.'

Sandra Next Door was still scowling when they were greeted at the hotel reception desk by Rachael.

Jim, who had rather enjoyed the verbal sparring, regarded his favourite nemesis with equanimity and asked, 'Do you want to take your fangs out and explain?'

They both explained, giving a garbled account that quite possibly left Rachael wondering if she should call hotel security. As security came in the form of Martin, who was about a foot shorter than his wife and a few gym sessions shy of fighting his way out of a paper bag, Jim and Sandra Next Door had little to fear.

'Let me get this straight,' said Rachael. 'The Vik vigilante has been inspecting my sheets under a UV lamp and would like to know why I dropped acid with the TV gardening legend Alan Titchmarsh?'

'No, it was Harminder Singh who took the LSD,' said Jim.

'With TV gardening Alan Titchmarsh?'

'Don't be stupid,' said Sandra Next Door. 'TV gardening legend Alan Titchmarsh would never do that; any more than King Charles would pop into the village pub for a pint.'

'But he did!' exclaimed Rachael. 'King Charles, I mean. It was in the Gazette last week. He and Camilla were on their way to Balmoral in the helicopter and he was caught short. Hang on, I have it here somewhere.'

Rachael disappeared beneath the desk, and they could hear the sound of papers being shuffled. There was a muffled, 'Oh, bugger, I've dropped the invoices,' then a moment later, her hand appeared above the desk, waving a newspaper at them.

Jim unfolded the newspaper and found himself staring at a photograph of a grinning Bertie the barman wedged between King Charles and Queen Camilla. The headline read "Local Landlord Arrested for Allowing Pensioner to Smoke in Pub."

'You go away for a week, and this happens,' said Jim, disappointed not to have witnessed Easy trying to arrest Bertie.

'She's fair put on the beef,' said Sandra Next Door, nodding at the photograph. 'She better watch out, or she'll never fit into her coronation dress.'

Rachael stood up behind the desk and smoothed down her skirt.

'I thought she'd given up smoking,' she remarked.

'I suppose that would explain the size of her backside,' said Sandra Next Door thoughtfully.

'I think she's a fine-looking woman,' Jim declared. 'For her age.'

Both Sandra Next Door and Rachael stared at him. They stared for so long that Jim began to suspect that he'd said something wrong. The fact that neither of them was blinking was the deciding factor. He'd definitely said something wrong.

'What?' he asked.

'For her age,' said Sandra Next Door. 'Would you have said that about a man? He's a fine-looking man for his age.'

'Well, no, but I don't generally comment on how men look. Not that men can't be good-looking, but I'm...'

'A total sexist!' crowed Sandra Next Door.

'Jesus, no. I didn't mean that. I'm a feminist,' Jim protested.

'Is that because some of your best friends are women?' asked Rachael.

'But you said about her weight!'

Jim's voice had gone up an octave and he was gesturing wildly at Sandra Next Door.

'That's different,' she explained, enunciating her words as if talking to an idiot. 'I'm a woman and I understand how she'll feel about wearing that dress.'

Jim threw his hands in the air and gave a loud harrumph.

'Women! If you need me, I'll be in the car.'

When he'd gone, Sandra Next Door gave Rachael a happy little grin.

'Game set and match to me, I think. Right, about this vigilante.'

She found Jim in the car, as promised, five minutes later. He was fiddling with his phone.

As she crawled into the passenger seat, he said, 'I can't get hold of Penny. Did she say where she was going?'

'You need to get a proper car. This one's too high. I've just flashed my underskirt to Mrs Innes at the bus stop. Why are you calling Penny?'

'I was going to lodge a formal complaint about you. Have you any idea where she is?'

'No. She's probably out of signal range. You know what it's like. The UK government has a target for full coverage across the country in the next seven years, so we should expect a decent signal around the turn of the next century.'

'I'll try again later,' said Jim.

Sandra flipped down the vanity mirror and bared her teeth at her reflection.

Rummaging in her handbag for a lipstick, she said, 'Rachael and Martin aren't the vigilantes, by the way. Since the honeypot hotel article, their bookings have gone through the roof. The New Pitsligo Friday Orgy Club has them booked out for the first two weeks of May. I offered to do a hotel inspection, but she said they're expecting the Inverkeithny Dogging Society off the afternoon ferry, so there's no time.'

'In which case,' said Jim, turning the key in the ignition, 'we'll visit Glossop. And I don't know why you're pretending to do your lipstick. We both know you don't have a reflection.'

The bickering continued for the few minutes' drive to the new estate on the edge of town, near Jim's house. Barry Glossop's house was one of the larger of the five designs that were replicated across several streets. Sandra Next Door's tongue gave a click of approval as she eyed the neat front lawn and the wheelie bin obediently situated just the right distance from the end of the drive, ready for the Monday morning collection. There was little to distinguish the house from its neighbour, and Jim could see that the uniform blandness and absence of untidy vegetation appealed to her. She seemed quite cheerful as she marched up the drive.

This cheerfulness quickly evaporated, however, when the gossip columnist answered the door. The man was an unshaven, bleary mess who, judging by the hairy beachball overhanging his belt, had reached middle age still clinging to the firm belief that he was a medium up top and a thirty-two down below.

They explained the reason for their visit, and he gestured for them to come in, walking away and leaving Jim to close the door behind them. They found him in the living room, slumped on the sofa with a can of Heineken balanced on his belly.

'Sit down,' he grunted. 'I'd offer you a cup of tea, but quite frankly, man refuses to make tea. You're welcome to help yourselves, although milk on the turn is a turn-off, say most Brits.'

Jim looked around. The curtains were closed and the only light in the room came from the television, which was tuned to an English football match. Strewn around the room were empty takeaway cartons and beer cans. He pushed a pile of newspapers to one side and placed a pair of toenail clippers on the arm of Barry's chair, then sat down.

Sandra Next Door stood, rigid, in the doorway and Jim could see that she was working up to something. It was there, in the set of her jaw and the slight whistle coming from her nose each time she breathed out.

'I am not sitting down in this pigsty,' she growled. 'Jim, get my suitcase from the car.'

Ah, there it was. Jim frowned at her and shook his head. No, he wouldn't sit here while she cleaned. He would not spend any longer with Glossop than was necessary. The man was a snake. One that had just eaten something very big and had a huge lump in its belly like in the pictures on Facebook. Although Jim preferred the pictures of dogs. And Gordon liked the ones of weird vegetables. Sometimes Gordon would send him a picture of a really good carrot willy. What if Gordon was never his friend again? How would he even find out about Jesus potatoes? Jim's stomach felt like someone had put vindaloo in a tumble drier. He didn't like it. It was very uncomfortable and unfamiliar and made his eyes leak. He wiped the corner of one eye and, making a supreme effort to ignore his stomach, turned his attention back to the conversation.

'Bleached blonde babe begs to get down and dirty,' Glossop was saying. 'Barry Glossop, twenty-three, says the sexy sixty-something couldn't wait to get her hands on his tinnies.'

'Oh, for goodness' sake,' Sandra Next Door snapped. 'Do you still have the letter from the Vik Vigilante?'

'No, I gave it to the police, and in a shocking example of police harassment, Sergeant Martisha Wilson, thirty-six, told the victim that it was his own fault for being an arsehole in the first place.'

'Sexy sixty-something agrees. Did you at least manage to get a good look at the vigilante? You told your employer that it was a woman.'

Glossop lifted his beer, scratched his belly button then gave his finger an experimental sniff.

'In an article in the Gazette, Barry Glossop, the thirty-two-year-old most eligible bachelor on the island, was misquoted as describing the Vik Vigilante as having a jaw-dropping cleavage. We would like to correct that statement and offer an apology to any vigilantes affected by this article. Barry now says the cleavage may not have been the cause of any mandibular sagging, and now he comes to think of it, there may not have been any cleavage at all.'

'You're saying it could have been a man or a woman?' Jim asked.

'The five-foot-seven part was true, but I'd have to go back to my sources for the rest of it,' said Glossop. He closed his eyes for a moment then opened them. 'Sources in the Glossop community have confirmed that the balaclava appeared to be home-knitted.'

Could the man at least make the effort to talk like a normal human being? Jim could feel a soupçon of frustration being added to the tumble dryer.

'Does the Glossop community have anything else to add, or is that it?' he asked, conscious of a slight edge to his voice.

Glossop must have sensed it too because he visibly bristled.

Removing the tin of beer from its perch, he struggled to his feet and said, 'Island vet or heartless git? Seventy-nine-year-old Jim Space triggered outrage today when he implied that Barry Glossop, beloved veteran journalist, had held back information during the investigation into the Vik Vigilante.'

Sandra Next Door moved forward and placed a hand gently on Glossop's arm.

'When did you last leave the house?'

Bugger me with an electric typewriter, thought Jim. She sounds almost...nice. What's going on? She's not going to invite him to come with us, is she? He didn't have to wait long for an answer.

'It seems to me,' Sandra Next Door added, 'that you're not okay.'

'It's been a while,' Glossop admitted. 'Traumatised man hibernates in homely hideaway.'

'I expect that being made to eat your own newspaper would leave scars.'

Glossop gave her a miserable little nod.

'Man's anus in tatters after three-day newspaper expulsion marathon.'

'Well, sixty-something blonde bombshell advises man with ring of fire to get back to work. It'll take your mind off things and the routine will do you good. If you have any friends, speak to them about how you're feeling.'

'I'll be okay.'

Sandra Next Door gave him a tight smile and removed her hand from his arm.

'I'm leaving my suitcase with you,' she told him tartly. 'I'll be back tomorrow, by which time I expect this place to be clean and tidy.'

Without further prompting, Jim went to the car for the suitcase. He was relieved to get out of there. The man smelled like a bag of old cheese puffs and Sandra Next Door was being kind. It felt like everything was out of kilter today.

He tried to phone Penny again, to ask if she thought that Sandra Next Door had had a stroke, but the call once more went to voicemail. He added a dash of worry to the tumble drier. Not enough to make him return to the ankle bracelet idea he'd proposed that time she went for a quick shopping trip to Aberdeen and returned two days later with a monstrous hangover, a new hairdo and enough bags to fill the recycling bin twice over. No. Not that much worry. Just enough to make him want to keep trying her.

CHAPTER 17

Sergeant Wilson was beginning to regret taking a civilian along. It wasn't that she was worried about Weasley getting hurt or mixed up in something serious. It was all the confiding. The Sergeant didn't mind being Auntie Sergeant Wilson to the primary school kids. No, they were easily bribed with sweeties to shut up when they started telling her about how wee Bobby McNosebubble had wiped his bogies on their homework. So far, she'd wasted an entire bag of wine gums on Fred, and the woman was still going on about George having a secret love child. The Sergeant had wondered why she'd been strangely keen to come to the mainland and now realised that it was either to get away from George or, and this seemed the most likely explanation, it was because she liked torturing poor, defenceless police Sergeants.

Fortunately, thanks to the tide and a fair wind, the ferry had reached Aberdeen in record time, and the Sergeant got a break while they collected the hire car. But the minute the seatbelts clicked home, it had started again.

'It's not so much the money. Or even that Dirty Dolores could be telling the truth, although I doubt Gordon would have touched her with even Jim's todger. No, it's the lying. Nearly two years he's kept it quiet. Two years!'

Sergeant Wilson decided that as there was nothing else to do, she may as well treat this like that time she'd let Easy play I Spy, only with slower driving and fewer flashing blue lights. She did like to give the lad a challenge. I spy with my little… whoomph…it had disappeared in the rearview mirror before he could finish. Right, about this lovechild thing and putting up with Fred. What was the phrase she was looking for? Play along. Aye, she'd play along, and she'd play nicely too. Because she had people skills.

'Put yourself in George's shoes,' she said. 'You're fat, beardy and ginger…'

'And?' Fiona prompted.

'No, that's it. The man has suffered enough.'

'You're really rude about the ginger thing. I find it very offensive.'

'Unfortunately for you, you can't divorce me.'

'I don't plan on divorcing George. Gordon. I don't plan on divorcing Gordon.'

'Then stop moaning and help him sort it out.'

'But I'm hurt.'

'And when I've finished playing my violin, I'll batter you to death with it. We all know that Jim's right and Dirty Dolores is lying her orange wee face off. We all know that George is a cowardy custard who couldn't find his own manhood in a box of dildos…'

'And?' Fiona prompted again.

'Sorry. I got carried away with wondering how big the box would need to be. Just accept that he's been a twat and help him sort it out.'

'Simple as that?'

'Simple as that.'

Fiona went very quiet, and Sergeant Wilson was just beginning to believe that she might get some peace when…

'But I'm hurt!'

'Oh, for fuck's sake.'

Sergeant Wilson let the angst become a gentle drone in the background while she got on with the important jobs of driving and trying to remember where the Fraserburgh chip shop was. There was something else she was supposed to think about. Something to do with Easy. Oh, that was it. Richard Less. Easy had phoned while she was on the ferry to say that there were seventy-two of them on the Police National Database, and he hadn't even started on the Ricks, Rickys and Dicks. He'd snickered at that last one and Sergeant Wilson had had to remind him that he was a professional fucking police officer, the wee nyaff.

She wondered how Fanny Features was getting on with the friends and family connections. The woman had been suspiciously quiet.

'Phone Fanny Features and put her on speaker,' she instructed.

'It's a bit awkward, what with the Gordon not speaking to Jim situation,' Fiona said.

'Just for a minute, pretend we're all adults and that a murder is more important.'

'Fine,' Fiona sighed.

She scrolled through her contacts and selected Penny's name. After a few rings, Penny's voice came through the speaker.

'Hello. This is Penny Moon. I can't take your call right now but–'

Fiona hung up and dialled again, with the same result.

'Stupid woman,' said Sergeant Wilson. 'I left her in charge. How dare she be out of signal range when I need to speak to her? Try Space Cadet or Curtain Twitcher.'

Fiona called Eileen.

'Hello. You're through to Eileen Bates–'

'Oh, for fu–. Nae another voicemail.'

'Is that you Sergeant Wilson?'

The Sergeant's eyes flicked from the road to Fiona, who

she noted had moved on from wine gums to jelly babies and was biting the heads off with disturbing ferocity.

'How does her voicemail know who I am?'

'It's me, Sergeant Wilson. Eileen.'

'Well, answer the phone like a proper person. Do you know where Fanny Features is? I can't get hold of her.'

'No. I've been trying to call her as well, but it's just going to voicemail. Is there anything I can help you with?'

The police officer gave a growl of frustration. This was very inconvenient. How was she supposed to get any police work done if Fanny Features kept disappearing? Och, she'd have to make the best of it. Use her kind, friendly nature to gently tease out the answers. Hopefully, Space Cadet would manage to stay sensible for five minutes.

'Start talking, Arsewaffle. Did you find anything useful at Brodie's cottage?'

The silence stretched for so long that Wilson barked at Fiona to check the connection. Before she did, however, Eileen's voice returned, faint and nervous.

'Erm, no?'

'Are you sure? You don't sound too sure.'

'Erm, no?'

'Is that no you're not sure or is it no you're not not sure?'

'I'm not sure.'

'Are you not sure about being not sure or are you not sure about being not not sure or are you not sure about whether you're not sure or not not sure?'

'I'm not not sure,' Eileen yelped.

'So you're sure?'

'I don't know what the question was.'

Eileen sounded close to tears.

'Did you find anything useful at Brodie's cottage?'

'Ooh, erm, maybe.'

'I'm smelling kippers here. Fred, are you smelling kippers? Or it could be haddock. Whatever. Something smells fishy.'

'I did have a shower this morning,' Fiona mumbled.

'No. It's wafting down the phone.' The Sergeant sniffed dramatically. 'Possibly salmon. Space Cadet, do you know why I'm smelling something fishy?'

'Okay, okay,' said Eileen. 'God, you're scary good at this.'

'I've said it before, and I'll say it again–'

'They don't call you Polygraph fucking Wilson for nothing,' Fiona and Eileen chanted in unison.

'Exactly. Come on then. Out with it.'

The nervousness crept back into Eileen's voice, and she all but whispered, 'Penny said not to tell you. We found a photo album and some cards. The photos have names on the back. Penny thought we could use them and the cards to build up a picture of Brodie's relationships.'

'And why were you not supposed to tell me?'

'I can't remember. It was something to do with Lisa the journalist being in bed with Fudmuppet.'

'Fudmuppet has a girlfriend? She must have a face like fried roadkill if she's that desperate.'

The Sergeant ignored Fiona's muttered, 'Beauty comes from within,' and continued her interrogation.

'What's this about her being a journalist?'

'She's not sleeping with him. She's going to give him all the credit for solving the case. But it's fine because Penny's going to get her on our side, so she won't do that. As long as you don't find out about Lisa and Fudmuppet trying to hog all the glory, you won't be annoyed with him. And as long as Lisa doesn't find out you're trying to get one over on Fudmuppet, he won't be annoyed with you. And nobody gets annoyed with me and Penny and Mrs Hubbard. I think. It's all very complicated and we're working with Lisa.'

'Jesus, do you lot have timeshares in one brain cell? Aye, I want to solve it before Fudmuppet. Aye, I want to utterly humiliate and destroy the man. Unravel his DNA strand by strand and have it with a Bolognese sauce and a nice chianti. Where was I? Aye. But I'm not going to do that at the expense of the old dude murdered while he was cleaning other people's ice cream and snot off a lighthouse window.'

'Okay, okay. I got some people you're not supposed to know about to do some things that you're not supposed to know about. We couldn't find the older ones in the photographs, but we found a few of the younger ones.'

'Ooh, gimme, gimme, gimme.'

'I took the ones that the algorithm identified as the strongest matches, then I used an ancestry website to connect them and build a partial family tree that links back to the man I think is probably Brodie.'

Sergeant Wilson growled her frustration again.

'I am so bored that my eyeballs have drilled through the back of my head and fucked off to Banff with my prefrontal cortex. Get to the point.'

'I'm getting there,' said Eileen. 'Eesh, you're so impatient.'

'What did you just say?'

'Nothing. Do you want to know who Brodie was?'

'Is it Richard Less?'

'No. He was Kenneth Mathers.'

Sergeant Wilson's mind went back to the printout that Easy had given her earlier.

'That's interesting,' she said. 'Because I think we might be on our way to visit his daughter.'

CHAPTER 18

Martia Mathers looked even more drained in real life than she had in the printout. She stood clutching the door of the granite semi near Fraserburgh's seafront, hip bones jutting through the cheap, blue nylon of her dress and her hair a tangle of greasy tresses around a face that belonged to a woman thirty years her senior.

She didn't seem surprised to find the police on her doorstep.

'It's about Dad, isn't it? I saw it in the papers. I thought you'd show up eventually.'

'Aye. I'm sorry for your loss. Can we come in?' Sergeant Wilson asked.

'If you like.'

Martia didn't bother with the offer of tea, but she seemed quite happy to sit with them in the living room and answer Sergeant Wilson's questions.

'I'm trying to understand your Dad's background. On the island, he called himself William Brodie. Do you know why that is?'

'Not really. I wasn't even aware that he'd changed his name. He and Mum split up when I was eleven. She wouldn't talk about it. She'd only say that he wasn't very well in the head and had to go away. He sent cards and money for Christmas and birthdays, but I never saw him again after that. Mum told me it was for the best.'

'Where were you at...' the Sergeant rifled through her notebook, then quoted the time and date of Brodie's death.

'I'd have been here. I had an appointment for a blood test that day, but I couldn't make it. Flu.'

'Can anyone confirm your whereabouts?'

'No. People generally stay away when you have the flu. It was just me and Tank here.'

Sergeant Wilson turned to see a tiny tortoiseshell cat stroll into the room. It regarded the visitors with some suspicion, evidently deciding whether or not they met its high standards. Then it came to its conclusion, flicked the visitors a dismissive glance and stalked over to the windowsill, where it proceeded to clean its backside. Sergeant Wilson wished she could do the same with Fudmuppet, but she didn't think the police station windowsill could take her weight.

'You live alone, then?' she asked, turning her attention back to Martia.

'Yes. Mum left me this place when she passed.'

'I don't mean to be indelicate,' said the Sergeant, ignoring Fiona's snort beside her. 'How do you manage the upkeep? I know you've had struggles of your own, so are you working now?'

'Disability benefits. I have MS. Something else I inherited from my mother. It's the relapsing remitting kind, and I'm just coming out of a relapse now. I thought the flu would make things worse again, but I seem to have got away with it.'

'So, you couldn't have—'

'Killed Dad? No. I barely had the strength to lift a cup of tea last week. The past month, even. I'm still exhausted now, although the numbness is fading.'

Sergeant Wilson thought about this for a moment. They

could check with the doctor, of course, but it was unlikely that Martia Mathers would have been able to immobilise her father, strip him and rig up a pulley to stick him to the glass. After hauling the equipment up all those bloody steps.

'Can you think of anyone who would have wanted to harm your father?' she asked.

Martia considered the question for a few moments, then replied, 'As I said, I haven't seen him since I was eleven. To my knowledge, neither has anyone else in the family, although I haven't seen them for years. I follow a few on Facebook, and they would have gotten in touch if he'd been in contact. Only my mother knew the whole story, but we all know he left under some sort of cloud. I don't think it's likely to be someone in the family who killed him. Maybe some of his old colleagues would know more. It's possible that he could have kept in touch with them even though he left a quarter of a century ago. I remember there was a guy called Richard that used to come round sometimes. Sorry, I don't recall his last name.'

'Where did your dad work?'

'Fingavel Engineering down by the harbour. It's still there, although they're probably not open this coming week. There's an Easter Festival and boat show at the harbour, and a lot of the businesses have given their staff the week off. The streets will be closed to traffic, you see.'

Sergeant Wilson made a note of this and then sat quietly for a moment, scratching her head with her pen while she tried to think of her next question. Fiona got there first.

'I understand that you might not know this, and please don't be offended by my asking, but was your dad involved with drugs?'

So, Fred had been listening to the briefing on the ferry after all, thought the Sergeant. And nae just sitting there like a ginger zombie, licking her wounds and eating police wine gums. Could you claim wine gums on expenses? Never mind, she'd come back to that very important question later. First, she wanted to hear what Martia had to say.

'I'm not offended,' the woman sighed. 'I'm proud to be clean. I don't remember there being any sign of Dad taking drugs. I've met enough junkies and dealers in my time to know the signs.'

'But could he have been involved in handling them?' Fiona asked.

'Conceivably, yes. I'm telling you, I didn't know the man as an adult. He could have been up to anything. We were never short of money when he was around, if that's any help. My mum had a fine collection of jewellery, and this house was bought and paid for. Of course, she sold the jewellery after he left. Otherwise, I'd have been going to school in bare feet. Look, I'm sorry, but I'm really tired. Do you think you could come back tomorrow?'

'No need,' said Sergeant Wilson. 'We've covered most of it. Just one last thing. The friend of your father's. It wasn't Richard Less, was it?'

Martia ran her fingers through her hair and then slumped back in her chair.

'That sounds vaguely familiar, although I can't be sure. There used to be a photo album with pictures of all the family parties, but it disappeared. I think Dad probably took it with him. It's sort of comforting, really. The thought that whatever happened to make him leave, he still wanted to remember us. If you find the album amongst his things, maybe there will be a picture of Richard in there.'

Fiona reached out and put a hand on the woman's arm.

'Thank you. I know this couldn't have been easy.'

'Actually, it was. It's like speaking about a stranger.' Martia looked down at the hand for a moment, then back up at Fiona. 'It's quite sad, isn't it?'

'Families come in all sorts of shapes and sizes,' said Sergeant Wilson.

She had no idea what that meant, but it sounded like a

good thing to say, and it seemed to do the trick. Martia gave her a weak smile. The Sergeant stretched her lips and bared her teeth back at the woman.

'When you're up to it,' she said, 'tomorrow morning if possible, could you drop a list of family members into Fraserburgh police station? From what you say, they're probably not involved, but it'll help us to officially rule them out. And if you remember anything more about Richard, please get in touch.'

Sergeant Wilson handed Martia her card, and she and Fiona made their way back into the street. As soon as the door closed behind them, the Sergeant gestured for Fiona to follow her.

'There's a chip shop just up here. I'll buy you a fish supper.'

'I'd prefer a battered sausage.'

'I'm sure you would, but I'm fed up with talking about George today, so we'll sit down, have our tea and do a debrief.'

They were soon ensconced in the Fish Bar and Diner, home to the best battered haddock that Sergeant Wilson had ever tasted. The diner was surprisingly large and modern, a far cry from the three rickety tables that Margaret had crammed into the back room of O Fryer of Scotland on Vik. The wood-panelled walls were freshly painted and festooned with photographs of fishing boats from days gone by. A selection of sea-related knick-knacks lent interest, and a large brass wall clock, in the style of a traditional tide clock, gently ticked the minutes away as they waited for their food to be served. Steam misted the windows, the warmth of the place and the tantalising smell of frying fish blending to create an atmosphere of a salty cocoon.

'Martia's story made me think that you're right about letting things go and helping Gordon straighten this mess out,' said Fiona.

'Well, that's good. Because Martisha's story did fuck all.

Can we talk about the case before you put me off my chips? We can wait until tomorrow before we chase down the rest of Brodie's family. Between the work Eileen's doing and whatever Martia gives us, we'll be off to a good start.'

'What about this Richard Less?' Fiona asked. 'Eileen has the album. We could probably ask her to identify him. If she can share his photo with Easy, that might help Easy narrow things down on the police computer.'

'If she shares it with Easy, Fudmuppet will find out about the album.'

Fiona brushed an imaginary crumb off the table as she considered this.

'Fudmuppet probably already knows you've asked Easy to trace Less. If what you say is right, he's not interested in Pat Hughes' gossip. I doubt he'll take much interest in where a photo came from.'

'You might be right,' said the Sergeant grudgingly. 'My current theory is that Brodie and Less were up to no good, so tracing Less is more important than the painful downfall of Fudmuppet. I'm leaning towards burglary or drugs. Aye, nae as an alternative career when Fudmuppet fires me. Burglary or drugs would be the two things that might explain Brodie's wealth. Because he wasn't just flush with cash when Martia was little. This afternoon, I overheard Fudmuppet saying he had near a million in his bank account. Ye dinna get paid that much for wipin' bogies off a windae.'

'If Fudmuppet decides that the photo album is important evidence that he should have, you'll hand it over?'

'Aye, okay,' the Sergeant grumbled. 'Let's call Space Cadet. And I'll also get Easy to check for a spate of burglaries around about the time Brodie left. Now, pass me your fork. My boob's itchy again and I can't reach it down the arm of my stab vest.'

Fiona gaped at her.

'Use your own fork!'

'Don't be disgusting. I'm about to eat my chips with that.'

Ignoring Fiona's outraged "Oi," Sergeant Wilson grabbed the fork and stuck it down the armpit of her protective vest, scratching furiously while she used the other hand to scroll through her phone contacts.

'I told you to stop answering the phone like that,' she barked, when Eileen had finished her cheery introduction. 'I need you to do something important. Go back through that album and look for a photo of someone called Richard. Then see what you can find out about him. Aye. Richard Less. He was in cahoots with Brodie. No. How the fuck would I know what they were doing? I don't care what you think of my psychic abilities. I'll tell you what's in your future. I will put you in the police shoplifters database and rub my hands with glee next time you go to the mainland. Aye. Thank you. And when you're done, pass the information and a copy of the photo to Easy.'

She hung up abruptly and dialled her right-hand man. The elderly couple at the next table had gone, and she and Fred were the only customers, so she put him on speaker.

'I thought you were off doing something with a river,' Easy said. 'Dunderheid was on the phone for you. I didn't tell him about you eyeing up DCI Moffat in case he got jealous because you used to fancy *him*. Anyway, I could only get the orange Kit Kats, and I remembered to put the padlock on the biscuit tin before I went home.'

'I wasn't phoning about the biscuits,' said Sergeant Wilson.

'Oh. Because you usually phone around this time for a chocolate biscuit briefing ahead of the next day.'

Sergeant Wilson rolled her eyes heavenward with as much drama as she could muster. It wasn't as much as she would have liked. She was weakened. Starving. She'd been waiting an age for her damn chips. What were they doing? Picking the tatties out of the fields?

'This is more important than biscuits,' she said. 'Eileen Bates is going to pass you some information about Richard

Less, and a photo of him, I hope. I want you to get back to me as soon as you find him on the computer. I'll clear your overtime with Dunderheid. The other thing I need you to do is search for a spate of burglaries around the Broch twenty-five years ago.'

Once again, she hung up without so much as a goodbye. Then she stood up, intending to find someone and ask whether the cook had gone out with a couple of fishing rods and a picnic because that was surely the only plausible explanation for why she hadn't had her haddock yet. The staff were spared her outburst, however. A young waitress appeared with two plates, overflowing with chips, and apologised. Sergeant Wilson still had half a mind to tear the lassie a new one, but Fred came over all holier than thou and said she'd made a vow to be thankful for what she had.

'I've created a monster,' said the Sergeant.

Fiona lifted a chip from the plate and pointed it at her, grinning.

'Cause nobody wants to see Martia no more; they want Shady, I'm chopped liver. Well, if you want Shady, this is what I'll give ya.'

'I have no fucking idea what you're talking about. Get on with eating your chips before they get cold,'

'Martia Mathers. Marshall Mathers? Eminem?' said Fiona. 'It's been going round my head since you told me we were visiting her. Never mind. Do you have to phone Dunderheid now?'

'Why would I phone Dunderheid?'

'Easy's overtime.'

'Oh, that. Och, I just sign it off as Superintendent Christie and it always goes through.'

'Doesn't Superintendent Christie mind?'

'No idea,' said the Sergeant through a mouthful of fish. 'He doesn't exist. I've been doing it for so long that he has his own badge number and budget. How do you think I got so many tasers?'

'I thought you swapped with Tayside for a box of crime scene tape.'

'That's just what I tell people. It's been harder since he got promoted last year, though. He has a very busy calendar. I had to employ a civilian member of staff to look after it.'

'Isn't she suspicious that she's never met him?'

'Och, no. Ruth gets paid to sit on her arse in an empty office all day, eating Tunnocks Wafers and turning down all the meeting requests. Christie sends her an email now and again, telling her she's a vital cog in the machine or some such management bollocks.'

'And these emails, do they lack any punctuation and contain the odd swear word?'

'That they fucking do. Now, eat your chips. We have a long journey back. There's no late ferry tonight, so I persuaded Simon Benson to give us a lift home in his fishing boat. He's parked up the road at Peterhead.'

'Docked. Boat dock,' said Fiona, biting into her battered sausage.

'I don't care if he's flying a fucking magic carpet, as long as he gets us home. Look at this.'

Sergeant Wilson waggled her phone at Fiona. On the screen was a text from Eileen.

```
Found Richard Less. You are not going to
believe who he is.
```

CHAPTER 19

Penny slowly staggered to her feet and turned to meet the hard-eyed gaze of the man with whom she least wanted to cross paths ever again. The person she had dismissed as her imagination playing silly buggers when she'd spotted him on the ferry yesterday.

Donald Wallace stood before her in all his arrogant glory. This time, however, the drugs kingpin had ditched the designer suit in favour of jeans and a life jacket. Beside him stood the three goons, all of them dressed in identical black and one of them clutching a crowbar. They were the same shaven-headed primates she'd met last week, except all the more intimidating because there was no pub full of witnesses this time.

'What are you doing here?' she asked, trying to keep the nervousness from her voice.

'I should ask what you're doing here,' Donald drawled, a smirk playing at the corners of his lips. 'Meddling in my business again? I only helped you the first time because of Mindy. This time I'm feeling less sympathetic.'

'No, you didn't,' Penny said defiantly. 'You wouldn't have helped us at all if Mrs Hubbard didn't have the goods on you.'

Donald's smirk disappeared. The week before, he had reluctantly helped the Losers track down one of his dealers, who was now a witness in a murder case and very inconveniently out of office.

'The old bag's not here now,' he sneered. 'Who's your little friend? Another loser?'

Penny straightened her back and thrust out her chin. She could feel her fingernails digging sharply into her palms.

'She's a journalist. And leave Lisa out of this.'

'So, yes, another loser.' Donald's voice became low and menacing. 'Quite a pretty one, too. How about you come down here, sweetheart, and let me take a proper look at you?'

Lisa didn't move from her perch. Instead, she crossed her arms over her breasts and stared unflinchingly down at the man, seemingly regarding him with interest. The sort of interest a child might pay to an unusual insect or a white dog turd.

The superior smile had returned to Donald's face, and if Penny's knees hadn't been wobbly and sore right now, she'd have launched herself off the platform and slapped it right off. Or at least, that was what she told herself as she all but bared her teeth at the man.

Noticing her body language, one of the goons laughed, until Donald quelled him with a single glance.

'Alright, let's satisfy your curiosity,' he said. 'Open the crate. Go on. It won't bite you. Darren, give...Lisa, is it? Give Lisa a hand with her crates.'

Penny's hands were trembling as she turned back to her enormous crate and attempted to grasp the lower edge. Tugging hard, she braced herself for what she might find. The makeshift door moved forward. Then up. And up. Penny almost closed her eyes. Up. Up. What the hell?

Before her stood a series of large copper pots and pipes.

'Aye,' said Donald. 'You thought it was going to be smack, didn't you?'

Penny started to speak, but no sound came out. She tried again.

'What is it?'

'It's a meth lab!'

She didn't know what to say. Her entire knowledge of meth labs came from Mrs H, whose addiction to American cop shows had equipped her with a surprising amount of expertise in serious crime and a fine collection of US law enforcement acronyms. Penny took a step back, recalling Mrs Hubbard's retelling of Balltown Vice episode five, where a mysterious explosion behind a restaurant led Detective Maxwell Steelgrave to some tweakers. She had no idea what tweakers were, but she did know that meth labs were highly volatile. She'd be DOA if this thing went kaboom.

She looked behind her, eyes darting left and right while she tried to assess whether she could make it to the tunnel or the cave entrance before Donald's goons could catch her.

Donald's smile grew wider.

'Dinna fash yersel', lassie. It's a micro-distillery. Look behind the crate. See the small barrels there? What you're looking at is Caskstone Cave whisky. I took it over from the previous owner after he met with an…unfortunate event.'

Penny's panic subsided, although the fear and the wariness remained. Donald Wallace did not reach the top of his chosen career by being a nice guy. He was a dangerous man. The last time they met, he had tried to pressure her into taking him on as her business partner so that he could launder his dirty money through Losers Club. He did not take kindly to Mrs Hubbard's threats to reveal information about him if he didn't back off. The fact that Penny was his daughter Minky… darn it, must not call her that in front of him…the fact that she was Mindy's friend would make little difference if he thought she posed a threat to his livelihood.

'Why is it here?' she asked.

Donald had just opened his mouth to reply when a loud crack resounded throughout the cave. The goon that Donald had called Darren was standing by one of the smaller crates, the lid at his feet. He gestured with the crowbar, telling Lisa to look inside. Tentatively, she took a pace forward. Then she stepped back, her brow furrowed in confusion.

'It's water,' she said. 'Big bottles of water.'

With some difficulty, she hauled a large, clear plastic bottle from the crate and set it down on the platform with a thud.

'Exactly,' boomed Donald, clapping his hands. 'Pure Caskstone mineral water from a spring deep within the Scottish cliffs. That's why I asked how much you value your lives. This stuff is highly exclusive, and those in the know swear by its restorative powers. One drink and you'll feel rejuvenated. You, dear ladies, are looking at something more valuable than drugs, and it costs next to nothing to produce. Come on down here and I'll explain. Come on. Don't be shy.'

The goons on either side of him stepped forward, and Darren put a hand on Lisa's arm. It seemed that coming on down was non-negotiable.

Penny exchanged frightened glances with Lisa. Then the other woman allowed herself to be led towards the edge of her platform, and Penny began to pick her way on unsteady legs back down the rocks to the ground.

As her feet touched the floor of the cave, Penny's focus narrowed. She was hyper-aware of her heart hammering against her ribcage. The scuffing of her feet against stones and sand seemed to be coming from far away. Perhaps the blood rushing in her ears was drowning it out. She didn't know. Her vision had narrowed to Donald and the goons. She shuffled forwards. Was this it? Would they grab her? Drown her? Was she to die in a cave?

She took her phone from her pocket, cursing herself for not thinking of it before. She could call Jim. He'd rescue her. She looked down at the screen, bright in the fading afternoon light. No signal. Shit. Nobody knew she was here. Had Lisa told anyone about the trapdoor? Unlikely. Shit, shit, shit.

Penny had no choice. She moved towards the goons and

waited to be grabbed. From the corner of her eye, she saw Lisa jump down from her platform and come to a wary halt. Both of them were as tense as each other.

Nothing happened. Well, not quite nothing.

Donald waved the goons back and turned away, ambling towards the mouth of the cave, where he perched himself on a rock and waited for them to catch up.

Penny hadn't noticed before, but a small, orange RIB had been pulled onto the beach. Donald removed his life jacket and threw it, letting out a small sigh of satisfaction as the thing teetered on the edge of the vessel and then slid inside.

'Pull up a rock and sit yourselves down,' he said with an amused smile.

The two women did as they were told, perching on a large rock to his right.

'I love it here,' he told them. 'Used to explore the cliffs as a boy. When I think of the chances I took! I'm lucky to still be here. It's how I found the place. There's no way up or down that cliff unless you like a good climb, which I did. Brodie and his pal were using the old tunnel to smuggle in drugs, and a third guy had been running a whisky still in the cave for years. It was all small change stuff. If you think about it, they could have done a lot more with the place.'

Donald gestured towards the cave and chuckled at his own wit.

'Brodie was well placed to take in a lot more than he did, what with the tunnel being under his house and this bay being hidden from all but the most adventurous. Yet for some reason he didn't. Told me he couldn't risk getting caught. Had to stay under the radar.'

'Did he say why?' Lisa asked.

'No. And if you report on any of this, I'll shove one hand down your throat, the other up your arse and then I'll shake hands in the middle. Aye?'

'Aye,' said Lisa meekly.

'Where was I? Brodie and his pal. I let them get on with it

and never told a soul. Later on, when I was a bit more advanced in my career, shall we say, I considered making them take in some of my wares, but I have my own setup, and there was no advantage to me in bringing my gear here, only to have to move it again to the mainland. I was more interested in the still. That was where the money was. As a lad, your man with the still took me under his wing and showed me what to do. I'd run errands for him, and he'd give me a bit of cash.

'I didn't have much in the early days. It was only after the girls were grown and I moved to the mainland that my Uncle Isaac brought me on board. These days, I'm loaded, of course. I never forgot this place, though.

'Eventually, I came back and made the guy an offer for his still. Naturally, he refused. He was making a pretty penny selling whisky to the pubs on the island. They'd put it in their empty branded bottles, sell it and pocket the difference.'

'Just out of curiosity,' said Lisa. 'Why are you telling us all this? The drugs, the illegal booze, none of it reflects well on you. For all we know, you killed Brodie to get your hands on his smuggling operation.'

'Jesus, woman. I've already said it was small-fry and of no interest to me. I didn't kill Brodie. Penny will tell you that I'm only interested if there's a benefit to me.'

Penny nodded.

'Classic psychopath,' she said.

'Hey, that's a bit harsh,' Donald complained. 'But aye. Anyway, the old dude with the still popped his clogs. Natural causes, before you ask. His family had been distilling whiskey for centuries, and even though he wouldn't sell the thing to me, his son was glad to get rid of it.

'The man had made good whisky using the fresh water that comes into the cave. The tunnel was packed with barrels. All I had to do was sell the stuff and make more, so I upgraded the equipment. By this time, Brodie and his pal were getting on a bit. Moving product was a young man's game and they'd lost interest. I put them to work on the whisky business and paid them a tidy sum too. I think they still took in some packages on the side, but only the odd shipment.'

'I don't want to be rude,' said Penny, 'but Lisa has a point. Why are you telling us this?'

'I'm getting to it,' said Donald, a touch of irritation bleeding through. 'The short answer is publicity. I have improved the whisky, and it's now bottled professionally by Lochlannach Distillery under the Caskstone Cave brand. Because we produce such a small amount, it's very rare and very valuable. We're talking thousands of pounds for a bottle.

'I added the Caskstone Water to the business last year. I was intending to sell it to complement the whisky, but I gave some sample bottles to Mrs Hubbard for Elsie's wake. Johnny Munroe and his Hollywood pals declared it the next big thing, and now I find myself making even more from the water than the whisky.

'The irony is that the whole thing is legit. I needed a legitimate business for…let's just say cashflow reasons. Then suddenly, I'm making more from it than I ever did from Uncle Isaac's operation. As soon as he's out of the jail, I'm going to concentrate on this full-time. But for now, I'm stuck juggling both.'

'The big bottles in there,' said Lisa. 'They're just water?' For real?

'Aye. We ship them to the mainland, where they're checked and properly bottled for sale. What I want you to do, journalist lady, is write an article. Get me some publicity for my water. Scotland's best-kept secret, whatever. You, dear, are still here because there's something in it for me. I'm not too sure why I'm keeping the other one around.'

He glared at Penny, but she didn't shrink from him, as he was no doubt expecting. She simply stared calmly back. She knew exactly why he was keeping her around. He still had a hankering for a share in Losers Club.

'With Brodie dead, doesn't that present a problem for you going forward?' asked Lisa, now in full journalist mode.

'It does, so you'll agree that the man was more useful to me alive. And his pal's in the wind, too, which is just as inconvenient. I only came by today to check on things. See where we are in terms of stock. Unfortunately, there isn't much, so I'm going to have to draft in help. And we can't use the tunnel to shift stuff for a while because the polis are all over the cottage. That's why we came by boat. I assume the polis told you about the tunnel, Penny. I heard that you have your nose firmly planted between Sergeant Wilson's arse cheeks. Now, there's another bonnie lass. I bet it smells rare in there, does it?'

Lisa shot Penny a sharp look, and Penny visibly cringed. She hoped that the other woman took it as a reaction to Donald's crude joke because the last thing she wanted was for Lisa to know exactly how close she and the Sergeant were.

She could hear the false note in her voice as she laughed, 'Ooh no. I don't know where you heard that. Lisa found the tunnel, and we're sure the police don't know about it. As for Sergeant Wilson, I don't have much to do with her at all. Terrible woman. She attends Losers Club, but she's not part of the inner circle. The core group, the gang if you like, is Jim, Eileen, Sandra Next Door, Mrs Hubbard–'

'Oh, aye,' said Donald, giving her a sour look. 'I'd forgotten about Mrs Hubbard. I hope you don't have your nose in there. Probably smells like burnt mothballs.'

He stood up and brushed the back of his jeans.

'Can I count on you both to say nothing about the location of the Caskstone business or the tunnel? At least until I've sorted this damn mess out. And I want first approval on the article before it's published. No mention of my alternative line of work, got it?'

Lisa nodded, her eyes full of enthusiasm. Penny could see why this would be an interesting story for her. Gangster turned distiller and water supplier to the stars. Please, God, never let her find out about Mrs Hubbard's continuing involvement with the Hollywood Knitting Club. Nobody needed Scorsese's attempt at a Fair Isle jumper splashed across the front pages.

'If that's us agreed, said Donald, signalling to his goons, 'we'll be on our way. Can I give you a lift back?'

Penny almost said yes, but with a sinking heart, she remembered that she'd bolted Brodie's door from the inside. They would have to take the tunnel back. Otherwise, nobody would ever get into the cottage again.

'No,' she said with a sigh. 'But if Darren could give us a leg up to the tunnel entrance, that would save some time.'

She turned to go but was brought to a halt by Lisa, who said, 'Just one final question. Brodie's pal. Do you have a name?'

'Well, that's a whole other story and not one for today. It'll be dark soon and I want to get back to Port Vik before Mindy sends out a search party. I knew him as Richard Less, but others call him by a different name.'

CHAPTER 20

Jim lifted the brass knocker and let it fall with a heavy clunk. He did it again. And again. There was something about the weight and shape of the thing. It felt quite satisfying to let it drop like that.

'Sandra Next Door?' said a voice behind them.

Sandra turned and her normally dour expression transformed into a delighted beam, directed straight at the person behind them.

The person in question was a stubble-chinned six-foot-three Amazon in a gold lamé boiler suit. She was carrying a blue, plastic lunchbox, and her wellington boots were liberally splashed with what smelled like…Jim had to think about this for a moment. It smelled like if you put rotten cabbage and fermented herring in a blender. Looked like it, too.

'Iona,' Sandra Next Door said. 'Meet Jim. Jim, Iona.'

'Pleased to meet you,' said Jim, holding his hand out for Iona to shake.

Iona ignored his hand, saying in a broad Aberdeenshire accent, 'Sorry. I've been out seeing to the pigs. The last thing you want to do is shake hands with me. God, I once played Snap with Bieldy, and he said he couldn't get the stink off him for a week. The man is prone to exaggerate. It was only three days. Come on in. I'll get changed out of my boiler suit, make us a cup of tea and you can tell me the reason for this surprise visit.'

Iona's farmhouse wasn't a traditional stone building. The original farmhouse had been so extensively damaged in a storm that repairing it was more expensive than converting it into a pig shed and building a new farmhouse next door. The new house was a glass and wood monument to modern architecture, and Jim couldn't help a small pang of jealousy. It was exactly what he would build if he had to start afresh.

'I have a few sows about to give birth,' Iona explained, ushering them through the boot room into a glossy, modern kitchen. 'It's a bit early in the year for it, but what can you do? It's yon big beast, Toby. He's a randy bugger. Never mind. I'll get them into the farrows this coming week, and we'll have a bonnie batch of babies by the next. I'm that busy, you're lucky you caught me. Sit yourselves down at the island. I'll be back in ten.'

Iona took exactly fifteen minutes. She came back, freshly showered, wearing a pair of jeans and a pink jumper bearing the logo "Shake my Balls." After the lamé jumpsuit, Jim hadn't expected something quite so ordinary. Although he did want to ask about the balls. He wouldn't. The version of Penny that he kept in his brain was telling him not to do it. But he really wanted to.

She saw Jim staring and asked, 'What? You look like you've never seen a bingo jumper before. Did Sandra Next Door nae tell you? I have two passions in life: pigs and bingo. I do the calling on Friday and Saturday nights. Professor McKenzie made the jumper for me.'

'I don't know Professor McKenzie,' Sandra Next Door said.

'Aye, you do. The cardiologist on North Street.'

'Oh, Cosmo. I'd forgotten about him. He won first prize at the Vik Show last summer for his knitted zoo. I liked the alpaca in alpaca wool. Very clever. The man is a genius with a ball of yarn.'

'I thought you said he was a cardiologist,' said Jim.

'Oh, he is,' gushed Sandra Next Door. 'Makes the best cardigans this side of Huntly. Of course, there's Mrs Forbes in Ellon, but she's not a patch on him.'

'What's he a professor of, then?'

'Knitting! He's famous for it. I'm surprised you haven't heard of him.'

Jim had never seen Sandra gush before and had to admit he was slightly disturbed by it. Would the real Sandra please stand up?

Iona had been busying herself with kettle and teabags while they chatted. Jim was secretly hoping for a biscuit. It was nearly teatime, and his tumble-drier belly was starting to shout for its next load. Even a Rich Tea to take the edge off would be welcome. No such luck.

Setting three mugs down on the cool marble surface of the kitchen island, Iona pulled up a stool.

'Lovely as it is to see you both,' she said, 'I doubt you popped by unannounced without a reason. What can I do for you?'

'We're looking into the Vik Vigilante,' Jim explained. 'Your name came up as someone who...and I'm not suggesting that this is anything to do with you...your name came up as someone who might have a grudge against Alec Carmichael. Something to do with the Freemasons.'

Iona frowned, then her face cleared, and she laughed uproariously.

'That was ages ago. I already got my own back. Banned his wife from the bingo for cheating.'

Sandra Next Door gasped and put a hand to her heart, scandalised.

'Did she really cheat? Mrs Carmichael always seems so upright. She and her cronies rule the Highland Dancing sub-committee for the Show. They're very particular about kilt lengths.'

'Well, *somebody* carefully altered the numbers on her bingo card, and I'm sure it was a coincidence that those new numbers were called.'

'I thought Alec Carmichael was the one that refused to let you wear the apron,' said Jim. 'Seems harsh that she was the one who suffered.'

'He was just the straw that broke the Cameltoe's back. She'd been a pain in the behind for years. Every weekend, I'd put on my best show, and she'd sit there making snarky comments.'

'Oh, that's terrible,' said Sandra Next Door, momentarily forgetting that snarky comments were her bread and butter.

Iona unconsciously mirrored Sandra Next Door, putting her hand on her own chest.

'I know. But dinna worry. Everybody was fair scunnered with her. Let me tell you, you've never heard the like of the big cheer that went up when she walked out the door. The next weekend, Mrs Hay brought me a plate of peppermint slice to say thank you. And that's why Professor McKenzie knitted me this jumper. So, there you have it. Now you've ruled me out, who's next on your list?'

'There's only Brian Miller left,' said Jim. 'The Vik Gazette said his taxi wheels were stolen. Pat didn't have any gossip on him other than what everyone already knows.'

'That's your source?' Iona laughed. 'Pat Hughes? You better watch out for her. You're a big lad and she likes them that way. Tried it on with me at the Donaldsons' ceilidh. Said she'd never had a man in a skirt before, cheeky vratch. We were surrounded by them! I had to tell her I was more Gay Gordons than Dashing White Sergeant just to get rid of her. Would you not be better with Mrs Hubbard? Her gossip's far superior.'

'Mrs H is busy doing something else at the moment,' said

Sandra Next Door. 'Can you think of anyone else who might have had a grudge against the vigilante victims?'

Iona gave the question due consideration, sipping her tea while she thought.

Eventually, she said, 'Alec Carmichael? Everybody. To tell you the truth, I think Miller took his own tyres. Ask Kenny Bates at the garage when they were last replaced. I bet you it was fifteen years ago. A new set of tyres from the insurance is probably worth more than the car. You're wasting your time there. Singh and Glossop, not a clue. I don't know them.'

Jim and Sandra Next Door left shortly afterwards, conscious that their host wanted to watch Countryfile before doing a final check on the sows. Iona promised to call them should she think of any more likely suspects, but they both knew that the investigation was dead in the water.

Sandra Next Door crawled onto the front passenger seat of Jim's car for the last time that day, and he slammed the door, instantly cutting off what was by now her standard complaint about there being no need for cars with high seats. If he was rich, he thought sourly, he'd buy a Humvee just to piss her off.

They were quiet on the drive back to Sandra Next Door's house, each thinking about what they'd learned that day; both of them silently picking over what Pat Hughes, Harminder Singh, Reverend Green, Glossop and all the other victims and suspects had told them.

As Jim pulled up in front of her bungalow, Sandra Next Door said, 'It might help if we sit down together and go through what we know. Something might jump out at us.'

She sounded weary, like the fight had gone out of her. Jim looked at his watch and gave a small start. No wonder she was tired. It was getting quite late. He realised that he hadn't thought about Penny since they were at Glossop's house, almost two hours ago.

'Come in and I'll make us something,' said Sandra. 'We

can pick over the investigation while we eat. How does a sausage sandwich sound.'

'Aye, that would be grand. Give me a minute while I try Penny again.'

Sandra Next Door simply nodded and went into the house, leaving the front door ajar for Jim to follow. She was definitely feeling ground down, he decided. Normally, she'd have closed it behind her and left him to knock and beg for his supper.

He dialled Penny's number and was about to hang up when she answered.

'And where have you been, young lady?' he intoned, adopting his sternest voice.

'Sorry,' said Penny. 'No signal. I have got so much to tell you.'

She sounded breathless, like she was walking outside.

'Where are you?' Jim asked.

'Car park next to Brodie's cottage. Listen, meet me at my mum and dad's, and I'll fill you in on what's been happening.'

'I'm at Sandra Next Door's. She's making me something to eat.'

'It better not be another sausage sandwich. You've had about six already today. Please tell me it's not a sausage sandwich.'

'It's not a sausage sandwich,' said Jim obediently.

There was a short pause. He knew that Penny was debating whether to press the matter, but she must have decided to let it go.

'Well, just come over when you're done next door,' she said. 'How's your investigation going?'

'It isn't. That's why we're having not a sausage sandwich. We're going over it and comparing notes. I'll see you in about an hour. Please be wearing your sexiest nightie. You know, the one that says you're a bad girl.'

'It says I'm a *bed* girl!'

'Aw, you've gone and spoilt it now. What about the knickers with the—'

'Shut up,' Penny laughed. 'I'll see you later.'

Smiling happily to himself, Jim hung up and went to sit at Sandra Next Door's kitchen table, staring longingly while she bustled between cooker and fridge. He could have helped, he knew, but she seemed to be doing a fine job, and he'd only annoy her by getting in the way. Or using a tampon instead of a tea bag.

Ten minutes later, two cups of tea were steaming gently on the kitchen table, and one Jim was sighing contentedly. This was the best sausage sandwich he'd had all day, and that was saying something. There was plenty of competition. Sandra Next Door had found a large notepad, and they were going through the interviews they'd done.

'Reverend Green doesn't like Alec Carmichael,' said Jim, making notes as he talked. 'He confirmed that the parish newsletter was hacked, but he was away on a church retreat at the time. No access to the internet, so it couldn't have been him.

'Dirty Dolores. She's a victim and a known liar. She gave a few names, one of them being Edna Mains and the other being Sophie Hendry, the girlfriend of one of the footballers from Glossop's WAGS and Hags article. Edna has COPD and needs a mobility scooter, so she's out. Sophie's a possibility, I suppose. Nothing else from the football team.

'Glossop wrote an article about the McCullochs. They were away on some dancing thing at the time. Carmichael's neighbours, the Hee-Hawes, were in Hong Kong.

'I did wonder about Minky. Dolores is seeing her son and, from what Penny says, I don't think she's a fan. But as she told us about Dolores in the first place, she's an unlikely suspect. We could visit her tomorrow if you want.'

Sandra took up the baton and began making notes in a neat hand under Jim's untidy scrawl.

'No. I think you're right. Let's leave Minky out of it for

now. Rachael and Martin – we thought they were affected by another of Glossop's articles. However, it was to their advantage, so there's no motive. My Geoff Next Door is on the list due to arguing with Carmichael. We've established they sorted things out between them, so I'm scratching him off even if you don't agree.'

'There's something about Geoff Next Door that I didn't tell you,' said Jim, squirming awkwardly in his chair. 'Pat Hughes said he knew about the wife-swapping ring and erm.'

Jim stopped, unsure as to how to proceed. Sandra Next Door was scowling at him again, all traces of the nice but alien Sandra gone.

'Spit it out,' she barked.

'She said he asked them to take you.'

'Take me where?'

'No, take you. As in, take you.'

'Like in a dirty movie way.'

'No!' shouted Jim, horrified. 'Have you as a member. Include you in their activities.'

'Good. Because I was about to wash your mouth out with soap.'

'Good?' Jim's gasp quickly became a snort of laughter. 'I know you're a sexy sixty-something, but I'd have thought you were far too hygienic for wife-swapping.'

Sandra Next Door flushed a deep pink. She leaned an elbow on the table and clutched her forehead, her eyes fixed on her cup.

'Not good about him offering me to the…you know what I mean. He didn't do it. He just wouldn't,' she spluttered. 'Pat bloomin' Hughes. As if my Geoff would. Well. That woman needs a lesson in the truth. If I were the vigilante, she'd be top of my target list.'

'Sorry,' said Jim, not wanting to be the cause of another major argument. 'She did provide a lot of useful and accurate information too. Forget I said anything. Where were we?'

Sandra Next Door was silent for a few moments, then seemed to gather herself.

She straightened up and said, 'Glossop. We got nonsense from him. Even the description of the vigilante being a woman was wrong. The only thing we established was that they wore a balaclava and were about five-seven. And Singh wasn't much better. You said you thought it might be something to do with the high teas.

'Then, last but not least, Iona. She's not entirely in the clear, but she struck me as honest. I believe her.'

'Me too,' said Jim glumly.

He cast an eye over their notes.

'We could speak to Brian Miller, Minky and Sophie Hendry in the morning. I think we're clutching at straws, though.'

'I agree,' said Sandra Next Door. 'Let's sleep on it. Fresh minds in the morning might make all the difference.'

Despite her attempt at cheerleading, Jim could hear a note of melancholy. Or was it desperation? Whatever it was, Jim left the house head down, feet dragging, and the door that would normally be shut firmly behind him was instead closed with a gentle, click. He had never spent so much time alone with Sandra Next Door before, but he had to admit that they'd made a good team. Just not a very successful one.

Aye, well. There was always tomorrow. For now, he thought, looking longingly over Sandra's garden wall, Penny's bedroom light was on, and he knew she still had those knickers in her suitcase.

CHAPTER 21

Penny was awoken by the urgent beep-beep beep-beep of her phone. Beside her, Jim lay on his back, his long limbs taking up more than two-thirds of the available space. She rolled over, and sensing the movement, a large lump under the duvet stirred. It must have been cold during the night. Timmy had crawled beneath the duvet and curled up at Jim's feet. For just the briefest moment, Penny felt that all was right with the world. Her babies, her parents, her dog and her Jim were all tucked up safely under the same roof. Then she felt the raw throb down below, where the sexy knickers were attempting to give her an involuntary episiotomy, and decided to get up.

Grabbing the towel she'd hung on Len's exercise bike in the corner of the room, she blew a kiss at the space on the wall where the poster of Chesney Hawkes had hung until she'd removed him to her own house. The leftover pieces of Blu Tack and the slow encroachment of other people's things made it feel like this was no longer her room. No doubt, one day soon, her mother would declare an urgent need to decorate, and all traces of Penny's youth would be painted over.

A small part of her wanted to move back into this time capsule. It was very comforting, and she was grateful to her parents for absurdly preserving this piece of her past with its lumpy bed and scarred wallpaper. However, she had her own house now, just a few miles away. Wherever she had lived, Valhalla had always been home home. Yet, with the kids, the dog and the big galoot snoring in the bed over there, home home had moved. She hadn't noticed it, but home home had slowly become her cottage by the harbour in Port Vik.

The big galoot grunted and muttered something about barbecue sauce. Dreaming of a pulled pork bap perhaps? Penny smiled to herself. He had been spending more and more nights at her cottage recently, and she had been wondering if it was time to discuss him moving in. His place was much bigger than hers, but she was reluctant to uproot Hector and Edith again. They needed somewhere that they could always call home too. After the summer, Edith would be off to university and Hector would begin his baking apprenticeship. There was precious little time left to build memories with them in her nest by the sea, but she wanted them to always have somewhere to come back to, just like she'd had.

Resolving to make everyone pack their suitcases ready for their return to the cottage that morning, Penny headed off to the shower.

Len was installed at the table, coffee and poospaper before him, when she ambled into the kitchen fifteen minutes later.

'Thank goodness you're here, Pennyfarthing,' he said. 'I need some help with the crossword, and you need to have a word with your mother. She twerked on me last night.'

'Morning, Dad,' said Penny, opening the back door to let Timmy out. 'Give me a clue.'

'Well, she moves her bottom a lot. Sticks it out. And she's been talking about a Taylor Swift. I have no idea what a Taylor Swift looks like. I offered to find my bird-watching binoculars so she could show me, but I said to her, "Mary, I am not taking you anywhere unless you stop sticking your bottom out." We'd be the laughingstock of the bird-watching community.'

'I meant a crossword puzzle clue, Dad.'

'Oh.' Len turned the Vik Gazette to the back page and ran his finger down the columns of letters. 'Here we are. Sixteen down. Move, clap and start to enjoy this intimate thrill. Two words. Three letters then five.'

'What was Mum doing when she was twerking on you last night?'

'You want the details? Right. Well, first she moved her bottom out. Then it went up a bit. There was a lot of jiggling, which I quite liked. Then she–'

'No, I meant that it's the answer to your crossword clue. Lap dance.'

Len took his spectacles from where he'd tucked them into the vee of his woollen tank top. He slid them over his nose and peered closely at the puzzle, muttering under his breath. Then with a flourish, he scribbled the answer into the small, white squares.

He seemed about to give Penny another clue but was interrupted by Hector and Edith, who were determined to make pancakes. Hector put himself in charge of the process and this soon led to bickering, with Penny chasing them off to pack their things while she poured neat circles onto the heavy, cast-iron girdle that Mary had inherited via Mrs Hubbard from Elsie. She hadn't intended to cook that morning, but she rather enjoyed the slow pace of pouring and watching the bubbles appear on the rising batter. It gave her time to think about Elsie and how all the woman's friends had received something to remember her by. Mary had never been close to Elsie, but Len had. The two of them had connived to bring "special medicine" to the elderly islanders, with Len growing the plants in his shed and Elsie trundling around Vik, delivering it in her library van. Penny doubted that the new librarian, Mrs Harples, would be quite as enterprising. The woman's lips had spent so much time pursed in disapproval that she had to steam-iron them straight to crack a smile.

'Do you think you'll ever start your special medicine gardening business again?' she asked her father.

'Probably not,' Len replied. 'You need a reliable distribution network for that sort of thing. I talked to Gordon about it. He delivers veg boxes to a lot of my former customers. But he thought Fiona wouldn't be too pleased. Now they have Ellie-Minty, they can't take that sort of risk.'

Penny put a hand on her father's shoulder and kissed the top of his head.

'It's for the best,' she said. 'Pancakes. How many do you want?'

A Hopper family breakfast was a glorious, noisy thing, with all five humans and one dog vying for the syrups and spreads, laughing through mouthfuls of doughy sweetness as melted butter ran down their chins. Penny had left Jim to sleep. Despite the sexy twinkle in his eye last night, he'd been tired and left rather subdued by his lack of progress with the vigilante. A lie in would do him the world of good.

Edith was midway through a tale about how her friend Jessica had become trapped in the chemistry lab at school, when Penny's phone rang. She checked the screen and saw to her surprise that it was Fiona.

'Excuse me, I'll just...' she said, pointing to her phone and then the door.

She moved to the hallway and answered, a small knot of anxiety in her stomach. Was Fiona calling to berate her about Jim?

'Hello?' she said tentatively.

'Hi, Penny. Have you or Jim heard from Gordon this morning?'

'I can check with Jim, but I haven't. Why? Is everything okay?'

'I don't know. Simon Benson gave me a lift home from Peterhead in his boat last night and–'

'Sorry. Peterhead? What were you doing in Peterhead?'

'Sergeant Wilson and I went to talk to Brodie's daughter.'

'His daughter?'

'Can you stop asking questions and listen, please? Brodie's name is Kenneth Mathers. He has a daughter in Fraserburgh called Martia. She doesn't think he was killed by any family members, but she mentioned that he had a friend called Richard Less.'

'Less? Jim told me that Pat Hughes thought Brodie might be Richard Less.'

'He's not. But Eileen has discovered who Richard Less is and Sergeant Wilson will be speaking to Fudmuppet this morning. If Less is the killer, then the case is over. I'm more worried about this vigilante thing and Gordon.'

'Who is Less? Donald Wallace knows, but he–'

'Never mind that now. As I was saying, we got a lift back to the island with Simon. He had some old copies of the Gazette in his boat, and he gave them to me. Very handy for composting. Gordon was reading the ones we'd missed while we were away last week. All of a sudden, he sat bolt upright, shouted that he knew who the vigilante was and ran out the door. He still had his Homer Simpson slippers on. He's taken off in the van to God knows where and left his phone here. I thought he might have gone round to Jim's, but I can't get hold of Jim either.'

'Jim's not at home,' said Penny, her brow creased in consternation. 'We're at my parents' house. I don't know if Gordon would have come looking for him anyway. You know they're not speaking?'

She wasn't sure if Gordon had told Fiona about the reason for his and Jim's falling out, so she was choosing her words carefully.

'It's okay,' said Fiona. 'I know about everything. Gordon and I had a big talk about it when I got home last night, and we're fine. We're going to see Dirty Dolores this afternoon and demand a DNA test. I don't agree with how Jim went about things, but I do agree that Gordon should have told me about it right at the beginning. I suggested he speak to Jim today and be pals again. They're a pair of twats, but what can you do?'

'I'm so relieved,' said Penny. 'And so glad you worked it out.'

'We're getting there. It'll take time before I can trust Gordon again. But one thing I do know. There's no way on earth he slept with that woman. As it is, I'm stuck here on the farm with Ellie-Minty and no transport. I'm worried that the eejit will do something stupid and tackle the vigilante on his own. Do you think Jim could go out and look for him?'

'No bother. I'll wake him up and send him on his way. He'll ring you when he has news.'

'Thanks. And tell Jim thank you from me.'

Penny woke Jim with a plate of pancakes and a cup of tea. His face briefly lit up until she told him the reason she'd disturbed him.

'Look for Gordon?' he asked. 'I don't know where to start.'

'You can start by going through Dad's old copies of the Gazette to see if you can spot whatever made Gordon get up and go. He still had his Homer Simpson slippers on!'

Jim pulled himself into a seating position and shoved Penny's pillow behind his back.

'He loves those slippers, Penny. He wouldn't risk wearing them off-carpet unless it was an emergency.'

'I know,' she said. 'Fiona's worried he might try to tackle the vigilante on his own. You have to figure this out, Jim.'

She laid a pile of newspapers on his lap and balanced the pancakes on top.

'The kids and I are going back to mine. Eileen has figured out who this Richard Less character is. All I know is that it isn't Brodie. I'll go round to Eileen's once I've got everyone settled back home, so if you need me, you know where I am.'

Penny left Jim going through the newspapers and herded her brood into the car, ready for their joyous return to the cottage. There were big Granny hugs and kisses for Hector and Edith, and everyone behaved as if Penny were whisking the kids off to Mars for a few years, as opposed to a few miles down the road, where Mary met her friends, went to her clubs and shopped practically every day. Penny rolled her eyes when the sweetie tin came out.

'A wee something for the journey, my darlings,' Mary said, handing Hector and Edith a selection of pan drops, pear drops and sugar mice. Then she looked Penny up and down appraisingly and added, 'None for you, Chunky. You're looking a little too…well-covered.'

As usual, Penny paid no heed. She merely acknowledged her parents' goodbyes with a cheery toot of the horn and set off.

It was a short journey. Ten minutes or so saw them parking in their little garage in the lane. Everyone who lived in the harbour houses used their back doors. Front doors were for visitors who were unaware of the lanes that criss-crossed behind the rows of pretty pastel-painted cottages. Since she was a child, it had been Penny's dream to live in a pink one. Originally a two-up two-down, an extension at the back of her home now accommodated the kitchen below and a third bedroom above, leaving room outside for the small lawn which Timmy liberally decorated each morning. All her little family's needs were taken care of in this place, and Penny adored it.

Chattering loudly in their excitement to be home, Hector, Edith and Penny hauled their suitcases from the car and made their way down the path to the back door. So distracted was she that it was only when she went to put her key in the lock that Penny noticed something amiss. The door was already ajar. The jamb was splintered, and it was clear that some sort of tool had been used to force entry.

She felt her stomach lurch. Her happiness of a few seconds before instantly evaporated and was replaced with a shot of adrenaline that sent her heart racing. Hector and Edith were crowding in behind her, and she instantly flung out an arm to prevent them from pushing past her and going into the house.

'Stay there,' she hissed.

'What?' the twins said in unison, starting to protest.

'We've had a burglar,' she whispered. 'They might even still be in there. I'm going to check. You go into the lane and call Sergeant Wilson.'

'Mother,' Hector started to say, but she quelled him with a murderous glare; the sort of mother glare that communicated in a way no words ever could that she meant it – really, really, disobey-me-and-you're-toast meant it.

Hector had been on the receiving end of that glare only a few times in his life but knew from bitter experience to take it seriously. He shut up and got his phone out.

She left her chicks outside, their worried faces peering anxiously through the kitchen window. Waving her hand in a futile gesture to ward them off towards the lane, Penny cautiously peeked into the hallway. All was quiet. Nothing moved.

Her stomach muscles ached with tension, and her brain was frantically signalling for her to retreat, now, go back. Yet she couldn't go back. She needed to be sure.

Slowly, she opened the dining room door, cringing at each tiny creak of the hinges. It was empty. It appeared untouched. Penny let out the breath she'd been holding, then breathed in deeply through her nose.

The dining room was the easy one. There was nothing much in there. Now came the hard part.

On she went, to the living room door. This stood slightly ajar, and even before she reached it, she could see that things had been disturbed. With a single finger, she pushed. Silently, the door swung back. Penny's stomach muscles sagged.

The doors of her antique cabinet hung loose, its contents spilled across the floor. The ugly lamp that her mother had given her as a housewarming gift lay on its side, the pink shade torn and battered, as if someone had kicked it. The few DVDs she owned were scattered on the sofa, their boxes lying open and empty. She went to touch the photograph of her and Jim, which now rested in the fireplace, happy smiles obscured by shattered glass, but she withdrew her hand, reluctant to taint potential evidence.

The initial shock faded, and Penny began to take in the smaller details. The signed copy of her favourite book, The Juniper Key, had been tossed aside, its spine broken. The plant on her windowsill, half dead from a week without water, had been moved. She sniffed. Something smelled wrong. Unfamiliar. A smell that didn't belong.

Penny backed out of the room and crept to the bottom of the stairs. Normally, she clattered up and down without a thought. Today, they were an endless, carpeted slope disappearing into the gloom above. She put a foot on the bottom step, wincing in anticipation of a creak that never came. Next foot. Up. Next. Up.

Her breathing was fast and shallow now, coming in short gasps. Her eyes never wavered from the top landing, straining in the dim light to catch any movement.

The only sound was the ticking of the hall clock below, every few seconds marking another step.

Up. Tick. Tick. Tick. Up. Tick. Tick. Tick. Up.

Near the top now.

She gripped the banister with claw-like fingers, thrusting her shoulders forward, instinctively pitching her weight into the stairs as her lizard-brain prepared for a push or a shock.

Crouch, Penny, crouch, she told herself. Smaller target. They'll aim high. You'll be low.

She squatted on the top step, one hand on the floor, leaned forward and peeked into the upstairs landing. Empty.

Such light as there was came from the bedroom doors, which stood half closed. All was still. Eerily so. She should have taken a weapon. Her mind went to the poker by the fireplace. But it had no longer been by the fireplace. It had been lying among the scattered books from the bookcase.

Okay, Penny. Stealth time is over. No weapon and four doors, all close together. Fuck this burgling bastard. You can't let him slip past you. You aced the self-defence classes. You can do this. Come in fast and hard. Boot the doors in like a one-woman SWAT team. But what if he's under a bed? So, he's under a bed, you idiot. Keep him there. But what if he's in a wardrobe? Punch his lights out. You've got this. Big girl pants on. Ready? Go.

Her knees, still complaining from yesterday's adventures, reluctantly obeyed. She stood up and quickly bashed the bedroom doors, bam-bam-bam, sending them bouncing on their hinges. Her head moved left, right, left right, eyes darting to and fro, alert to any signs of the intruder. Nothing stirred.

Feeling like a ninja, she spun on the ball of one foot and lashed out with a leg, kicking the bathroom door. It flew open, revealing…nothing.

Penny didn't stop to draw breath. She ran into her bedroom and flung the wardrobe door open, all the while keeping an eye on the landing outside. Then she dropped to the floor and checked under the bed. In an ideal world, she'd have sprung up and dashed to the next room, but she was an ample-bottomed woman in her mid-forties who preferred the mild part of "mild to moderate exercise." The result was less spring, more roll and stagger.

She repeated the process in Hector and Edith's rooms, then lay on Edith's floor, a panting puddle of sweat and tears. There were no monsters under the bed, but all three rooms had been ransacked and their contents thrown haphazardly across beds and carpet. She felt violated. And there it was again. That smell. The smell of someone else. A stranger who had ripped apart her little haven.

Shit. Hector and Edith. She had to tell them she was safe.

If they'd heard her crashing around up here, they might come looking for her.

She retraced her steps to the back door, where she found her little cherubs, wearing an AirPod apiece, feet tapping to the bass.

Penny's first instinct was to scream at them. Had they called the police? Why hadn't they stayed in the back lane like she'd told them to? Instead, she took a beat. Sank down to sit on the back step. Reminded herself that the most important thing was that the kids were safe.

The kids sat down on the ground beside her, and Timmy crept over to lie with his nose on her lap. Then together they waited for the police.

It wasn't a particularly long wait. PC Easy Piecey arrived, flushed with excitement and full of explanations about Sergeant Wilson being busy and how he'd taken full advantage of her absence to "go full-on blues and twos."

'Lights, sirens, pedal to the metal,' he boasted as Penny ushered him into the living room.

He did a lot of tutting and scribbling in his notebook. He managed to knock over and smash the one remaining whole vase. He asked her if anything was missing. She didn't know. The big stuff was still here, but her telly was a hand-me-down from her parents and hardly worth stealing. Easy made some more notes and did more tutting. Then he phoned Sergeant Wilson to ask her what he should do next.

While he was making his call, Penny lingered over the rough piles of mangled paperwork. The folders that had been neatly stacked in the cupboard had been hurriedly emptied, their contents tipped out and mixed up. Using a pen, she poked at a few. There was that smell again.

'Can you smell something…I don't know…not weird, just different?' she asked Easy when he hung up.

'I dunno. First time I've been here. What does it usually smell like?'

Penny didn't reply. She just sniffed. Something was tickling the back of her brain. Something very unexpected. Something that didn't make sense. Yet.

'I have to go,' she told Easy. 'I'll take Hector and Edith to Eileen's. No point in telling you to lock up, when you leave, I suppose. Just pull the door to. If someone else wants to break in, they'll have to tidy up before they can decide what to steal.'

'But Sergeant Wilson says you're to stay here,' Easy protested. 'She says she has some very important news, and you're not to—'

But he was talking to himself. Penny was gone. She hadn't even said where she was going! PC Easy Piecey stood alone in the strange house, with only the ticking of the hall clock to mark the seconds until Sergeant Wilson arrived and banned him from the biscuit tin for a week.

CHAPTER 22

Jim sat on Penny's bed, the newspapers spread across the faded blue and yellow faux-patchwork duvet cover that stood as testament to her terrible taste in the mid-nineties. The matching wallpaper border and curtains were probably the height of fashion at the time, as was the stained pine wardrobe; a deep orange relic whose next home was surely a skip. Laurence Llewelyn-Bowen called, young Penny. He wants his TV heyday back. Whatever happened to Carol Smillie, Jim wondered. Now, there was a lass. Not a patch on Lorraine Kelly, of course. Although he suspected that Gordon would disagree. This would be a good topic of debate for the next time they went to the pub… or didn't. His heart did a sad little flip at the thought of Gordon.

He picked up his phone to google Carol Smillie then laid it down again. He was letting himself become distracted. He needed to focus on his mission – find Gordon, ignore any angry shouting, tell him to go home and put on a decent pair of shoes. But, och, he couldn't find the article that had set the man off. Perhaps Sandra Next Door could help.

Jim lifted his phone again, this time to call Sandra.

She must have recognised his number on her phone because she answered with a curt, 'What?'

'Gordon has figured out who the vigilante is, and he's gone out in his Homer Simpson slippers. Nobody knows where he's gone.'

There was a pause on the other end of the line, then, 'Oh, that's very serious. He loves those slippers. He'd never wear them outside the house.'

'I know! Apparently, he saw something in one of last week's Vik Gazettes. I've been going through them, and I can't see anything.'

'Bring them over,' said Sandra Next Door. 'Two pairs of eyes are better than one.'

Jim didn't need to be asked twice. He gathered the newspapers together, and with a cheery goodbye to Mary and Len, let himself out the back door and hopped over the low wall separating the neighbours' properties.

'Were you planning on getting dressed at all?' asked Sandra Next Door, eyeing his striped pyjamas with some disgust.

He'd borrowed them from Len, so the legs were about six inches too short and didn't quite meet the tops of Mary's Ugg boots that he'd hurriedly donned before setting out. Thank goodness for tall, big-boned women, he thought, otherwise his ankles would be freezing in a pair of trainers.

'I was busy!' he protested, hands on hips, ready to do battle with his nemesis.

'Aye, I can see that. You've got half a pancake stuck to your front. Come and sit down. I'll get a cloth.'

They sat at the same table where they'd pondered the case the evening before, only this time it was awash with old copies of the Gazette. The notepad in which they'd scribbled their conclusions still lay in the centre, open to Sandra Next Door's notes. Jim's eyes fell on the neatly penned lines about Glossop:

"Attacker 5'7" wore balaclava."

But that wasn't all the gossip columnist had said, was it?

'Glossop said the balaclava was hand-knitted,' Jim murmured.

Then he locked eyes with Sandra Next Door.

'Bugger me with a four-ply Shetland. Hand-knitted!' he exclaimed. 'We've been looking at this all wrong. We were ruling people out when we should have been reading between the lines.'

He stabbed a finger at the note Sandra Next Door had made about Harminder Singh:

"Something to do with high teas?"

'There are connections here. They're subtle, but they all lead back to one person. Let's start with–'

His flow was interrupted by the buzz of Sandra Next Door's phone. She checked the screen, and her expression turned to one of bemusement. Holding up a finger to stall him, she answered the call. Jim could only hear her end and felt a moment's sympathy for Penny, who had had to endure many such calls.

'Yes. Oh my! Yes. Really? No. No. Yes. Yes. Okay. Cheerio.'

'That was Iona,' she told Jim once the call had ended. 'She's had a note from the Vik Vigilante. It says that revenge moves in mysterious ways.'

'I'm not surprised,' said Jim. 'It seems that we've been used by the vigilante. This whole time, the clever bugger has been stringing us along.'

'Stop talking in riddles and get on with explaining,' Sandra Next Door snapped. 'We're in a hurry, remember?'

'Aye, well, you're the one taking phone calls.' He held up a hand as if to protect himself from a blow. 'Okay, okay. Where do I start? The high tea. I asked Singh if he had any disgruntled customers, and he was evasive. Looking back on it, I think he was worried about being overheard, which meant that some of those disgruntled customers were in the garden centre at the time. There was certainly one disgruntled customer.'

'Pat Hughes,' Sandra Next Door said, her lip curling at the mention of the woman.

'Aye, she was not happy about those cucumbers. Moving on to Dirty Dolores. She was doing tanning injections on the side and, going by what we heard about Sophie Hendry, Dolores isn't very careful. When we were in the garden centre, I was thinking to myself how Pat Hughes was the Port Vik equivalent of Mrs Hubbard, only shorter, darker-skinned and about twenty years younger. Darker-skinned. She mentioned she'd been on holiday, so it didn't strike me as odd at the time. But when you start putting it together.'

'Dirty Dolores must have given her too much tanning injection,' said Sandra Next Door. 'Hide at home for a couple of weeks then tell folk you've been on holiday. Ha! I hope she ran out of loo roll.'

Jim gave her a complicit grin.

'You're all heart, Mrs Next Door. Then there's Sophie Hendry's waxing accident. Pat knew about that because she told Ally Morrison, who told Sandy Dewar that Sophie got a free wax after the WAGs and Hags article, and Dolores made a mess of things. As Pat was the source of the gossip, she probably knows Sophie. Another reason to go after Dolores.

'Next, the hacking of the parish newsletter. Pat mentioned that she'd always been good with computers. Slim, I know, but add it to the rest and you start to get the picture.'

'Then there was what she said about my husband offering me to the wife-swappers,' Sandra Next Door pointed out, beginning to eagerly grasp Jim's emerging theory. 'She said she didn't know much about the wife-swappers.'

'You told me she'd made it up. I think your words were that he'd never do such a thing,' Jim pointed out.

Sandra Next Door flushed a little at this.

'I spoke to Geoff Next Door last night,' she admitted. 'He knew what Carmichael and the others had been up to and made some off-colour joke to Carmichael about selling me to them so he could get more time on the golf course. Pat could only have known that if she was close to one of the wife-swappers. It's not the sort of joke you generally repeat outside of those in the know. Not unless you want the whole island to find out about your activities.'

'Just out of interest, how much was Geoff Next Door asking for you?' asked Jim, suppressing a smile.

'Pat Hughes isn't the only vengeful woman on the island,' she said, giving him a meaningful look.

Jim took the hint and continued to expound his theory, telling her, 'She probably overheard Sergeant Wilson teaming Gordon and me up with you and thought she'd throw a wee dig your way. Which brings us to Iona. In my opinion, Pat deliberately sent us in the direction of the person who had scorned her advances. She would have known that Iona got her own back by kicking Mrs Carmichael out of the bingo. I imagine it was the subject of much gossip at the time. Yet Pat didn't mention it when we were discussing Carmichael. She only mentioned a possible grudge.'

'You're right,' said Sandra Next Door, picking up a newspaper. 'And somewhere in one of these, there must be an article written by Glossop that offended Pat Hughes. But it's all very circumstantial. We're basing this on tiny snippets. We don't know for sure that it's her.'

Jim waggled a knowing finger at her then tapped his temple, and she shot him a look that said stop buggering about and tell me what you're thinking.

'One of the things that Pat's known for is her array of colourful cardigans.'

'She's won the knitting competition at the Vik Show several times,' Sandra Next Door agreed. 'Ah, I see where you're going with this. Glossop said the balaclava was hand-knitted.'

'Bingo, as Iona would say. I would guess that a knitting pattern for a balaclava isn't the sort of thing you have lying around.'

'You could probably get it off the internet.'

'Or from a professor of knitting,' Jim suggested. 'Worth a try?'

'I'll call Cosmo McKenzie.'

While Sandra Next Door spoke to the expert, Jim nipped back to Penny's parents' house and got dressed. He knew where to go for Gordon now, but he'd be buggered if he was turning up at that randy witch's door in his pyjamas. He threw water and toothpaste in the vague direction of his face, then leapt back over the wall to find out whether Professor McKenzie had hammered the final nail into Pat Hughes' coffin.

'He gave Pat the pattern,' Sandra Next Door confirmed. 'I didn't think we should go round to Pat's on our own, so I phoned the police station. I spoke to a DC Khan, and she said that Sergeant Wilson and Easy are at Penny's.'

Jim felt a slight loosening in his bowels.

'Penny?' he gasped. 'What about Penny? Hector and Edith. Are they okay? Why would the police be there?'

'Something about a break-in. If Sergeant Wilson's there, Penny and the kids will be fine. The Sergeant may be an idle, foul-mouthed cow, but I've seen her in a crisis. She's good.'

Jim felt somewhat reassured by Sandra's words. She was right. Penny was okay. Penny had to be okay. The kids were okay. Because if anything happened to them, Jim would tear the world down. He would cover the sun and fill up the seas. He told himself to stop. Not a healthy train of thought. Don't imagine anything. They're all fine. Go and get Gordon.

Sandra Next Door took her car keys from a hook on the side of the fridge and said, 'I'm driving this time. I have a sensible vehicle.'

Jim looked at her aghast.

'You're not coming. Pat Hughes is a maniac. You might get hurt.'

Sandra reached behind the kitchen door and retrieved a sweeping brush. Jim couldn't resist the thought that sprang unbidden to his mind.

'Oh, your broomstick. I thought you meant we were taking your car.'

Sandra Next Door didn't reply straight away. Instead, she maintained eye contact with Jim as she slowly lifted a leg, placed her foot on a kitchen chair and snapped the broom handle over her knee.

'Nobody gossips about my Geoff Next Door and gets away with it. I'm coming, and you can't stop me.'

CHAPTER 23

Pat Hughes lived in a secluded house at the end of a long, tree-lined street in the posh part of Port Vik. It was difficult to reconcile such genteel opulence with the gossipy wench that worked in the post office, Jim mused. He adjusted his grip on the bag in his hand and slipped through the gate, looking around him cautiously.

Professor McKenzie had given Sandra Next Door the address, cautioning her that Pat had a ferocious dog called Brutus. Jim had confidently declared that he knew exactly how to deal with this. He had seen all the movies. He'd do what they always did to the Dobermans…Dobermen?... in films. This was child's play. Much to Sandra Next Door's chagrin, he'd raided her freezer for a couple of thick steaks, before crushing up Geoff's sleeping pills and lacing the defrosted meat with the results.

So it was that their stealthy approach to Pat's home was accompanied by the tell-tale crinkle of a supermarket carrier bag. If worst came to worst, he decided, he could always use the thing as a cudgel. Sandra Next Door's steaks were surprisingly heavy.

The house wasn't as large as its location and garden would suggest. In common with many houses on Vik, it appeared to have been built in the 1950s bungalow style, using granite imported from Aberdeen. A long dormer window spanned the roof and two large bays were set either side of a polished oak front door.

The door on the front of the small garage was closed. Jim tried it. Bugger. Locked. He hadn't noticed Gordon's van parked nearby, but who knew what was behind that door.

He and Sandra Next Door went through the wrought iron gate at the side of the garage, squeezed past the wheelie bins and picked their way along a path to the back garden. As they went, he noted with a sense of foreboding that all the curtains in the downstairs rooms were closed. Sandra Next Door was clutching the broken handle of her sweeping brush, holding it out before her like a child with a wooden sword. He hoped they wouldn't need it.

They were both tense, eyes and ears tuned for the dog they'd been warned about, yet all that greeted them at the back of the house was a pastoral scene of rhododendron bushes and untidy flower beds awaiting spring's warmer caress to reveal their glory. If Jim had expected to find Gordon tied to a chair in the sunroom, he was out of luck. The curtains here were also firmly closed, with not so much as a hairline crack between them.

Jim tried the back door and found it locked. The rattle of the handle, however, did set off a round of barking from somewhere deep inside the house. Odd, it sounded far more high-pitched than he'd anticipated.

He stepped back to consider his next move. Behind him, Sandra Next Door did the same.

'I'm going to knock on the front door,' she whispered. 'I can't cope with creeping around. Let's just see what she has to say for herself. If she's even in, that is.'

Inside, the dog continued its high-pitched yapping, and they heard a muffled voice say, 'Brutus. Shut up.'

The voice came closer, telling the dog, 'You'd bark at a

falling leaf, you would. What's wrong? Do you want out for a pee?'

Sandra Next Door and Jim simultaneously jumped back and bolted behind a tree as they heard the lock turn in the back door. They stood stock still, Jim clasping Sandra in front of him, both holding their breath while they listened to the back door open and then close. It felt like far more than half a minute had passed before Jim cautiously poked his head around the side of the trunk.

'Fucks' sake,' he whispered.

'What is it?' Sandra Next Door asked.

'Brutus. He's about the size of one of my trainers.'

'Good. If we can get past him without setting him off again, I don't think she's locked the door.'

Jim gave her shoulder a gentle squeeze of acknowledgement and began to edge out from behind her.

Cautiously, they both emerged from their hiding place and slowly moved across the lawn, keeping their eyes fixed on the small, white furball that was sniffing the grass.

Then it looked up.

They froze.

Brutus stared at them as he conducted a quick threat assessment.

Sandra Next Door and Jim stared at Brutus as they did the same.

Everyone reached their conclusions at the same time.

The dog bared its teeth, its lip curling in a vicious snarl. It was no longer yapping. The growl was low and vibrated with vicious intent.

Sandra Next Door squeaked, and Jim muttered all the swear words he didn't dare use in front of Penny. He looked behind him, checking whether the tree had any low-hanging branches they could climb. There were none. Not strictly true. There were none within Sandra's reach. He briefly considered climbing the tree anyway and leaving her behind.

Eileen would have been speechless with wonder when, divining his intent, Sandra Next Door said, 'Don't you dare.'

The furball took a step closer, now directly facing them, hackles up and wee legs quivering with tension. Jim's wee legs were quivering too, although this might have more to do with the sugar rush he was still experiencing from his morning pancakes. Six Rich Teas at Sandra's kitchen table hadn't helped. Plus, he needed a pee. Perhaps he could pee on the dog and make it go away.

As all these thoughts ran through his brain in an uninterrupted stream of nonsense, the dog made its move. Barking as though it were being strangled by a set of bagpipes, it charged forward, its sharp little teeth making a beeline for Jim's leg.

Later, he couldn't explain why he did what he did next. Sheer panic, he supposed. Instead of running away, in a single motion Jim dashed straight at the creature, swept it up and dumped it in the carrier bag.

Sandra Next Door looked on, astonished, as he held the writhing receptacle aloft and said, 'My, these bags for life are strong buggers, aren't they?'

Then he strode to the bottom of the garden, as far away from the house as possible, and waited for the snarling bundle to go quiet.

It didn't take long. The animal seemed to recognise its defeat and soon became still. He carefully laid the bag on the ground and opened the top, fully expecting another round of growls, but the animal was quiet. Too quiet.

'I think you've murdered Brutus,' said Sandra Next Door, leaning in to look inside the bag.

She gave it a gentle poke with her stick. The dog didn't move.

'Och, he's fine. I'm a vet. Trust me, he's just scared,' said Jim.

But a guilty little voice inside him said, 'Et tu. Jim. Et tu.'

He tipped the dog out of the bag. It lay still, its fur

streaked with a pink paste of steak blood and Geoff's sleeping pills.

'Look,' said Jim, pointing at its chest. 'He's breathing. He must have got some of the sleeping pills inside him. A mild sedative for humans can be more powerful for a wee dog.'

Sandra Next Door gazed down at the hound, her face a mask of concern.

'You've done it now. He's taken too much,' she said.

'Doubtful. He was too busy trying to bite his way out. I don't think he had time to lick the steaks.'

Jim felt Brutus' chest, wishing he had his vet bag with him so he could give the furry fella the once over. The heartbeat felt steady, though, and the breathing seemed regular.

'We can't leave him lying out here,' he said. 'We need to find somewhere safe to put him.'

They laid the sleeping animal on some empty sacks in the shed and quietly scampered to the back door, anxious to get into the house before Pat noticed the silence outside and came calling for her dog.

Jim grasped the handle, and at a nod from Sandra Next Door, pressed down.

The light from outside barely penetrated the thick curtains of the sunroom. Jim looked around at the dark lumps of furniture as his eyes slowly adjusted to the gloom. Chairs, a table, a lamp slowly took shape. No Gordon.

He gestured to Sandra Next Door to follow him and picked a path between the chairs, moving towards what he guessed was the kitchen beyond.

His guess proved accurate. Their path ran straight through a narrow galley kitchen. Jim's shoulder caught on the door of the fridge, and he suppressed a yelp of shock. So tense was he, so afraid of Pat suddenly appearing from one of the doorways ahead, that any unexpected movement or noise was likely to render him a squealing mess.

For fucks' sake, man, he told himself. Did you put your big boy pants on this morning? He agreed with himself that he had put on his big boy pants that morning. The ones that made Penny laugh because they said Big Boy right where it mattered. In that case, get a grip, he thought. She's nae likely to jump out of the fridge and clobber you with a fresh pint of milk, is she? She's a sneaky coward who doesn't know you're here. Probably. But it's dark. You can do dark. You get up in the night for a pee, don't you? Two doors ahead and to the right. That's one each. Plus the downstairs loo. Don't be an idiot, Jim. She's hardly got him in the loo. You're right, Jim. We'll skip the downstairs loo. What about the cupboard under the stairs? Now you're talking. Folk hide all sorts in there. They're not just for carrier bag collections, you know. He realised he was babbling and told himself to STFU. Then snickered at a sudden vision of Mrs Hubbard asking, 'What would be best for that one, dearie? A cream or a pessary?'

'Stop giggling,' Sandra Next Door hissed in his ear. 'And what are you doing with your hands? Are you having a fit?'

Jim was, in fact, doing the TV cop series of hand gestures that preceded a surprise raid, but quickly gave it up as a bad job. Not even he knew what he meant.

'You take the first door on the right,' he said. 'I'll take the second. Then we'll both take the cupboard under the stairs. I'm going in. Cover me.'

'Cover you?' Sandra Next Door snorted. 'What in? There's a tin of custard on the worktop back there. Would that do?'

'Just open the first door and go fucking in. Scream if there's a person in there.'

'Aye same to you. Without the unnecessary language, you heathen.'

Sandra Next Door turned the handle of her room and crept inside. Jim did the same with door number two. They both emerged a few seconds later.

'Dining room clear,' whispered Sandra Next Door.

'Living room like a fucking mausoleum to Royal Doulton, and I nearly dropped her mother's ashes in the fireplace,' murmured Jim. 'Who keeps ashes above the fire? That's like rubbing it in.'

Sandra Next Door judiciously ignored him, and they both turned to face the cupboard under the stairs.

The door looked very ordinary; a white wedge, almost head height at the higher end. But Jim's hackles were up. Some primeval instinct was warning him that something bad was behind that door. Maybe Gordon, trussed up like a chicken. He sent up a quick prayer. Oh God, please don't let him be naked, for I could never unsee that. Love, Jim. Amen.

'What are you waiting for?' asked Sandra Next Door, leaning forward and grasping the handle.

She turned and pulled. Jim held his breath. He leaned forward, his eyes straining to see what was behind door number three.

It wasn't what he expected. There was no collection of old shoes, bags for life and a vacuum cleaner. No used-once-a-year cooler bags, ancient backpacks with a pen and an old packet of chewing gum in the bottom or patches on the wall where stick-on hooks had fallen off years ago, never to be replaced. In the moment before he was blinded by light, Jim saw a set of stairs leading downwards.

'Darn. It's one of those automatic lights,' said Sandra, covering her eyes with a hand.

They stood for a moment, eyes closed, watching burning circles fade behind their eyelids.

Then a voice from below said, 'Brutus? I thought I shut the door. How did you get in?'

Jim swore under his breath and risked opening his eyes a fraction. They didn't like it, this harsh, yellow light, but he gave them no choice. He opened them some more and told them to man up like the rest of him.

There was nothing for it now. Any moment, Pat would come up those stairs. He took a deep breath. And another.

'Charge!' he roared, launching himself down the steps.

'What?' said Sandra Next Door, taken unawares.

Then she, too, was clattering after him, the heels of her pumps slipping on the smooth varnish.

Jim came screeching to a halt at the bottom, staggering forwards slightly as Sandra Next Door barrelled into him. There were two people in the basement room, and neither of them were naked. Jim breathed a sigh of relief.

Pat sat there, in a bright orange cardigan. Gordon was next to her in his underpants, his big, plush Homer Simpson slippers resting on a chair. In front of them was a sewing machine and a swathe of denim. They were both staring, shocked at the intruders.

'Hiya, Jim,' said Gordon, after a brief pause to gather his thoughts. 'Pat's the Vik Vigilante. She's just fixing my dungarees.'

'Jim. Sandra Next Door,' said Pat coolly, nodding at each of them in turn.

'But I thought...so, you're not in danger?' asked Jim, his mind reeling.

'Not in danger,' Gordon assured him. 'Better than ever, actually. Turns out Pat here doesn't fancy me. She just really likes dungarees. She's mad on sewing as well as knitting, and dungarees are a very complex challenge. I am a complex man.'

'But she's the vigilante!' Jim exclaimed.

'That I am,' Pat agreed. 'Or one of them, at least. I'll admit to Glossop and having a wee bit of fun with Iona at your expense, but I was on holiday when the other vigilante attacks happened.'

Jim sat down on a plastic storage crate, as much to give him a moment to think as to rest his legs.

'You really were on holiday, then? I thought Dirty Dolores had overdosed you with the tanning injections.'

'Ooh,' said Pat. 'Is she doing tanning injections? That's illegal.'

Jim could see her filing the information away for future use. Then something occurred to him.

'But the wife-swapping. You knew more than you were letting on.'

'Aye,' said Sandra Next Door. 'You have some explaining to do. Starting with why you brought my Geoff Next Door's name into it.'

She was still standing at the bottom of the stairs, clutching the broken broom handle in front of her, eyes glittering dangerously as she sneered at Pat. Jim felt a moment's satisfaction that, for once, he wasn't in the firing line. Pat's arsehole must be clenching like a jellyfish shagging an electric eel right now. Bugger. Did he just say that out loud? He did a quick check. Aye, everyone was staring at him, right enough. Well, most of them. Gordon was trying not to laugh. That was a good sign, wasn't it?

'I'm sorry,' said Pat, looking down to pick some imaginary fluff from her cardigan. 'It was just something my niece, Sophie, told me. I haven't told anyone else. I knew you were all friends, so I thought I'd pass it on to make you aware of the rumour. If it was me, I'd want to know.'

Sandra Next Door lowered the stick.

'Sophie? Sophie Hendry?' she asked, then turned to look at Jim, her expression quizzical. 'She's the one that Dirty Dolores…glued. If Sophie knew about Geoff Next Door's joke to Alec Carmichael, then she must be involved with the wife-swapping.'

'She was, but she only went once,' said Pat. 'Carmichael and his wife tried to get her to do something she didn't want to, so she didn't go back. That's why I said I knew nothing about it. I didn't want her name being dragged into things. 'She has enough on her plate already, what with her husband being off work with his back and her being made redundant. Poor lass. She's getting help, but it's taken its toll.

'That stupid WAGs and Hags article was the final straw. All the other football wives and girlfriends, including her best friend, started saying she was up herself, like she thought she was something special. They stopped talking to her just when she needed them most. She's a lovely woman. She didn't deserve it, so that's why I went after the man who should never have written the damn article in the first place.'

'You didn't go after Carmichael?' Jim asked.

'Why would I go after that pompous bucket of snot?' Pat replied. 'I have far better dirt on him than the wife-swapping. When he tried to pressure our Sophie into doing things, I said to him, I said, "I know exactly what you are and what you've been up to, so if you want to keep your reputation and your little wife-swapping secret, you'll leave my niece alone." I thought he was going to pee his pants.'

Gordon chose this moment to be struck by a flash of genius. He suddenly removed his slippered feet from the chair and stood upright, a pale line of belly poking from between his boxers and his Aberdeen Football Club T-shirt.

'I have it!' he declared. 'I know who the other vigilante is. It's...and I may be going out on a limb here...wait for it... wait...wait some more...it's Sophie!'

'Aye, we know,' said Sandra Next Door. 'Sit down. You're making the place look untidy.'

'It breaks my heart to say it, but yes, it's Sophie,' said Pat. 'She's not well. But you can't go around drugging people and assaulting them. It's not right.'

'As opposed to not drugging them and assaulting them,' Sandra Next Door observed.

'You've got something on your lip there,' said Pat. 'It might be drool. Oh no, I think it's just a bit of sarcasm that's dripped off your tongue. I didn't really harm Glossop. I only gave him a bit of a scare. Sophie didn't harm Singh or Dolores either, not really. But that was down to luck. It was only a matter of time before something went badly wrong. She was about to move on to the football crowd next. Not your Penny, Jim. Penny was always lovely to her. There's no danger of that happening now, though. We've sent her to a private hospital on the mainland for treatment. And don't worry, my vigilante days are over as well.'

'Just out of curiosity,' said Jim. 'What on earth did Harminder do to upset her?'

'Ah. Hmm. How do I put this? You know how Alec Carmichael was pressuring her to do things?'

'Aye.'

'Harminder Singh gave him the box of cucumbers.'

'I don't get it,' said Gordon.

The others didn't enlighten him. They simply watched and waited for it to sink in. From beneath a knitted brow, Gordon's eyes glanced right, then left. Jim could practically see the cogs turning. Finally, the brow smoothed, and the eyebrows raised.

'That's a flagrant abuse of vegetables!'

'She didn't do anything. No vegetables were harmed,' Pat assured him. 'But the whole experience was dreadful for her. If you ask me, she let that Carmichael off lightly. If she knew what I know about the man, she'd have done a lot worse.'

'What do you know about him?' asked Sandra Next Door.

Pat leaned forward and everyone else instinctively did the same, intrigued to discover whatever deep dark secrets she had been keeping about Carmichael.

'Well,' she said, licking her lips. 'I shouldn't be telling you this, and you didn't hear it from me, but…'

CHAPTER 24

Penny threw her shoulder against the front door of Brodie's cottage. It didn't give way. It must be locked, she thought. It was only greased yesterday, so it can't be sticking again. If anyone was inside, they would either have opened the thing by now or they were hoping she'd give up and go away. Well, that wasn't going to happen. This was her last resort. She knew who had broken into her house, and behind that door was the answer to why they'd done it.

Reaching into her pocket for her picks, she squatted down and began to work on the heavy old lock. It took her less time than it had yesterday. She was better able to judge the pressure needed and was more attuned to the mechanism now.

She felt the click and grasped the door handle, using it to pull herself upright. No need for stealth. She'd already announced her presence when she'd tried to ram the door. She didn't fear the intruder. Rather, she didn't understand why they violated her home. Also, she wanted to punch their lights out for upsetting her children. But realistically, she'd just deliver a stern talking-to. She took a deep breath, then with a muttered, 'Please don't let it be bolted from the inside,' she turned the handle and pushed.

In the living room, motes of dust danced in the solitary beam of morning sunlight that had struggled past clouds and the layer of grime that coated the windows. Penny looked around expectantly, but there was nobody there. For a second, she experienced a sense of anti-climax. Everything was as she'd left it the day before. Brodie's mug sat on his little side table. The wooden spoon with which Eileen had threatened Mrs Hubbard lay on top of a rickety bookcase. It was all in its place, except for one thing. The rug that they'd smoothed back over the hatch had once more been pulled to one side, and the hatch stood open.

Penny approached the opening and looked into the space below. The lights were on, but nobody was there. She felt a deep sense of unease. She hadn't planned for this. At worst, she'd anticipated some sort of slanging match when she confronted the intruder. Breaking into her home seemed such a senseless act. But this. Going into the tunnel. What was the point of this? Penny's bones were urgently communicating that something was deeply wrong.

She placed a foot on the first step, paused and then made her way down.

The journey should have seemed much shorter this time, but Penny went more slowly, conscious of the deep niches in the wall, built to conceal whisky barrels, large enough to hide a human being. Where she had felt confused earlier, she was now deeply wary. Her mind was working overtime to reconcile the incomprehensibly misguided actions of the intruder with their foray into a tunnel that was built purposely to facilitate shady deeds.

Sugar lumps, she'd forgotten to bolt the front door! Too late now. If anyone wandered into the cottage, they were in for a surprise. Although the consequences of her being the reason the world found out about Donald's secret lair didn't bear thinking about.

She stumbled along, the toes of her trainers catching on the uneven floor. She was trying to keep to the higher stones and avoid the stream that trickled between them, yet she could still feel the cold water seeping into her socks.

It was freezing down here. She had fled the house in such a hurry that she'd left her coat in the car. She pulled up the hood of her sweatshirt and dug her hands into the pouch in front. That would have to do. Harder to keep one's balance, but needs must when the devil drives.

The thought of the devil made the back of her neck prickle, and she glanced behind her, unable to shake the sensation of a presence lurking in this place, deep below the cliffs. All she saw were the strange shadows across the rough ceiling, cast by the string of lightbulbs as they were caught by tiny air currents that flowed past the beams.

Penny giggled nervously, wondering what Eileen would make of her skittishness. The sound seemed unnaturally loud and out of place, yet comfortingly human at the same time.

She imagined her friend tucking a hand into her elbow and telling her, 'Cordon bleu. There's no need to be scared, Rubber Duck. They're just magnifications of souls yet to pass over.'

'Manifestations,' Penny whispered, correcting her imagination.

Then she wished she hadn't. Things were spooky enough without her fevered brain adding manifestations to the mix.

She was nearly at the end now. The dank smell of ancient stone and algae had given way to the tang of sea air, and she could see the outline of the exit into the cave. Her feet scraped inexorably over the stones, shuffle, step, shuffle, step. Her eyes were fixed on the growing arch of light. It wobbled with every jolting stride as if she were viewing it through the lens of a hand-held camera.

Shuffle, step, shuffle, step.

And suddenly she was there, clinging to the rock and breathing the fresh air, her eyes sweeping across the cave.

'Come down,' said a voice below her. 'I heard you coming a mile off.'

Penny crawled down the rock, her feet scrabbling for purchase, until she slid the last few feet and quickly turned to face the person she had come to confront.

'What are you doing here, Lisa?' she asked.

'Just a little research of my own,' the woman replied.

Penny's eyes flicked to the large crate, which stood open. Its door had been smashed and shards of wood were scattered across the rock platform on which it stood. She noted that the small casks of whisky had been moved and placed to one side.

'Doesn't look like research,' she said. 'Looks more like you're helping yourself to Donald's whisky.'

'Can you blame me?' the journalist scoffed. 'It's worth thousands. Tens, maybe hundreds of thousands.'

'Why? Is the Ecclefechan Express not paying you enough?'

'Ecclefechan Express,' Lisa snorted. 'It doesn't even exist. I did work for the Press and Journal, but they let me go last year. Apparently, encouraging creativity in journalism doesn't apply to expense claims. I told you before, I freelance to pay the bills. I just didn't say what the freelancing involves.

Lisa gestured to the casks and added, 'Today, it's liberating whisky from a drug dealer. Oh, don't look at me like that. The man's a monster. It's not like I'm stealing from the innocent.'

'You're damn right, he's a monster,' Penny shouted, horrified that Lisa would take such a risk. 'He'll kill both of us when he finds his whisky gone. We're the only people who know about this place, and he was pretty clear that our lives depended on us keeping it that way.'

'Not if he can't catch me!'

'And what about me? And my family?'

She and Lisa were only a few feet apart now, jaws tense as their voices rose. There was a manic gleam in the other woman's eyes that Penny had never seen before. Lisa had one hand behind her back and used the other to sweep her hair back from her face. She gave a shrill laugh.

'You'll have to take your chances. Maybe have a word with your friend, Sergeant Wilson.'

'I'm sure *your* friend, DCI Moffat, will have something to say about this,' Penny countered.

'I've never even met DCI Moffat, you idiot. I knew his team was on the island and just used his name because I knew I'd have to explain why I had the keys.'

This made Penny pause and she took a step back, a sudden swooping sensation inside her acting as an early warning system that, in her anger, Lisa had just let something very serious slip.

'How did you get the keys?' she asked, her voice suddenly small and low, the outrage of moments before having been replaced by uncertainty.

'Fuck,' Lisa spat. 'I really hoped that it wouldn't come to this. Oh well, ho hum, what's done is done and all that. Confession time. My father gave me the keys.'

'Your…what? Brodie? Brodie was your father?'

'Well done. Round of applause for Penny Moon. Bit late, but she got there in the end. Yes, Brodie was my useless arse of a father. We had a reunion last week. It was all very tearful and unpleasant, but I needed cash, so I went along with it.

'You see, my sister inherited our mother's house. I was left nothing. Neither she nor my mother wanted anything to do with me, so I made my own way in the world. Then I saw a picture in the newspaper. Richard Less had done something charitable for his community and everyone was very pleased with him. Only he wasn't called Less now. He was in a suit and looked far more prosperous and pleased with himself. But he still had those beady eyes. I recognised him as Dad's friend straight away. The two of them had been thick as thieves back in the day. Quite literally. If it wasn't nailed down, they'd have it.

'Anyway, I came to Vik and watched Less until my father appeared. Family reunion, yada, yada, yada.'

Despite the chill in the air, Penny felt a trickle of sweat run down her back. Her cheeks were hot, and she could hear a slight buzzing sound. The air felt thin, like the time she and her ex had taken the kids up Mont Blanc. There was that same sense of discombobulation. Yet she needed to know.

Her voice was almost a whisper when it came.

'Did you kill Beacon Brodie? Did you kill your father, Lisa?'

The other woman's eyes were dead. No emotion. Simply a flat, 'Of course I did.'

'Why? How could you...'

Penny's voice trailed off as she contemplated the enormity of what Lisa had done.

'I needed the money. That's what I was looking for the day we met.'

'You didn't find it.'

'No, I didn't find it. He wouldn't give me any. I knew he would have loads in the bank, but Dad always had some good old-fashioned cash stashed away for a rainy day.'

'Presumably, you already knew about the tunnel,' said Penny. 'So why all the drama? Why bring me down with you yesterday?'

'To kill you, of course,' said Lisa, her tone implying that Penny was once more being an idiot. 'I didn't want you looking at that photo album. I wasn't sure if he'd kept any photos of me, but I couldn't risk you finding one and recognising me. But then we were so rudely interrupted by Donald Wallace. Just as you were breaking open the big crate for me.'

'So, I was right. It *was* you who broke into my house. I smelled your perfume. It took a few sniffs before I recognised it. Chanel Coco Mademoiselle. I looked for you at the hotel first. Then I realised you must be here. I couldn't understand why you'd done it. And why you'd trashed the place. The photo album was never there, you know.'

'That's why I let you find me here. Where is it?'

Penny felt a moment of panic. She couldn't let this woman

go after Eileen. Lisa was a bigger psychopath than Donald, and that was saying something.

'I gave it to Sergeant Wilson,' Penny lied, but the slight hesitation had cost her.

'Aye, right. Who did you give it to? The truth.'

'Sergeant Wilson,' Penny insisted, her voice an octave higher than she would have preferred.

Lisa stared at her dispassionately, then shrugged.

'I'll just go round all your friends until I find it. As you're of no use to me now, we may as well get this over with. I won't be gentle. This is the best bit.'

She took her hand from behind her back. In it was the crowbar that the goon had used to open the smaller crates.

Penny tried to take another step back, preparing to defend herself, but there was nowhere to go. Behind her was the rock wall she had scrambled down minutes before.

She stepped to the side. She was too late. The crowbar came swooshing towards her. She ducked and felt it graze her hair before it landed with a clang on the rock.

Ooh, that must have hurt the wrist, Penny thought, as she darted away. Lisa ran after her, giving her no time to think. Instinctively, she headed for high ground. In a feat of adrenaline-driven agility, she sprinted up the rocks and onto the platform housing the smaller crates. Lisa had obviously been rummaging through these because many of them were open.

She leaned into a crate just as Lisa reached the edge of the platform. The woman seemed about to climb up, but Penny grabbed one of the water bottles and threw it at her. It glanced off Lisa's shoulder, knocking her backwards. Penny lobbed another one, and Lisa stepped away, wary now.

God, Jesus and all the angels, I know I don't keep in touch, and I'm rubbish at going to church or any of that religiousy stuff, but please help me now, Penny prayed. There were only so many bottles of water, and they were very heavy. Lisa would soon realise that all she had to do was wait for Penny to either run out of bottles or become too tired to chuck them.

It soon became apparent that Lisa *had* realised this. She'd dart forward, Penny would throw, she'd dart back. It was only a matter of time.

Realising that she was only delaying the inevitable and that nobody was coming to rescue her because she truly was an idiot who hadn't told anyone where she was going and they didn't know about the tunnel so how could they even guess and there wasn't even a bloody phone signal so she couldn't even call them…and breathe, Penny, breathe. Realising all of these things, she looked around, desperately trying to formulate a new plan. Lisa was going to kill her, and despite every part of her recoiling at the thought, she was going to have to kill Lisa back. Or first. That was it. She was going to have to kill Lisa first.

Oh, God, Jesus and all the angels forgive me and look after Mum, Dad, Jim and my kids.

Oh, Hector and Edith. Through the mayhem that was taking place in her brain, one thought came loud and clear: I can't believe that the last time I will ever see them was when I rushed them through Eileen's porch.

She flung another bottle, giving herself a moment to think. If she could make it to the other platform, there were pipes and pieces of broken crate that she could use as weapons. It was the getting there that was the problem. But when you couldn't get around something, you had to go through it.

Penny didn't stop to query the flash of inspiration. She grabbed two water bottles to make herself very heavy, tucked them under her arms and launched herself over the edge of the platform, straight at Lisa.

Believing she had the upper hand, the other woman had become complacent and wasn't expecting such a bold move. Penny landed squarely on her chest, and they both went down in a tangle of limbs. The crowbar flew out of Lisa's hand, skittering across the stones and sand, but she was fast, far faster than Penny. She pushed Penny off her and struggled to her feet. Knowing that she could never reach the crowbar before Lisa, Penny followed through on her plan. Ignoring the pain, she scrambled on hands and knees towards the rock steps to the big crate platform.

She pulled herself onto the lower rock and used the next one to lever herself upwards so that she could run up the rest. But the few seconds delay had made all the difference. Penny heard rather than felt the blow to the back of her head; a whoosh of air followed by a sickening crunch that, like a clicking jaw or a hard swallow, sounded far louder internally than it must have externally. Something warm ran down her neck. She tried to continue her climb, but her legs seemed to have forgotten that her brain was in charge. In fact, they were entirely disconnected from the rest of her, and she watched in wonder as her feet slipped backwards and the rock zoomed towards her nose.

Penny's arms were still feebly pushing, but instead of trying to get away, she slowly pushed herself over, rolling onto her back. If these were her final moments, she wanted to hold the important things in her mind. Jim, Edith, Hector, Mum, Dad – they were all there together, smiling down at her. Through the veil they cast, she could make out Lisa, spittle flying from the corners of the woman's lips as she let out a triumphant roar and lifted the crowbar, preparing for the final blow. But Penny was already gone, borne away by the manifestations of the people who mattered, into a warm, dark, safe place.

Funny, she thought, as her mind began to drift in the darkness, the only one of you talking here is Jim. But then he never did know when to shut up.

CHAPTER 25

Pat leaned forward and everyone else instinctively did the same, intrigued to discover whatever deep dark secrets she had been keeping about Carmichael.

'Well,' she said, licking her lips. 'I shouldn't be telling you this, and you didn't hear it from me, but…Alec Carmichael's real name is Richard Less.'

'But you said,' Jim began, but Pat held up a hand to stop him.

'I know, I know. I know that I said my friend recognised Brodie as Richard Less. The Richard Less thing slipped out in front of Sergeant Wilson before I could put my brain in gear. Then I realised that I'd opened a can of worms. If anyone connected Less to Carmichael and they found out about Sophie being the vigilante, they might accuse her of killing Brodie. So, I muddied the waters. Stupid, I know, but as I say brain was not in gear. I genuinely do want Brodie's killer caught. I can't protect Sophie anymore, so I may as well see that dreadful man brought to justice.'

'I think we can all agree that your plan was highly successful,' Gordon confidently declared. 'Not one of us had a clue that Richard Less is Alec Carmichael.'

His phone beeped and he checked the screen.

'It's a text from Eileen. She says that I'll never believe this. Richard Less is Alec Carmichael. Oh well. At least you tried, Pat, at least you tried.'

'When you said brought to justice, what did you mean? Did Carmichael...Less kill Brodie?' asked Sandra Next Door, refusing to be diverted by Gordon, who was tentatively running a forefinger back and forth across Pat Hughes' back in some weird show of solidarity.

'No. I don't think he has it in him. What I meant was that he and Brodie were up to no good. First, they were smuggling drugs. Then they were smuggling whisky. I saw it with my own eyes.'

'How? What? Where?' asked Jim, before settling on, 'How?' on the basis that it was vague enough to cover most things.

'Up a tunnel under Brodie's cottage,' Pat said. 'It runs from under the floor of his living room down to a cave that you can only get to by boat.'

'How do you know this?' asked Sandra Next Door.

'Because my husband was the one who used to make the whisky, while Brodie and Less ran the drugs. He was a lot older than me and the whisky still in the cave was in his family for generations. Our son wasn't interested, so my husband took Donald Wallace under his wing. When he died, we sold the business to Wallace for a tidy sum. How do you think I could afford to buy this place on a Post Office salary? Brodie and Carmichael started working for Wallace on the whisky side of things. I only know that because Brodie told me. We'd known each other for a quarter of a century, and I was one of the few people he trusted.'

Jim already knew about the tunnel because Penny had told him the night before.

'Who was Brodie?' asked Sandra Next Door. 'If he wasn't Less, who was he?'

'Kenneth Mathers,' said Pat, Jim and Gordon in unison.

'I don't know the full story,' said Pat, 'but there was some trouble in the family to do with one of his daughters. He and Less were burglars and something went wrong during one of their jobs. It terrified him. Then the thing, whatever it was, happened with his daughter, and he convinced himself that he'd tainted his children, so he put everything in his wife's name and took off. The youngest was just about to start secondary school at the time, but the eldest was about sixteen, maybe a bit older. He tried to keep up with them both from afar, especially the younger one.'

She looked like she was about to continue, but her tale was interrupted by a sudden burst of music from Jim's pocket informing everyone that he was too sexy for his shirt. So sexy, in fact, that it hurt.

'Bloody Penny and her tunes,' he said, pulling the device from his pocket. 'Sorry, it's Sergeant Wilson. I better take this.'

He may as well have put the call on speaker. The Sergeant's tinny voice reached every corner of the basement.

'Thank fuck you don't have one of those stupid voicemail voices. Where's Penny? Bring her to me.'

'What do you mean, where's Penny?' asked Jim, feeling a small prickle of alarm. 'I thought she was with you.'

'Easy was supposed to be babysitting her until I got there, but remember the cat herding competition at last year's Vik Show?'

'Aye.'

'Imagine Easy is the one that fell asleep on the starting line and Penny is the one that was found a month later living in a wheelie bin behind a chip shop in Dundee. Where are you?'

'Sitting in a basement with a man in Homer Simpson slippers and underpants. Why has Penny gone a.w.o.l?'

'Her place was broken into. Easy said she was going on about smelling something in the living room, then she dumped the brats on Eileen and took off. I told him to make her stay put because I needed to warn her to stay away from that Lisa Jennings.'

'The journalist? What's she got to do with this.'

'She's Brodie's eldest!' Pat Hughes broke in.

'Who's that?' shouted Sergeant Wilson. 'Stop ruining my stories and mind your own business. I went with Fiona to speak to Brodie's other daughter, Martia, yesterday. She didn't mention a sister at the time, but she dropped off a list of family members at Fraserburgh police office this morning and Lisa Jennings was right at the top.'

'Shit. Penny's been working with Lisa on the case,' said Jim.'

'Aye, Eileen told me. If Penny's with Lisa, she's in danger. The woman has a history of serious mental illness and involvement in more than one murder. There's no time to go into it now. Do you think Penny could be with her?'

Jim thought back to the conversation they'd had in bed last night. Aye, not the sexy one, the other one. Although the sexy one had been good. She'd been dropping hints about some perfume she wanted. And he liked what she did to persuade him. Mind you, it would be a damn miracle if it stayed in his mind until Christmas. Och well, she always seemed happy with bed socks and a Toblerone anyway. Nevertheless, something she said last night was tickling the underside of his brain. What was it?

'The perfume,' he told Sergeant Wilson. 'She liked Lisa's perfume. Maybe that's what she smelled. If she did, then Lisa was responsible for the break-in and Penny would definitely want to talk to her. Unless it was Dirty Dolores, although she's too orange to leave the house at the moment.'

He glanced over at Gordon, but the man didn't seem to have been triggered by the mention of Dirty Dolores. Rather, he appeared to be losing a battle to wrest his dungarees from the clutches of Pat. Normally Jim would rush in to help, but this was not the time. Penny was the priority here.

Still pondering the theme of smelly people, he was struck by another idea.

'Iona Cameltoe! Smells very strongly of pig shit.'

'I don't care if your cameltoe smells of foot fungus and fairy dust,' said Sergeant Wilson. 'We'll assume she's gone after Lisa Jennings over the break-in.'

'Penny told me Lisa's staying at the hotel,' Jim said, mildly amazed that he'd retained so much information.

'Try the cottage,' said Pat through gritted teeth. 'Every hotel and B&B was fully booked by the Findochty Foot Fetishists last week. If she came to see Brodie, she might have stayed with him. Ouch. That was my boob!'

She had Gordon in a headlock, and he had just sunk his teeth into her right armpit.

'The cottage! I'll meet you there!' shouted Jim.

'No. You stay at your orgy in the basement,' Sergeant Wilson instructed.

'Tell her about the tunnel,' Pat groaned, ignoring Gordon's yelp of pain as she twisted his thumb towards his wrist.

'The cameltoe was already too much information,' the Sergeant tartly informed him. 'I can't sit here chatting all day about your anatomy. This is a police emergency.'

'It's an actual smuggling tunnel,' Jim yelled. 'If you let me come, I'll tell you about it.'

The Sergeant's reply was worthy of a politician explaining how he'd accidentally given his own company a lucrative government contract.

'There is a risk that you could be injured. I can't stop you from coming, but you must not get in the way of the police, and by that I mean me, doing my job. Tally ho, Wank Boy. And bring your cameltoe. It'll save me using the PAVA spray.'

She hung up and Jim stared at his phone screen, unsure whether he was allowed to come or not.

'Well? What are you waiting for? Get going,' said Sandra Next Door.

He didn't hesitate. He raced up the basement stairs, feeling in his pocket for his car key.

Behind him, he heard Pat Hughes say, 'I haven't heard Brutus barking in a while. He must be wanting in by now.'

He decided to let Sandra Next Door deal with that one.

At the top of the stairs, Jim turned right, ran through the galley kitchen and the sunroom, turned left into the garden, past the wheelie bins, through the gate and into the drive. Gordon hopped from the front door, his leg halfway into his dungarees.

Jim paused.

'Are you coming?'

'Aye.'

'Are we?'

'Aye.'

'Ye ken.'

'I ken.'

'Aye, well.'

'Pal.'

'Mate.'

Gordon clipped the straps of his dungarees and hobbled as fast as he could down the drive, emitting a short "ow" every time a sharp stone penetrated the bottom of a slipper.

CHAPTER 26

Penny's car was parked next to another vehicle in the lighthouse car park. Sergeant Wilson's new squad car sat at an angle opposite, skid marks leading up to its rear tyres. Easy must have passed his advanced driving test, Jim mused as he and Gordon hopped out of the Land Rover and made their way through the gap in the wall.

To their right, the door to Brodie's cottage stood wide open. Jim could see Easy bent over the bookcase, examining its contents. Sergeant Wilson was behind him, a foot raised, as if she were contemplating the wonderful target his backside made.

'It's under the rug,' Jim told her.

'Thank fuck for that,' said Sergeant Wilson, pointing to the open hatch on the other side of the room. 'For a minute there, I thought my detective skills had failed me.'

'Is it just you two?' asked Jim. 'I thought you'd have reinforcements from the MIT.'

'They're on the other side of the island. Fudmuppet found a fingerprint belonging to the school bus driver, Malcolm Kenny. The man did time for a murder back in the eighties and sells Batman comics on eBay. I told Fudmuppet he's barking up the wrong tree, but he wouldn't listen. Said he'd send a couple of DCs over when he could spare them, so it's just us. Ready?'

Jim, Gordon and the two police officers formed a small column and shuffled, single file, through the opening. They quickly reached the bottom of the stairs and turned left, following the string of lightbulbs that gradually receded into the distance, their light converging and blending to a dim glow.

For a moment, Jim allowed the others to bump past him as he stood still, mesmerised by the effect but was quickly brought back to reality by a sharp word from the Sergeant.

'Wank Boy. Do you want to save your girlfriend?'

The others were moving quickly ahead. Gordon was fighting a losing battle to keep his slippers dry. Of all of them, he seemed to be having the most difficulty staying upright as his soles skidded on the slimy green stuff that coated the stones.

Shadows loomed at them, and more than once, Easy hit his head on a beam or careened off at an angle, his shoulder connecting with the rock wall with a thud and a yelped, 'Ooh ya bugger.' When the gangly police officer slipped sideways and disappeared into one of the dark niches carved into the stone, Sergeant Wilson put up a hand and ordered them to pause.

'Speed is not our friend,' she declared. 'Easy, take your time and stop being a twat. If you break something, it'll cause me a lot of paperwork, and I can't afford to have you sitting in the office doing my paperwork for six weeks.'

Considering that she had delivered a fully comprehensive safety briefing, she began to pick her way more carefully over the stones.

It was very cold down here, and Jim's breath was coming in short puffs, small clouds dancing in the light before dissipating into nothingness as he laboured across the rugged surface underfoot.

There was a sense of controlled urgency to their progress.

Sergeant Wilson was quiet now, mutely thrusting out a hand every so often to keep the stumbling Easy upright. Gordon was panting with the effort of navigating the dips and protrusions in wet slippers, yet he remained uncomplaining, slavishly following the Sergeant's footsteps. Jim brought up the rear, occasionally clasping the back of Gordon's dungarees to steady himself or, more often, to prevent the man from tumbling into the stream that wended its way between the stones.

Then suddenly, the air changed, and they could see the end. Driven by a spike of adrenaline, Jim pushed forwards, but the Sergeant flung out an arm to hold him back.

'Police first,' she whispered. 'You can come when I say it's safe.'

She cautiously crouched and peered through the opening. Jim leaned in behind her, thick, wiry curls of her hair tickling his nose as he took in the cave beyond. He suppressed a small yelp when her elbow shot back, narrowly missing his crotch, but he didn't withdraw.

Below, Penny was standing on a rock platform, surrounded by crates, as she threw a bottle of water at Lisa, who darted away, batting at the bottle with a crowbar.

He found himself moving his head back and forth as if he were at Wimbledon watching a bizarre game of tennis, rather than standing in a tunnel entrance watching the woman who refused to be his future wife battle for her life.

The Sergeant must have felt him start forward because she stabbed him with another warning elbow.

'Stay. Be quiet,' she hissed.

Penny desperately looked around her and then bent back to the crate. She seemed to be taking longer this time, and Jim's heart pounded hard in his chest as he watched Lisa come close to the platform. Just as it seemed that the other woman was about to climb up, Penny emerged, rolling two bottles beneath her arms. She didn't hesitate. She launched herself straight off the edge. For a second, she seemed suspended in mid-air. Then Jim watched with mounting horror as she appeared to hurtle towards the floor of the cave.

The Sergeant was picking her way downwards, hands clinging to shallow grooves in the rock. Jim felt Easy push him to one side as the police officer made to follow.

The two women below were oblivious to the newcomers, both of them struggling to free themselves from the tangle of limbs on the ground. The crowbar had skidded away in the melee. Jim saw Penny's head turn towards it and silently urged her to get over there and pick it up. But he could see that she would never reach it in time. Lisa was closer and crawling towards it now.

With a supreme effort, Penny picked herself up and was lurching towards a set of makeshift steps carved into the rock by the other platform. It held a large crate containing some sort of machine. The whisky still he supposed. She was going for a weapon of her own. It was her only chance.

With a sinking heart, he saw her stumble. He saw Lisa come up behind her. He wanted to scream a warning. But the Sergeant had told him to be quiet.

Sergeant Wilson had reached solid ground now and was tripping over her own feet in her haste to get to the women. She wouldn't make it. Lisa was raising an arm. The crowbar glinted. The arm came down.

Jim felt sick as he watched Penny collapse, face down, on the rock. He should have shouted. He should have ignored Sergeant Wilson. He should be down there.

Then time slowed and everything happened at once.

Jim felt himself roughly pushed aside. His head collided with sharp stone. His eyes remained fixed on Penny, even as a large blue and red blur shot past him. Lisa raised her arm, preparing to strike the killing blow. Easy caught Sergeant Wilson's elbow as she tripped. Penny rolled over, her lips coated by the blood pouring from her nose.

All of this came into sharp focus before his vision was obscured by two large, dirty, yellow ovals.

Gordon soared towards Lisa with an incoherent bellow that echoed around the cave. Gravity and the padding that he'd acquired since the birth of his daughter gave him a heft that Penny could never have hoped to achieve.

Lisa looked behind her, but she was too late. Gordon's chin collided with her arm, knocking the crowbar out of her hand. His chest hit squarely between her shoulders, his knees following to sink into her thighs. With a scream of pure malice, she went down in a suffocating jumble of dungarees and belly fat.

Gordon's leap from the ledge at the tunnel entrance could only have taken a few seconds, yet to Jim, it felt an age. He shook his head to clear it and began to slither down the vertical rockface below, grasping at handholds in a vain attempt to control his descent. His coat rode up, taking his T-shirt with it, and he could feel sharp edges tearing into his flesh. The pain would come later, he knew.

His feet hit the sloping rock at the bottom, and he skittered down it, only flinging himself onto his stomach at the last moment when he realised that he was about to fall backwards onto the cave floor.

His inelegant descent didn't hinder his reaction time. The moment his feet landed on solid ground, he was off, leaping over boulders and kicking aside stones in his gut-burning, howling haste to reach the love of his life.

'Penny. Fuck. Penny.'

He ran to her, barging Sergeant Wilson and Easy out of the way, darting around the squirming pile of Gordon and Lisa.

'Penny. Fuck. Penny.'

He was on his knees, ignoring the jarring wallop of bone on rock.

'Penny. Fuck. Penny.'

'Don't move her!' Sergeant Wilson barked as his hand brushed back her hair and he bent to those precious, precious bloody lips.

'Can you hear me, Penny? I love you. The kids love you.

Hang on in there. No, don't go to sleep. Fight it. I'll get you posh chocolates. No more Toblerone. If you just stay with me. I'll put the bins out for you. Maybe even on time. I'll make you cups of tea in bed, and I won't laugh at you for always wearing odd socks or only eating the orange Smarties.'

He was babbling now, he knew.

'Please, please, stay with me, Penny. I can't lose you. You're not allowed to go. I need you to hold Timmy while I clip his claws.'

Her eyes fluttered open, and he heard her whisper, 'You never did know when to shut up,' before the darkness took her and left him sobbing in a bubble of pain that the outside world could not touch.

CHAPTER 27

Penny was lecturing Edith about spending more time studying for her exams and less time mooning after Dillon Clark when it happened.

Edith scowled at her and seemed about to say something. Then she simply melted. Around her, the cottage became indistinct, replaced by an odd brightness that made Penny want to turn away. Except she couldn't. The thing that had plagued her dreams was here, a nagging presence that plucked at her nerve endings and made her feel anxious. It pulled her towards the light, this thing, when all she wanted was to go back to the comfort of her little cottage by the sea. Her safe place. Where was Hector? He must be doing his Saturday shift at Jimmy Ghupta's bakery. Yes, that was it.

Jim's voice came to her from far away, somewhere beyond the light.

'I'll tell you what, woman, washing your knickers is far too complicated. Your mum caught me putting the sexy red ones in with the big, white granny ones and nearly beat me to death with a box of Persil.'

'Shut up, Jim,' she whispered.

There was a pause, then…

'Did you just say something? Shit. Nurse! Nurse! Where's the fucking buzzery thingy? Nurse!'

Penny's eyelids slowly raised, and she blinked, her pupils rebelling at the sudden brightness. Jim lay across her chest, an arm frantically scrabbling at something to her side. His head turned and his nose looked massive, swimming in and out of focus. She giggled blearily, the sound coming out as a halting hiss, then stopping abruptly as the slight movement set off a cacophony of pounding throbs at the back of her skull.

Jim was staring at her. There were tears in his eyes. Why was he crying? Penny wanted to reach out to comfort him, but her arm was trapped beneath his hips. She felt a small trickle run from the corner of her own eye. Now she was crying. Why was she crying?

'Bugger me with a bag of saline,' Jim hiccoughed, pushing himself off her.

She tried to smile, but the tendrils of darkness were wrapping themselves around her, lifting her back into the black place where her head didn't hurt. She didn't resist, even as Jim's hoarse cries for the nurse rose in pitch and volume. She just let herself be borne away by the shade, wishing she had the strength to tell him that she'd be back. Very soon, my love, very soon.

When Penny awoke the second time, she felt sharper, less like she was experiencing the world through a thin coating of marshmallow.

A man stood at the end of her bed. He was dressed in a dark suit and was smiling at her.

'Welcome back, Miss Moon,' he said. 'I'm Doctor Afzal. No, don't try to move. You've taken a nasty blow to the head, and any movement will feel like another one. Don't worry. We've pieced you back together again. Stay there...well you don't have much choice do you? I'll get your parents.'

He paused for a second, as if debating whether to mention something, then leaned in and said, 'If you could encourage your mother to go home, that would be grand. She's been practically living here for three days and instigated a wheelchair race on the geriatric ward that resulted in Mr Higgins' early demise. Dodgy ticker. Still, he won first place, so he went out smiling.'

The doctor left and was replaced by a nurse, who placed a button in her hand and gave her instructions to press it if she needed a shot of the good stuff.

'It won't let you overdose,' the nurse assured her, before glancing over her shoulder and turning back to whisper, 'but if Mary becomes a bit much, it'll take the edge off.'

Her parents came next, Mary leading the charge with a joyous, 'Chunky! Or should I say Humpty? They fixed your egg, get it?'

'They couldn't put him back together again,' Penny croaked, trying out her voice.

'Don't argue with me. I'm your mother. I know everything.'

'Hi, Dad,' said Penny, directing her gaze at the short figure in the blue cardigan.

He was wearing his favourite shirt, she noted; a soft, checked flannel number that Mary had more than once tried to consign to the clothes recycling bin outside the supermarket, only for it to be quietly fished out of the bag and hidden at the back of the wardrobe until a special occasion or another of Mary's clear-outs caused it to resurface again. Penny appreciated the effort which her dad had made on her behalf by wearing it.

Her mother, a whirlwind in chiffon scarves and a mandala-printed dress that Penny was sure was supposed to be worn over a swimming costume at the beach, swept over and planted a kiss on her forehead. The slight pressure made Penny wince, and she wondered whether it was time to press the button. Yet she held off. Jim and the kids would be on their way.

'Your father has saved all the crosswords for you, when you're up to it, and I've brought a selection of magazines,' said Mary, depositing a pile of Mosaic Monthly and Donkey Lovers Digests on her stomach.

Penny winced again, although not in pain this time. If her mother's enthusiasm had moved on to mosaics, it wouldn't be long before practically everything her parents owned was covered in a layer of grout and broken ceramic. She shot her father a sympathetic glance.

'We won't stay long,' said Mary, immediately belying this by settling into the chair by Penny's bedside.

Len took the chair at the other side.

He regarded his daughter appraisingly and asked, 'How do you feel, Pennyfarthing?'

'Sore,' Penny croaked.

'You gave us a scare there,' he told her, then reached across the bed and slipped his warm, dry hand into hers. 'If it hadn't been for Gordon, we'd have lost you.'

There was a moistness in his eyes as he gently squeezed her fingers. Penny gently squeezed back.

For the first time, she tried to remember what had happened, but could only picture Lisa, head thrown back and mouth an open, dark maw as she wielded the crowbar.

'Gordon?' she asked. 'What happened with Gordon?'

'He's a hero,' Mary declared. 'He jumped off a ledge and flattened that evil woman before she could hit you again. My only criticism is that he didn't flatten her enough. She's handcuffed to a bed down the corridor. The doctor told me to stop poking my head round the door and laughing at her every time I go past, but Sergeant Wilson said it was fine.'

'She lost an eye on the button of Gordon's dungarees,' said Len. 'That evil woman, not Sergeant Wilson. The Sergeant broke an ankle tripping over a rock. She has Easy wheeling her around everywhere, poor lad. The doctor's putting her on crutches tomorrow, as much for Easy's sake as anything.'

Her parents filled in many of the details she'd missed until there came a tap on the doorframe, and Jim's head appeared.

'Is it nearly time for our turn? They're only letting a few of us in at once so we don't tire you out.'

Penny's smile reached from her lips to her heart.

'Come in,' she rasped. 'Tell everyone to come in.'

Jim disappeared and she could hear a muttered discussion taking place on the other side of the doorway. Then he returned, followed by Hector, Edith, Gordon, Fiona, Sandra Next Door, Eileen and Mrs Hubbard. They all crowded around Penny's bed, their voices blending to an excited hubbub that turned her insides to warm caramel on a gooey brownie.

'I hear I have you to thank for saving my life,' she told Gordon.

His face was bruised, and when he smiled, she could see a gap where once there was a tooth.

'Spur of the moment,' he assured her. 'Spur of the moment. My slippers are ruined. But I don't like to talk about it, so we'll say no more.'

Penny then listened patiently as he proceeded to give her a blow-by-blow account of his actions. There was some good-natured teasing from the others when he described how he had been commended by Sergeant Wilson for the best sitting on a suspect that she had ever seen.

'You only sat on her because you'd burst the backside of your dungarees again,' laughed Eileen.

'She should think herself lucky that you're past your commando phase, dearie,' said Mrs Hubbard, who was sitting on the end of the bed, nibbling at a chunk of cinder toffee that she'd brought for the invalid.

She was in high spirits because, following a campaign by Mary and her friends, the McCullochs had been thrown out of the dancing competition, leaving the Hubbards as the de facto winners.

'You and Jim are friends again?' Penny asked turning back to Gordon.

'Aye. We had a long talk about it before we got in the car to come and rescue you, didn't we mate?'

He turned to Jim, who was emptying a bag of Maltesers into his mouth.

He chomped quickly, grabbing a cup of Penny's water to wash them down, and said, 'Aye. In-depth.'

'Good talk,' said Gordon.

'Aye.'

'Do ye…'

'No.'

'Fine.'

'Aye.'

'Aye.'

Jim picked up the small paper bag that Fiona had brought and, examining the contents, told Penny, 'We've agreed that there was fault on both sides. I'm sorry. Gordon's sorry. We're still best mates and we don't need to talk about it again. What the fuck are these sweeties?'

He jumped as Sandra Next Door smacked him over the back of the head.

'Enough of the language,' she said.

'Fine. What are these sweeties? They look shite.'

He ducked as Sandra Next Door aimed another blow his way.

'Grapes,' Fiona said, with a snort of exasperation. 'Gordon and I have been to see Dolores, and I feel quite sorry for her. Mason's father is…was Alec Carmichael. He was very abusive, according to her and told her that if she breathed a word about him being Mason's father, he'd turn her over to Donald Wallace. She was terrified. She was pregnant and had no money, so she panicked and said Gordon was the father. She knew he was blind drunk that night and wouldn't remember a thing. The two of them never, never, well, nothing happened. Anyway, she's paying us back by helping out one day a week at the farm.'

'Was Alec Carmichael?' asked Penny. 'You said *was* Alec Carmichael.'

Fiona was about to reply when she was interrupted by a voice from the doorway.

'We found him buried under the grass at the bottom of the cliff,' said Sergeant Wilson. 'Hello Massive Mary, Pocket Len, spotty youths, turdnuggets. That doesn't include you, George. As a fellow sitter on folk, I have upgraded your status from turdnugget to snotsocket. You may thank me later.'

She was sitting in a wheelchair, for once dressed in a woollen jumper rather than her habitual body armour. The lower half of one leg was encased in plaster and propped up, and behind her stood Easy, looking pale and tired under the harsh hospital strip light.

'Richard Less is no more,' said the Sergeant, chuckling at her own joke. 'Lisa Jennings, whom we have all agreed to call That Evil Woman from now on, has admitted that she killed him and his wife after she'd bumped off her father.'

'So, he didn't run away with the wife-swapping ring?' said Penny.

'No. They're all on a beach in Lanzarote. Her Evilness invited the Carmichael-Lesses round to discuss her father's financial affairs and laced their tea with the stuff she used on dear old Dad.'

Penny thought back to the depression in the grass that she'd assumed was the beginning of a cliff path. Despite everything she'd learned, she felt a pang of sympathy for the couple. The husband may have been a bad man, but neither of them deserved a horrible death and a shallow grave at the bottom of a remote cliff. She shuddered at the realisation of how close she'd come to joining them.

'Did That Evil Woman say why she killed her father the way she did?' Penny asked the Sergeant. 'She could have bumped him off quietly and it would have been weeks before anyone noticed.'

'Fork,' said Wilson, ignoring Penny's question.

Easy patted his pockets and produced a fork, handing it to his boss.

'You'll get it back in time for your dinner,' she assured him, poking it down the plaster cast and emitting a groan of satisfaction that had Jim and Gordon snickering like a couple of schoolboys watching a naughty movie.

'She wanted him found,' the Sergeant said once she had finished scratching. 'She wanted him to have a big, dramatic, humiliating ending. She blamed him for what happened all those years ago, and the fact that her mother and sister would have nothing to do with her.

'When she was sixteen, she pushed her best friend off a cliff. She only did a few years for culpable homicide because she was young and managed to convince everyone that it was an accident. Brodie knew it was no accident and that she was evil. He caught her torturing wee Martia.

'Easy managed to find the records for a spate of burglaries just before Brodie and Less left Fraserburgh. During his last burglary, something went wrong and a man was strangled. We don't know if it was Brodie or Less who did it, but according to Pat Hughes, the man was haunted by a bad deed and became obsessed that he was the reason that Her Evilness had turned out the way she did. He was terrified of doing the same to Martia, so the big cowardy bastard ran away.'

'Pat Hughes is the Vik Vigilante,' said Sandra Next Door. 'She's confessed everything to the police.'

'Only because you told on her, Thatcher,' said Sergeant Wilson, pointing the fork at her least favourite turdnugget. 'If being a grass was a criminal offence, you'd be on fucking death row by now. Anyway, Brodie, sob story, tortured soul and all that. Ultimately, I think that not getting done for murder had a lot to do with him and Less scarpering to hide out here. But what really chews my nipples is that he didn't even send his wife and kid a few quid to keep the wee one in school shoes.'

'He had money,' said Penny. 'That Evil Woman said she was after his money. He had loads in the bank plus some cash stashed away somewhere. She never found it.'

'If he had cash,' the Sergeant replied, 'we haven't found it either. Now, enough blethering. Have I ever told you about the time I stayed in this very room? Piles like them grapes that Wank Boy's eating over there. Oh, that's disgusting, Wank Boy. Somebody has to clean that bin. You could at least have spat it into a tissue first.'

Later, when everyone had gone and only Jim remained, Penny said, 'Thanks for washing my knickers. I heard you grumbling about it.'

'Whites and reds. 'You should stick to black, navy and dark green like me.'

'But then my knickers wouldn't be nearly as interesting.'

'True,' said Jim, taking her hand in his and kissing it tenderly.

He was sitting on the chair beside the bed, his body twisted sideways so that he could rest his head on her belly.

'If you hadn't pulled through,' he said, 'what would have happened?'

'I suppose the kids would have gone to my mum and dad. You'd have taken Timmy, though, wouldn't you?'

'Aye. We'd all have been broken up into separate pieces. I don't want to be a separate piece. I used to, but not since I met you. Penny, you and the kids and Timmy, you're my world now. My dad has moved on with his life, and that's fine. But my life begins and ends with us, our wee family.'

Penny's breath caught in her throat as Jim raised his head, tears once more pooling at the corners of his eyes. He clutched her hand a little more tightly, and she could almost see the waves of raw love coming off him.

'I can't be a separate piece, Penny. Please, will you just damn well marry me?'

EPILOGUE

Pat Hughes opened the door to her basement and slowly went down the stairs, one hand holding the banister, the other clutching Gordon's torn dungarees. Ahead of her, Brutus scampered down the last few steps.

'It'll only take five minutes on the sewing machine, then we'll be off to bed,' she told the little dog.

Brutus wasn't listening. He was sniffing the crate that Jim had sat on earlier, growling at the unwelcome scent of the man.

'Och, come here,' said Pat, laying Gordon's dungarees beside her sewing machine.

Brutus ignored her and continued his low, throaty rumble, so she strode over and scooped him up.

'Naughty doggy,' she said. 'The nasty man has gone and there's nothing in there for you. Look.'

With her free hand, she leaned over and popped the lid of the crate. There really was nothing of interest to Brutus inside. He would have little use for the pile of fifty-pound notes, stacked in neat bundles and wedged tightly into every corner of the crate.

Pat sighed and absently rubbed the dog's ear.

'Martia Mathers, that awful policewoman said. Brodie's

daughter. I suppose this rightfully belongs to her now. Although, I don't expect she'd mind me having a wee bit. If we never tell her. Eh, Brutus?'

Gently, she put the dog down on the floor and placed the lid back atop the crate. It closed with a firm click, and Pat straightened, smiling down at her best friend in the world, who was staring up at her, his head cocked to one side.

'Dungarees,' she said. 'And while I'm sewing, I'll tell you all about what Mrs Harples, the new librarian, has been getting up to in her spare time. Only, don't let on that it was me that told you.'

AFTERWORD

I hope you enjoyed this book. If so, I would be grateful if you could take a moment to pop a review or a few stars on Amazon.

You can hear more about my books and get access to exclusive material by subscribing to my newsletter via my website, https://theweehairyboys.co.uk . You also can drop me a line using the contact information on the website or treat yourself to a signed copy of one of my books.

Did you know that there's a Losers Club on Facebook for fans of the Losers Club series? Yes, you really can join Losers Club, although our fellow Losers are far more interested in cake and chocolate biscuits than diet sheets. I think it is best described as a warm, friendly and creatively bonkers place. Please do join us.

Other than this you can find me at:

Facebook Growing Old Disgracefully (blog)

Yvonne Vincent - Author

Instagram @yvonnevincentauthor

Threads @yvonnevincentauthor

X (Twitter) @yvonnevauthor

Tik Tok @yvonnevincentauthor

Amazon Yvonne Vincent Author Page

Until the next adventure.

Yvonne

ALSO BY YVONNE VINCENT

Losers Club

The Laird's Ladle

The Angels' Share

Sleighed

The Juniper Key

Beacon Brodie

The Losers Club Collection: Books 1 - 3

The Losers Club Collection: Books 4 - 6

The Big Blue Jobbie

The Big Blue Jobbie #2

Frock In Hell

You can find all of these via my website at https://theweehairyboys.co.uk or on Amazon.

Printed in Great Britain
by Amazon